DEVIANT REIGN

KNIGHT'S RIDGE EMPIRE

TRACY LORRAINE

Theo's nellect ♡

TRACY
LORRAINE

Editing by Pinpoint Editing

Proofreading by Sisters Get Lit.erary

Photography by Wander Aguiar

1

THEO

"**E**mmie."

The pure undiluted fear in my voice echoes around me as time seems to slow to a stop.

Blood soaks her white school shirt faster than I thought possible as my heart jumps into my chest.

"Fuck. No. Please. No," I mutter to myself as I race forward, although I swear to God that someone's hit fucking pause on my life.

It's like one of those nightmares where you just can't get to where you want to be. No matter how much you want it, you just can't do it.

Panic, adrenaline and dismay flood me, but finally, I fall to my knees in front of her.

Pain shoots up my legs, but I don't feel it.

"Emmie," I shout. "Emmie."

Her eyes are closed, her lips parted.

If it weren't for the memory of that stupid fucking shot I just took, then I'd think she was just asleep.

But she's not.

I acted on instinct, allowing my anger to take over instead of thinking rationally.

I used my heart instead of my head.

The exact opposite to everything Dad has ever taught me.

Leave your feelings at home, soldier. When there's a gun in your hand and an enemy is in sight, you have to use your head. Otherwise, people get killed. You get killed.

Rolling the fucking prick who thought it would be a good idea to touch something that belongs to me out of the way, I quickly inspect her for a bullet wound.

When all I see is a rip across the shoulder of her shirt and a minor graze on her skin, I breathe a massive sigh of relief.

Tucking my arms beneath her limp body, I push up to my feet, holding her close to my chest.

"You fucking shot me," a deep, pained voice rings out a second before heavy footfalls come to a stop behind me.

"I'll fucking shoot any motherfucker who touches my wife."

His eyes widen as he presses his hand to his shoulder, blood oozing around his fingers.

"Cirillo," a commanding voice booms. "I called you here to get your girl. Not to shoot my fucking brother."

My spine stiffens, my teeth grind and my grip on Emmie tightens protectively.

I know they have a history. A quick scroll through both of their social media accounts told me that weeks ago, and it only added to the reasons I wanted to hate her.

She was in bed with the enemy. Literally.

We might tolerate the Wolves, allow them to run their pathetic little business in the estate, but the blood between Archer and me has never been exactly... friendly.

He sees me as a threat.

I see him as a weak little prick.

"Whoops," I say, turning to face him with a smirk tugging at my lips, masking how I'm really feeling right now while my girl is bleeding in my arms.

She might be in a better state than Dax, but any amount of blood from a gunshot is too fucking much for my wife.

Archer's brow lifts, the muscle in his neck pulsating with anger.

"He was touching something that belongs to me." I hold his eyes firm, ensuring he hears every word that I'm about to say. "You might be a part of Emmie's past. I can hardly erase that. But rest assured, you're not going to be a part of her future. She's Cirillo now. And I'm taking her back where she belongs."

I take a step forward, my gun beside Archer's foot catching my eye.

Women make you weak.

Love makes you weak.

Dad's voice echoes in my head as I stare at it.

I dropped it. I fucking dropped it when I ran for her.

You're the Cirillo heir, Theodore. Heirs do not make mistakes. Ever.

Tension ripples around the room as I hold my head high and close even more space between us while Dax mutters behind me about getting patched up like a pussy.

3

A couple more of Archer's boys stand behind him, trying to be threatening but I don't even grace them with eye contact.

They're nothing. And they're all going to let me walk out of here with my wife and forget any of it ever happened.

They know full well that if they don't, they'll all be in cuffs and in the back of a paddy wagon before the sun comes up for their less-than-legal business practises.

"Emmie belongs here. She's Lovell through and through."

"Nah." I tilt my head to the side patronisingly. "She was just slumming it until her white knight arrived to show her how a queen should really live."

His jaw tics as he looks down at her.

"You care about her. I appreciate that. But you called me, remember? You know exactly where she belongs."

He holds my eyes for another two seconds but has no argument.

I just wish I fucking knew what game he was playing.

Why call me to come take her home and then argue with me about where she belongs?

Is it just his pride talking?

Is he just trying to look like a big man in front of his boys, when the reality is that he's just riding his big brother's coattails?

I watch as he lowers down and his fingers wrap around my gun. Mine twitch in my need to stomp on his fucking hand to stop him from touching it.

"You're right," he concedes, standing and holding

my piece out between us. "She was always too good for this place. For the shit hand she'd been dealt. I'm just not sure how being bound to you is actually any better."

"Then I guess it's a good thing none of that is your concern anymore, Wolfe. Now," I say, finally looking to his backup, "if you'll excuse me. I'm going to take my wife home and let her sleep off whatever the fuck you and your den of wolves have plied her with."

"Emmie doesn't do drugs," he states confidently, trying to win this pissing contest by proving he knows her.

"I know. But in case you hadn't noticed, she's fucking passed out in my arms right now, and I'd put money on it that it's not from your cheap-arse booze."

"A-acid," Dax blurts from behind me. "S-she... we... took acid."

My fingers curl around my gun as the need to spin back around and take a better shot burns through me.

"You're lucky she's in my arms, Daxton," I growl, taking it from Archer and holding his eyes. "Sort your boys out, *boss*. They're a mess. And we don't like mess on our turf."

I step toward him, but he doesn't move.

"And," I add, "if I catch any of your boys dealing anywhere around Knight's Ridge, I'll personally deliver them back in no fewer than one hundred pieces. You got that?"

"We don't—"

My eyes narrow and he swallows his words.

"You're right. You don't. Excuse me."

I don't wait for him to move, I just barrel straight through him with my shoulder.

His loyal servants helpfully jump out of my way,

allowing me to walk out of their little kiddy playhouse with my woman, vowing to both of us that I'll never give her a reason to step foot in this shithole ever again. The only person who stops me is a girl who looks completely fucking wasted, but she's clearly still a little with it because she holds out a bag I recognise as we pass her.

"Look after her," she slurs, her eyes dropping to Emmie for a beat before I turn my back on her.

I find my car exactly where I left it with the door thrown wide open, which is a fucking stupid thing to do in the middle of Lovell.

Thankfully, there aren't many Maseratis on this deadbeat council estate, so almost everyone should know who it belongs to and stay the hell away.

Ignoring the driver's side, I march around the hood and pull the passenger door open, gently lowering Emmie into the seat.

"It's okay, Hellcat. I've got you," I say, cupping her cheek and wiping away some of her smudged makeup.

Damn, I wished I was the one to make her look like that.

The knowledge that it was another guy who's caused her lips to be so red and swollen makes me want to storm back into that place and burn it to the ground with every motherfucker inside.

A soft moan rumbles in her chest as I cup her cheek, and she leans into my touch as if she recognises me even while she's out cold.

"We're going to get that cleaned up, okay? Then I'm taking you home."

Honestly, I want to say that my intentions are pure and that I'll take her to her dad's to sleep this all off, but seeing her with another guy has only fuelled my need to keep her to myself again, and I'm not sure I'm going to be able to ignore it and be selfless enough to give her what she'd want.

Dropping a kiss to her creased brow, I tug the seat belt around her and close the door, more than ready to head out of this fucking estate.

The second the engine rumbles to life, I floor the accelerator and leave everything behind in my dust.

I only make it to the end of the road when my phone rings through the speakers.

Without missing a beat, I connect the call.

"I've got her," I say before he has a chance to speak.

"Bring her fucking home, Cirillo," Dawson growls down the line, the threat in his voice making the hairs on the back of my neck stand on end.

I can only imagine how he felt having to ring me tonight when he couldn't get a hold of his daughter.

But fuck, am I glad he did. I was even more relieved to get my second call of the night from someone I'd rather not speak to who announced her exact location.

"Yeah, I need to make a stop first."

"What for? You promised you'd bring her straight here."

"Trust me, D. I'm looking after her."

"Cirillo," he warns.

"She needs..." I swallow hard, glancing over at her with blood staining her shirt. Most of it isn't hers, but it still rips me to shreds that I hurt her.

"We'll be there as fast as we can," I say, bailing on confessing that I almost shot her until he can see with his own eyes that she's okay.

I cut the call off before he can reply, something that

I'm sure I'll pay for later. But fuck it. Emmie is my first concern right now.

I'm sure I could take her old man should it come to that.

He's old, after all.

The traffic is almost non-existent at this time of night and I fly through the city, heading toward the only woman I trust to ensure that Emmie is as good as new in no time.

Given the choice, I think Gianna would have moved to the other end of the country to get away from Stefanos when their marriage went south, but she couldn't bail on Alex and Daemon. She might not have agreed with their intentions of joining the Family like their father and grandfather before them, but she understood it and ensured she was close enough for when they needed a breather from this life.

The street lights are fewer and fewer as I head into the Essex countryside and cars become few and far between as we get closer.

My fingers grip the wheel painfully as the anger that surged through me when I found her mid-orgasm with another guy continues to linger.

Hearing her call my name helped a little. Add the knowledge that she was tripping on acid and I'm halfway to understanding, but the image of his hands on her is something that's not going to leave me anytime soon.

She shuffles beside me and I look over, hoping that she's going to come to before we get to Gianna's.

"Hellcat?" I ask.

I'm rewarded with another groan.

"You awake, babe?"

She stills, and I'm forced to look at where we're going once more.

"It's just me, Em. You're safe."

She scoffs, telling me that she's awake enough to be aware of the situation.

"You're the most dangerous of them all, Theodore."

Looking back at her, I find that her eyes are still closed.

"Why am I with you?"

An unamused chuckle falls from my lips. "I told you, Hellcat. I'll always find you."

"Great," she mutters, her head falling to the side as if it's too heavy to even consider holding her up. "Where are we going?" she asks, but lights coming up behind us catch my eye in the mirror.

"U-uh..." I hesitate, keeping my eyes on the quickly approaching vehicle.

I've paid zero attention to other cars since we left the city. I have no idea if he's been tailing me for a while or if it's just some dickhead boy racer making the most of the nearly deserted country roads.

I tell myself it's the latter, but that doesn't stop my heart from racing and my palms sweating a little.

Something's wrong.

I feel it.

"Theo," Emmie snaps. "Where are we going?"

"W-we're... uh..."

She must open her eyes because a quiet shriek passes her lips.

"Why am I covered in blood, Theo?" A panic that I'm not used to hearing from her fills her voice.

"It's okay, babe. Most of it's not yours."

"Most of it. Is that meant to make me feel any better?"

"Uh..." I look back to the car behind, noting that it's almost closed the space between us. "Shit."

"What? What's wrong?" she asks, reading me better than I've given her credit for.

"I'm not sure but— Shit. Hold on," I shout a second before the car slams into the back of us, forcing us forward.

"Theo, what the hell?"

"I don't know, babe. Just hold on, yeah?"

I have no idea if she agrees or not, because she doesn't say anything and I'm too busy focusing on losing whoever this cunt is.

Pushing my foot down, I take the road as fast as I can, but it's winding and it's pitch fucking black out here, and I don't know it well enough to go at breakneck speed to lose this arsehole.

"Fuck," I hiss when he hits the back corner, making the car spin out.

"Fucking hell, Theo. What the fuck is going on?"

"I don't know. Just—"

"Hold on. Yeah, I got that," she snaps, suddenly sounding much more sober than when she first woke up.

Unable to keep up my speed with the corner coming up, I slow a little, but the stupid prick either has a deathwish or knows these roads like the back of his hand, because he pulls out and drives right beside me.

I glance over quickly, but all the windows are blacked-out, giving me no chance at seeing who's driving the obviously modified truck, seeing as it's keeping up with my fucking Maserati.

"Theo, he's gonna—"

My heart thumps in my chest as I slam my foot on the brake in the hope that he's not about to do what Emmie is fearing, but I'm too slow, and the truck crashes into my side, sending me shooting off the road and into the darkness of the trees.

"Shit," Emmie screams.

I twist the wheel, desperately trying to get back some kind of control, but we're going too fast for me to have any kind of effect.

"Oh my God," she screams again when the bonnet dips down and the arse end of the car lifts.

My instincts take over and I reach for her, needing her to be safe, to protect her, but I lose my grip on reality after the first tumble and the world around me gets even darker.

2

THEO

"Emmie," I moan, my muscles bunching as her fingers trail down my abs. "Fuck, Hellcat. I need your mouth on me."

"Patience, boss," she purrs, looking up at me with the biggest, hungriest eyes I've ever seen.

My cock jerks, desperate to be set free and plunged into my wife's needy throat.

"Fuck yes," I bark when she wraps her fingers around my belt and slowly begins unbuckling it. "Killing me, babe."

Her lips damn near burn when she presses them to my stomach, peppering kisses around the indents of my six-pack, her tongue teasing along the lines and working its way lower.

Reaching out, I thread my fingers into her hair, trying not to push her down but knowing that I'm already failing.

"You're not in charge right now, Cirillo. Push me and you'll get nothing."

"Emmie," I groan as she pops the button.

She laughs as I lift my hips to help her drag my trousers over my arse.

"Needy little soldier, Theodore. Anyone would think you didn't fuck me in the shower already this morning," she growls, nipping at the skin right above my waistband before dipping her tongue beneath it.

"Can't get enough of you, Hellcat."

"Know the feeling, boss. Addicted to your cock."

Fucking finally, she tugs both my trousers and boxers down over my hips, freeing my dick.

Her eyes widen in delight like they do every time she sees me naked and ready for her.

Precum is already glistening on the tip, and just the thought of her licking it off makes my balls begin to draw up.

If she doesn't fucking hurry up, I'm gonna just blow like a kid looking at his first porno.

Slowly, she licks her lips before her teeth sink into the bottom one as she stares at me hungrily.

"Suck me, Hellcat. I want to watch you choking on my cock. I wanna see my cum covering your tongue."

A growl rumbles deep in her chest at my dirty words.

Her eyes flick up to mine for a beat before she leans forward so she's on her hands and knees, giving me a great view of her arse in that barely-there lingerie she wore especially for me.

Fuck, my wife is pure fucking fire.

Her full lips part and her tongue sneaks out, ready to taste me.

"Yes, babe. Yes. Yes."

I gasp, my eyes flying open as I sit forward.

My heart is racing and my cock is hard as

fucking steel, but she's not here. She's not on her knees before me in nothing but a scrap of black lace.

"Fuck," I breathe, scrubbing my hand down my face and over my almost week-old scruff.

But the second I take in my actual surroundings, everything comes crashing down around me.

"Emmie," I shout, turning to the passenger seat.

My heart drops into my feet.

It's empty.

"EMMIE," I scream, frantically looking around in the darkness for her.

"EMMIE!"

My fingers fumble with the seat belt, but I get it open after a few seconds. Sadly, the door isn't so successful.

"Fuck. Fuck."

My entire body screams in pain and I attempt to pull my legs from the footwell and crawl over the centre console to the passenger door.

If she's not in here, then it must open.

She'll just be out there calling for help.

Please. Fucking please let her just be calling for help.

I want to believe it, but the dread sitting heavy in my stomach stops me from allowing myself to do so.

That truck. It wasn't some random attack.

They wanted this.

Whoever they were set out to fucking run me off the road.

But why?

And where the fuck is Emmie?

"EMMIE," I boom again as I slam my hands against

the door, putting all my weight behind it to force it open. But it doesn't fucking move.

The window is shattered, same as the back one, and I figure it's how she's escaped.

"Fucking hell."

I manage to get out without slicing my body up too badly, but when I get to my feet, I quickly discover that my legs don't actually want to hold me up. I also find that I'm alone.

"EMMIE," I shout as loud as I can. But the only thing I hear is my voice echoing through the trees and a couple of birds flapping away in fright.

"FUUUUCK," I scream before collapsing in a heap on the ground.

I have no idea how long it takes for headlights to light up the side of the road where I'm sitting feeling utterly hopeless.

None of the calls I've made to Emmie have even connected, and there's no sign that she was ever here. She was, though. I know she was.

And knowing that she's gone cuts me like a knife right through my heart.

What I said to D was meant to be the truth. I was going to bring her home safe.

But how am I meant to do that now?

And how can I turn up on his doorstep without her?

Pushing to my feet, I lift my hand to the thumping pain that's radiating from my head from where I must have hit it against the wheel as we tumbled.

"Holy shit, man. What the fuck happened?" Alex

barks out, rushing over with his brows pinched as he looks from me to the mess that is now my car.

The sight of it makes my chest tighten as I think back to my reaction when Emmie crashed it all those weeks ago. That was nothing, looking at my poor baby now.

Wincing as my fingers hit the cut on my head, I pull my hand away and look back at Alex.

"Some cunt ran us off the road," I snap, fury burning through my veins.

I'm gonna find whoever those motherfuckers were, and I'm going to put a bullet through their heads for this, especially if my suspicions are correct and they've taken something that belongs to me.

"Us?" he asks, looking around for who I might be with.

"Emmie," I mutter, kicking the ground in frustration.

Alex's lips part before he looks around once more.

"Where is she? Don't tell me she ran away from you." There's an edge of amusement in his tone and it pisses me the fuck off.

Despite the pain raging within me, I have him backed up against a tree and my hand around his throat faster than he can compute.

My nostrils flare as I glare at him, my breaths racing over his face.

But as much as I crave seeing my own anger reflected back at me—a reason to fight, to expel some of this frustration, this fury that's bubbling up inside me faster than I can control...

It's just not there.

"Do it if you think it'll make you feel better," Alex

offers, keeping his hands hanging limply by his sides. "It's not going to bring her back though."

My fingers tighten around his throat as his words wash through me, but he still doesn't react.

"Fuck," I breathe, releasing him and pushing back, bending over and resting my palms on my knees.

Silence ripples around us as I suck in breath after breath, trying to work out what the hell happened tonight.

I didn't think things could get worse than me having to see another man's hands on my wife, but this... this... "FUCK," I scream, my voice echoing into the night.

"Why are you even out here, T?" Alex asks after another long silence.

Spinning to face him, I reach up and shove my hands into my hair, sending pain shooting down my spine.

If he notices me flinch, then he doesn't say anything.

"I thought you were going home to beat the shit out of a punching bag after being booted from training?"

I think back a few hours ago and it feels like it all happened a million years ago.

Fucking Emmie in that empty classroom, skipping out on the rest of the day until I turned up at training, knowing that Coach would rip me a new one. But it turned out that showing my face and then throwing my weight into anyone who came my way and breaking our goalkeeper's nose wasn't what he wanted either.

Motherfucker kicked me out of training and has benched me for the rest of the week. At least he's not taken Friday's game from me... yet.

"I did," I mutter. "Then I got a call to say that

Emmie was off her head at some Wolves party in Lovell and I went to get her."

He stares at me, waiting for me to continue.

"She was with fucking Niall Daxton," I spit out, my fists curling as the image of him grinding down on her as she came hits me once again.

Alex's brows rise, knowing me well enough to know that I wouldn't have let that ride.

I might never have confessed to him how I feel about Emmie after everything that's gone down between us, but I don't think he needs me to.

It might only be Seb who truly understands, but they all get it. Either that or they're just so used to my obsessions over the years that they just let me do my thing and hope I don't take it too far.

I fear that this might be bordering on that, though.

"I shot him," I finally confess.

"Jesus Christ, T. You shot a fucking Wolf?"

"I grazed her too." Guilt floods through my veins that I physically hurt her. That I made her bleed, and not with her begging me for it while she was dripping for my cock.

No. She was fucking wet for *him* instead.

The roar that rips from my throat and echoes through the solitude around us doesn't sound like it belongs to me. And if it weren't for the agonising pain in my chest that accompanies it, then I wouldn't believe it was.

"You were going to Mum?" Alex guesses.

"It wasn't bad, but fuck. She was fucking bleeding, and she was tripping on acid and fuck knows what else he'd given her."

He stares at me for a second, sympathy oozing

from him, but there's no way he can comprehend how I'm feeling right now. How much I despise myself for what I've done. Even if some of it was out of my control.

I'm meant to be looking after her.

I'm meant to protect her.

We may never have said our vows, but I'll be fucked if I'm not going to uphold them anyway.

She's my girl. My wife.

My world. My everything.

Even if she doesn't want it.

"Come on," he says, taking a step toward me and throwing his arm around my shoulder, making me wince in pain once more. "You need patching up. You've probably got a concussion too."

"I'm fine," I argue, although I know it's a lie. I hurt like fuck and I can't ignore the blood that's trickling down the side of my face and dripping from my chin.

"Sure you are, boss," he mutters, but I don't miss the mocking in his tone. "Did you warn Mum you were about to drop in on her?"

"No," I confess, falling into his passenger seat without any argument.

"We'll call her on the way. I think that's going to need stitches."

"Oh my God," Gianna gasps when she meets us out the front of her house.

Alex had explained what the problem was as we drove here, but I don't think she really appreciated the state I was in. And as the minutes have passed, I'm finding it harder and harder to deny that I am actually okay.

Every time I move my head, a pain shoots down my neck, and my back hurts, but neither of those is anything compared to my head that's still streaming with blood. My grey hoodie is wrecked, as is Alex's passenger seat—not that he's complained about it yet. Can't say I'd have kept my mouth shut if the situation were reversed, mind you.

"I'm fine," I insist, but from the hard stare I get in return, I know I'm not fooling anyone.

"Alex, go to the bathroom. I'm going to need my kit from under the basin. And grab him a fresh set of clothes."

"You got it," he says, saluting her before moving into the house.

Her lips part, and I can already predict what she's going to say. She's patched us all up enough times that I can read her thoughts.

"You should—"

"I'm not going to the hospital, G. It's just not happening. Patch me up, then I need to get back to business."

"Theodore," she warns in her warm, motherly tone that always makes me feel like a child once again. "Alex is right, the force of the hit that caused that has probably given you a concussion."

She gestures for me to go ahead of her and I step into her home.

Warmth surrounds me, and it's not until the huge clock on the hallway wall catches my eye that I realise just how late it is and how much she probably doesn't appreciate our interruption.

Looking back over my shoulder, I grimace in pain before taking in what she's wearing.

"I'm so sorry for waking you for this," I say, my eyes on her robe and slippers.

"Nonsense, Theo. You know I'm here whenever you boys need me. Even if you'd be better off in the hospital," she mutters.

I take a seat on the sofa and she lowers herself down beside me, her gentle, warm fingers pressing against my head as Alex returns with her box of tricks and a bottle of vodka that he's swiped from her liquor cabinet.

"This is going to need stitches," she murmurs, more to herself than me.

"So stitch it. I can handle it."

Reaching out, I gesture for the bottle in Alex's hand, and after he's uncapped it, he takes a swig himself and passes it over.

"Make it hurt, G. I deserve it."

"I highly doubt that, Theodore. I've never met a sweeter boy in my life."

She winks at me and I bark a laugh, regretting it instantly when pain shoots down my spine.

It doesn't take long until my laughter is forgotten, and I'm soon gritting my teeth as she stitches me back together.

I stare across the room, keeping my mind on Emmie, on better times with her as I try to distract myself.

Gianna is right. I should probably be at the hospital and with a local anaesthetic for this, but fuck that. I'll take the pain if it means I'm able to get back out there and find my girl.

"We'll find her," Alex says firmly, obviously reading my mind.

I stare at him, the same question running around my head like it has since I woke up in my car.

Who wants her so badly that they'd go to that effort to get her?

3

EMMIE

A violent shiver rips down my spine and brings me to.

My head spins and my stomach turns over as memories from the day before slam into me.

Punching that stupid skank and watching with joy as her nose damn near exploded. Mr. Davenport's anger. My suspension. Letting Theo fuck me over the desk in one of the classrooms. But that image soon morphs to one with me and Dax on the sofa in the Wolves den.

The acid.

Fuck.

My eyes squeeze together tightly as I remember Theo standing in the doorway with a gun trained on me. The shot firing.

The pain.

"Shit," I hiss, sitting bolt upright, my eyes flying open. But nothing happens. No light floods my eyes, and I can't move my hands. "What the—"

"Ah, good. You're back with us at last, Princess," a deep voice rumbles from a distance.

My spine straightens and my skin prickles with goosebumps as I focus on the voice, desperately trying to place it.

"W-wha—" I swallow, trying to wet my dry mouth, but it does nothing. Sucking in a calming breath, I try again. "What do you want?" I snap, putting as much venom into my voice as possible.

A low, haunting chuckle comes from the guy who sounds a little closer now.

"Now there's the million-dollar question right there, Emmie Cirillo."

Hearing that name, acknowledging that whoever this fuck is knows about my life right now, sends a shock wave straight through me.

I shift, every muscle in my body aching, but I quickly discover that I'm not going anywhere. My hands are bound behind my back.

I wiggle my nose and blink my eyes in the hope of dislodging whatever is around my face, but it's pointless.

"You're a disappointment, Emmie. A fucking embarrassment, and a massive disappointment."

"Fuck you," I spit out, not giving a single fuck about who he is or his opinions about me.

He's silent for a moment before a familiar scratch of him rubbing a rough jawline fills the room.

"Unlike your husband, I'm not really into school girls."

My fingers curl, my nails digging into my palms behind my back, and my teeth grind in frustration as I try to bite back my words about Theo.

I don't want to show this arsehole that I care.

Hell. I *don't* care.

"What do you want?" I hiss, hoping that if I can keep him talking then I might be able to get a sense of who he is or what he wants.

I mean, I have some ideas. But quite frankly, I'm attached to more bad men than I can count.

This could be any of them.

I still as a thought of this being Theo hits me.

He wouldn't, would he?

But then I remember his face when I walked away from that classroom, the fury in his features as he trained that gun on me in the Wolves den.

It could be.

He's got enough minions who idolise the ground he walks on that he'd be more than able to organise this to punish me, to prove who's really running this show.

My heart aches with the possibility, refusing to believe that he could have something to do with this.

But I was in his car. It would have been easy to…

No.

I slam that line of thought down. He would never have run his car off the road like that to have me abducted. He'd have just dragged me here and probably taken great delight in tying me up and staring me dead in the eyes as he did it. Twisted fuck.

I blow out a breath. Even with ruling him out—loosely—I've still got a list of possible culprits.

"What do you want?" I ask, my voice losing its heat from earlier. I'm not sure snapping at him will get me anywhere, so I'm not going to waste the energy.

His response is a laugh that I'm sure the devil himself would be proud of.

"Right now, Princess? Nothing. I sincerely hope you enjoy your stay."

Heavy footsteps fill the room before a door slams closed, the loud bang reverberating through me.

"ARGH," I scream, my voice echoing off the walls around me as I attempt to vent my frustrations.

I scream until I've got nothing left. My body slumps down on the cold, solid floor.

Silent tears slip from my eyes, soaking the blindfold that's wrapped around my face and cutting off my sight before they finally slide down my cheeks, dripping onto the floor beneath me as my body begins to tremble with the cold.

My last thought before I slip into an uncomfortable and fitful sleep is of Dad.

Is he still waiting for me to come home like I promised?

If I actually manage to get out of this alive, he's going to fucking kill me himself.

A s I come to again, the familiar feeling that I'm being watched races down my spine.

Silently, I groan, not wanting to open my eyes only to find that they're still covered and that my wrists are still bound.

Snap.

My eyes fly open the second the sound hits my ears. A moment later, my arms move to allow me to pull them from behind my back.

They hurt like fuck after being tethered for so long,

and I wince as I wrap them around the front of my body.

Whoever just cut me free shuffles around the front of me and fingers brush my ear, making me jolt away from their touch.

"I can leave it on if you wish," he mutters, his voice so deep it sends a violent bolt of fear shooting through me.

Lifting my own hand, I drag the fabric from my face and immediately search him out in the dark room.

When my eyes land on the balaclava he's wearing, I'm barely able to hold in my frustrated laugh.

"Are you actually serious?" I hiss. "You're so scared of me that you feel the need to hide your face?"

"I'm not scared of you, Princess," he snaps, clearly unimpressed with my comment.

"That could be a mistake. But it also means that you're either scared of my father or my husband. Or both, maybe."

He comes to a stop in front of the open doorway, the light from whatever is outside this room pouring in behind him as he shakes his head, lifting his hand and rubbing at the back of his neck. The move causes his shirt to lift, and I get a very quick glance at the inked patch of skin it reveals.

"I'm scared of no one, Princess."

"Right. Of course not," I mutter. "That's why you feel the need to abduct me and hide me here."

He drops down on his haunches in front of me and reaches out, taking a handful of my hair before I get the chance to move. Ripping my head back and sending a shooting pain down my already sore neck, he stares right into my eyes.

"Watch your mouth, brat. It's going to get you in even more trouble than you're already in."

"Nothing new there," I quip before wincing when his grip on me tightens. I can only see his eyes and lips, but both of them are hard, his anger radiating from him. "What did I ever do to you?" I ask, forcing some lightness into my tone.

"Nothing personal, Princess."

"As I thought. You're just following orders, huh? And what is it you've been told to do? Come in here and mess me up a bit? Scare me? Hurt me? What's the endgame here? You going to send me back to Daddy broken and bruised to prove a point? Are you working for my grandfather? Or maybe it's my husband and my father-in-law you want. If that's the case, I should probably tell you that Theo's not going to be interested in what you do to me. He hates me."

He chuckles as if he doesn't believe me. Whatever. This arsehole can think what he wants.

I'm still not even convinced that Theo isn't behind all of this.

My heart aches as my stomach clenches with hunger.

I have no idea what time it is, how long I've been here, or when the last time I ate or even drank was.

"I need to pee," I tell the guy.

A smirk pulls at his lips as he releases me, roughly throwing me back against the wall. My shoulder collides with the unforgiving concrete but I refuse to react, to show him in any way that he's hurting me.

"Look around, Princess. Your castle has everything you could need. And if you're missing anything," he grits out, taking my chin in a punishing grip, "don't bother calling. We won't come."

When he releases me this time, I fly toward the floor, only just managing to catch myself before my cheek collides with the dirty, grey concrete.

"Arsehole," I mutter as he marches away before swinging the door closed and leaving me almost in complete darkness once more.

A little light filters in through the cracks in the door, and after a few minutes my eyes adjust enough to be able to make out a toilet in the corner—and more importantly, a tray beside the door. I can't see what's on the plate—it looks like a pile of mush—but there's a glass of water and I swallow, my raw throat desperate for it.

Ignoring my need to pee, I crawl over to the glass and down the lukewarm water in record time before staring down at the glass, wishing there was more.

My eyes flick to the plate which I now know holds dry, probably old bread, and my stomach clenches once more.

I fucking knew it was too good to be true when Dad said everything was going to be okay.

I knew things wouldn't just settle down and allow me to go back to a normal life. I'm amazed he believed it as well.

Or maybe he didn't and he knew this was going to happen.

Maybe he's right outside this building, waiting to storm in to get me back.

Maybe he and Cruz planned this. Theo too.

Falling back against the wall, I slam those thoughts down. There's no point trying to come up with some stupid idea that they're right around the corner and planning my elaborate escape.

My life might feel like a fucking movie at times. It would be easy to get swept away with the excitement of it all. But the reality is that Theo could be dead at his steering wheel and no one else knows that anything is even adrift. That I've been taken.

Images of how Theo looked the last time I saw him flicker through my mind, and a lump of emotion claws its way up my throat. He was slumped over the steering wheel, blood trickling down the side of his face, his arms hanging limply at his sides.

A sob erupts as I think about the possibility of him still being behind the wheel of his broken and battered baby, nose-down in a ditch.

Archer and Dax certainly won't be looking for me after what happened in the den. Although they might happily put a hit out on Theo after he shot Dax.

No one, not even a Cirillo, puts a bullet through a Wolf and gets away with it.

Another pained sob rips from my throat and my eyes close as exhaustion washes through me.

I knew that fucking smiley was a bad idea.

I just never could have imagined that I'd end up here.

4
———

THEO

I'm staring at the ceiling when the door to the room I was forced to stay in last night swings open, causing the space to illuminate around me.

"How are you feeling?" Alex asks, inviting himself inside.

I didn't want to stay here. I wanted to get back out there and do something to find her, to help her, to rescue her. But after the vodka, and then the painkillers Gianna almost forced down my throat once she was happy I didn't have a concussion, I was in no fit state to even leave the house, let alone drive or fight for my girl.

In all honesty, the painkillers have worn off and I'm in fucking agony, but that's not going to stop me from doing what I need to do today.

Flipping the covers off me, I sit up.

"Never been better," I hiss as the room spins around me.

Schooling my reaction so he can't see how hard every fucking movement is, I turn my back on him and start pulling on my clothes from last night.

"Here," he says before there's a dull thud on the bed behind me. "I brought you more clean ones."

"Thanks," I mutter, spinning back around and pulling them on instead.

He stands and watches me with his brows pulled, but he thankfully holds back the million and one questions that I know are on the tip of his tongue.

"I need coffee, then we're leaving. I need to find her."

He trails behind me as I make my way to the kitchen.

Thankfully, Gianna is already at the coffee machine and must have predicted what I was about to do when Alex came to get me, because she's got two travel mugs ready to go.

"How are you feeling?"

"Fantastic," I say, forcing a fake smile on my lips. "Thank you for last night."

She gives me a sad smile before walking over and inspecting her handiwork.

"It shouldn't leave too much of a scar," she says softly.

"I don't care about that."

"You should," Alex pipes up. "You're already ugly enough."

I glare at him across the kitchen but hold my tongue as he grins at me like a fucking idiot.

"You ready to go?" I ask once his mum has finished faffing with me.

"Yep, let's go and find your girl."

I'm almost out of the kitchen with my mug before he's even finished speaking.

"Move your arse or I'm going without you," I shoot

over my shoulder, swiping his car keys from the dresser by the front door.

"You're not driving my car, prick," he shouts before saying goodbye to his mum.

"Whatever."

Knowing he's right, and not stupid enough to risk another fucking car accident, I unlock it and drop into the passenger seat to wait for him.

"Where we going then, bro?"

I let out a heavy sigh, knowing that there's only one place we can go first.

I fucking promised her dad I'd get her home safe, and as much as I might not want to admit to the scary bastard that I've lost his daughter, I know I can't put it off.

After all, I'm pretty sure I'm going to need his fucking help.

Damn it.

"Her house."

Alex glances over at me as he backs off the drive.

"You serious?"

"You got any other suggestions?"

His lips part as if he has, but then he quickly closes them once more.

"He's gonna fucking kill you, man."

I shrug, resting my head back and letting my eyes close as he shoots down the street and back in the direction of the city.

My phone burns a hole in my pocket, but I leave it where it is for now. Calling in the troops is inevitable, but I need to talk to Dawson first.

If my suspicions are correct about who ran us off

the road last night, then he might have more intel than I do.

If he doesn't, then I guess we'll both go in all guns blazing to get our girl back.

Assuming he doesn't put a bullet through my head first, of course.

M y heart pounds so hard as I come to a stop in front of Dawson's front door that it feels like it's relocated all around my body. But I refuse to let my concern show on my face. That motherfucker is as blank and fierce as it always is.

"Any last words?" Alex helpfully asks from behind me a beat before I press my finger on the bell.

"Fuck off, wanker."

"Perfect. I don't even need to write that one down."

Heavy footsteps thump my way a few seconds before the door is unlocked and pulled open.

I don't say anything as Dawson glares at me. His lips part, ready to say something, but he doesn't seem to be able to find the words as he looks over my shoulder and only finds Alex waiting in the wings.

"I'm sorry, D. I didn't—"

He takes a step back and opens the door wider.

"You should probably come in."

I glance back at Alex. He hesitates as I take a step forward.

"Come on," I say. "We're gonna need all the brainpower we can get."

As I walk down Dawson's hallway, my eyes find Piper at the other end dressed for school. It's the first time I realise that I have no idea what the time actually is.

"Theo, are you okay?" she asks the second she sees me, her brow wrinkling in concern.

"I'll be better once we fix this shit," I tell her, following Emmie's dad into his living room.

He gestures for me to sit but he doesn't join me. Instead, he just paces back and forth on the other side of the coffee table.

"What's going on?" Piper asks, looking between the three of us.

"Someone ran me off the road and—"

"You were meant to bring her home to me," D barks out, his voice low and deadly as he takes a step toward me, his fists curled tightly at his sides.

"I know. I was. We just needed to stop to—"

"To what? What could possibly be more important than bringing her home, Cirillo?"

I blow out a long breath and drop my head into my hands, pushing my fingers into my hair and pulling until I realise my massive fucking mistake when the pain from my wound makes my eyes fucking water.

"I found her in the Wolves den in Lovell."

He glares at me before looking up at the ceiling as if he's praying for strength.

"She'd been taking acid. She was off her face."

Slowly, Dawson lowers his head. His face is a mask of fury and he directs it right at me.

"Because of you," he spits out. "She was off her face, trying to forget, because of you."

I swallow roughly, more than aware that his words are true.

"What happened at school yesterday, Cirillo? Why

was she suspended? Why did she run in the first place?"

"I know, D. I fucking know," I bark out, pushing from the sofa so I'm on equal footing with him. "But I had nothing to do with this. I was doing the right thing. I was taking her to get stitched up, and then I was bringing her home to you."

"Stitched up?" he gasps, the blood draining from his face.

"It was just a graze. Unlike the motherfucker who had his hands on her," I mutter.

His lips part, mimicking a goldfish, but he must decide not to comment on that and instead focuses on the issue at hand.

"Okay, so..." He scrubs his hands over his head before focusing back on me again. "You were run off the road?"

"Yeah. It was a black SUV. Blacked-out windows. I had no clue who was driving. When I finally lost control, we came off the road. Flipped a few times, I think." I shake my head, desperately trying to remember what happened between coming off the road and waking up with her gone. "I got knocked out." I point to my head. "When I came to, she was gone. No fucking sign of her."

"Her phone?"

"Still in the car in her bag. Dead."

"Fuck," Dawson hisses, pressing the heels of his hands into his eyes.

Piper rushes over to him.

"We'll find her, Dawson. We will."

She sounds so confident, I almost believe her.

When he finally lowers his arms, his face is full of anger and determination.

He looks like the brutal Reaper he no longer seems to have a desire to be.

But much like me, it runs through his veins, and I already know that he'll raise hell to get her back.

"I'm going to kill any motherfucker involved in this."

"You'll need to beat me there then."

His eyes hold mine, allowing me to see just how much he loathes me for being a part of his daughter's life. For being her husband.

"I know I fucked up, D. I fucking know. But I want her safe just as much as you do."

He's silent for a beat as if he's trying to hear the lies within my statement. He won't find them. I've never been more fucking honest in my entire life.

Emmie is mine. It doesn't matter whether she wants me or not. She's fucking mine, and I'll do whatever it takes to protect her.

"This has got my father's fucking name all over it," he growls, pulling his phone from his pocket and jabbing at the screen hard enough to crack the thing.

"You think it was Ram?" I ask.

"Don't you?" he spits out.

Whoever he calls answers almost immediately. "Get Link. I need you both here. Now. Emmie's gone."

A deep voice rumbles down the line, but Dawson quickly cuts it off.

"Just get here. We're getting her back. Today."

He ends the call and lowers his phone.

"Are you really serious about her?" Dawson asks me, his eyes holding mine steady.

"I am," I state, my voice not wavering at all.

"Good. Call your boys. We're gonna need all the help we can get."

"And the girls?" Alex adds smugly. "You know Stella isn't being left out of this."

"Call fucking Donald Duck if you think it'll help. Jesus," D mutters, running his fingers through his hair once more and storming from the room.

A crash sounds out somewhere deeper in the house, and Piper quickly rushes after him.

"Surely Ram hasn't abducted his own granddaughter," Alex mutters, dropping his arse down on the sofa and resting his foot up on the coffee table as if we've just turned up here to hang out.

"You'd like to think not. But you'd also think he wouldn't sign her over to an arsehole like me, and yet here we are."

"Ah, something we agree on."

I stare at him with a blank expression on my face.

"Why did I call you?" I mutter, reaching for my phone to get the others here.

I have no idea if they know something is wrong or if they just think we're skiving school. I soon get my answers when I discover I've got a stream of missed calls and messages from all of them.

Even fucking Daemon has called, and that never fucking happens.

"Because I'm your favourite and you knew I'd rescue your arse last night."

"Whatever. I needed your mother, not you," I scoff, hitting call on Seb's number and lifting it to my ear.

"Lies and you know it."

"Bro, get everyone to Emmie's dad's place," I bark the second the call connects.

"What's going on? Is she okay?"

"I don't know. Just get here, okay? And come ready."

"You got it, boss. I'm walking out of class right now." The moment he stops talking, I can tell he's telling the truth because a feminine voice drifts down the line. "Am I boring you, Mr. Papatonis?"

I don't hang around long enough to hear his response. Instead, I hang up and call Daemon back, knowing that he probably isn't at Knight's Ridge. And I find I'm right when he groggily answers the phone only a few rings later.

"Duty calls, man. Get your arse out of bed. Emmie's gone."

"Gone where?" he asks, clearly still half a-fucking-sleep.

"If I fucking knew that, I wouldn't be calling you to help us find her, would I? Come to her place."

"Fuck, man. I'll be there. Give me ten."

"Whatever," I mutter, hanging up on him as Piper rejoins us, concern for her stepdaughter written all over her face.

"We'll find her," she says to me. "Dawson won't stop until she's safe."

I nod at her, knowing full well that I'll be standing right by his side until we have her back where she belongs.

She makes us both a coffee while we wait for the others to get here, but despite thinking caffeine was exactly what I needed this morning, my mug goes untouched on the coffee table, getting cold just like the travel mug that's still sitting in Alex's car.

One sip and I knew my stomach wouldn't be able to take it.

The second the bell rings once more, I jump to my feet, racing out to the hallway as Dawson storms toward it.

"What's going—" Cruz's words falter when his eyes find mine in the living room door. "On? Why is Cirillo in your house?"

"Because Emmie got fucking abducted from right under his fucking nose."

I don't get a chance to blink before the motherfucker is on me.

His forearm presses against my throat, my back against the opposite wall as he glares down at me.

"What the fuck have you done to my niece, you stupid little prick?" he growls, his eyes darkening as I'm sure he imagines a million and one ways he could kill me with his bare hands.

My chest heaves as I fight to drag in the air I need while he squashes my windpipe.

"Leave it, Cruz. If it was Cirillo's fault, D would have put a bullet through him by now," Link states.

"I swear to fucking God, kid. If anyone so much as hurts a hair on her head—" He releases me just in time for me to finish that sentence for him.

"I'll fucking kill them if anyone has laid a fucking finger on my wife."

Dawson growls behind his brother as I say that final word.

Cruz's hold on me finally drops.

"I know you think it's all a joke. I know it looks like

a joke. But while our marriage might have started as a farce, what I feel for her isn't." The words fall from me far easier than I ever thought they would have.

"I've fucked up. I've hurt her. I've let her get away, even if it was with you." I look between Dawson and Cruz, knowing that they're the reason I lost her in the first place. "But I care just as much as you do. I need her safe just as much as you do."

"Doubtful, kid, but I appreciate your effort." Cruz looks me up and down once more, judging me as I stand here in a pair of sweats and a hoodie.

It's not exactly the uniform I prefer to work in, but I'm not wasting fucking time going home to pull on my armour.

"What happened?" he asks, nodding to my head.

"We were run off the road. I passed out. When I came to, she was gone, along with the car that forced us into the ditch," I say, giving him the CliffsNotes.

"Who was it?"

"If we fucking knew that, we wouldn't be standing here discussing it," I snap.

He takes a step toward me once more.

"Don't be a fucking smart-arse, kid. You might think you're all high and mighty, being daddy's little prince. But here, you're the bottom of the fucking ladder, even more so seeing as all of this is your fault. We wouldn't be—"

"Leave it, bro," D snaps. "Fighting with a kid isn't going to get us anywhere. You know as well as I do that Dad is all over this. For once, it's not actually Theo's fault."

A smug smile tugs at my lips as I glare back at Cruz.

"So... shall we figure out how to deal with your

daddy then?" His brows narrow at the sarcasm in my voice.

"Link, what have you got?" D asks, walking back into the living room and leaving the two of us taunting each other into a fight.

"It's still loading."

It takes a few seconds for his words to hit me, but when they do, I'm ducking around Cruz's big-arse body in the hope that my suspicions are right.

5
___

EMMIE

My body trembles with the cold, and I curl up in a ball to try to stave it off. It doesn't work, though.

Nothing works.

The cruel guy in the mask has never returned, and I'm not sure whether I'm relieved about that or not.

While he was here, he left the door open. After trying it more than once recently, I know it's locked well enough, and I have no chance of escaping unless it's through that door.

I glance over at it, willing it to magically open, to give me a small miracle.

But unsurprisingly, nothing happens.

Pushing my aching body up so I'm sitting, I wrap my arms around my knees as my stomach grumbles while the plate of bread taunts me from the tray he left.

I'm debating whether I'm going to have to just eat it when the click of the lock disengaging startles me.

Light streams into the room before a different guy

storms in, his face also covered. But the second he talks, familiarity washes through me.

"Let's go," he barks out, reaching out and lifting me to my feet.

But despite the fact that he clearly wants me to leave the room, my feet remain firmly in place on the floor.

He's not going to let me escape, so what horror is waiting for me outside that room?

"Emmie," he sighs. His voice softens despite his grip on my arm remaining unrelenting. "I'm not going to hurt you."

"Then why am I here?"

He slams his lips shut as his eyes bore into mine.

"What do you want from me?" I demand, slamming my foot down like a petulant child—not that I think it's going to get me anywhere.

"Come on." His other hand wraps around the nape of my neck and he pushes me forward, out of the room and into the blinding light of a hallway.

"Where are we?" I ask as he continues pushing me.

"You ask a lot of questions," he mutters.

"Wouldn't you if you were being manhandled by some masked cunt?" I spit out—much to his irritation, if the growl that rumbles from him is anything to go by.

"Careful, Princess. I could quite easily lock you back in that room and leave you to the wrath of the others."

My lips part to bite back again, but I quickly consider my options and close them once more. If he's actually intending on looking after me, then I should probably keep my frustrations over this situation bottled up for now. At least until that dick from earlier reappears.

"Where's the guy from before?" I ask as we approach a closed door.

"Called away. I got left to look after our new little pet."

He brings me to a stop at the door and releases his hold, allowing me to turn around.

"Give me something," I plead, holding his eyes, desperately trying to figure out who he is.

I know him. I fucking know I do.

But who?

Is he a Reaper? A Wolf? Cirillo?

Reaching out, he pushes the door open and nods into the room, allowing my eyes to drop to the ink on his neck. It looks to be the tail end of a snake that finishes behind his ear. It's pretty unique, but I still can't place him.

"We're not going to hurt you, Emmie. We just need... we need you on side."

"And locking me in a dark room is the way to do that?" I hiss.

"I'm not the one making the rules, Princess. Take your time, but don't try anything stupid. The window is locked, the glass is toughened. There's no point even trying. And if I think you are, I won't hesitate to drag you straight out and throw you back into that room."

I hold his eyes for three seconds, but he never backs down.

"Fine," I hiss, stepping into the room, although I can't deny that the clean, fully equipped bathroom before me isn't a welcome sight.

Glancing back at the guy, I let a soft, appreciative smile pull at the corners of my lips.

"Thank you."

"Be good, Princess. I'll be waiting."

With that warning hanging in the air, he closes the door and leaves me alone once more.

Only this time, I'm not in a dark, dank room.

Wasting no time, I race forward and turn the shower on as hot as it'll go before stripping out of my dirty, blood-coated school uniform.

It's not until I'm naked that I realise there's something else missing.

Lifting my hand, I press my palm against my chest where my necklace—my ring—should be.

"No," I sob, grief washing through me as I realise that I've lost a part of what Theo and I shared, despite the fact I mostly want to forget it ever existed. That ring symbolised more to me than our sham marriage. It reminded me of the couple of good times we had. Because there were a few.

A tear slips down over my cheek as I mourn my loss. Maybe it's how it should have always been. I should have taken it off the second Cruz escorted me out of that hotel and forgotten anything between us ever existed.

Maybe whoever these arseholes are, are doing me a favour.

My freezing skin burns and tingles the second I stand under the torrent of hot water. The wound in my shoulder hurts like a bitch, but I use the pain to ground me, to keep me fucking sane.

I have no idea where I am, who's holding me here, or why, but as I tip my face up to the stream, I forget all about it as the dirt, grime, and stupid decisions from the past however many hours washes down the drain.

Despite telling me that I could take my time, long before I'm ready to get out and return to the dark cell they seem to have decided is my room, there's a loud knock at the door.

"Emmie, you still in there?"

"No," I call back with a smirk.

"Time's up, Princess. I need to get you back to your room." There's a little panic in his voice that makes me smirk.

"Are you breaking the rules right now?" I call back once I've turned the water off.

"Unless you want us both staring down the barrel of a gun, you'll hurry your arse up."

"Jeez, keep your hair on."

"You don't even know if I've got any," he shoots back.

"Yeah, fair point," I mutter to myself, grabbing a towel that's hanging on a rail and drying myself off.

"You decent?" he shouts again before the handle twists down and a pile of clothes pushes through the gap.

"No, but that doesn't seem to be stopping you."

"I don't want to die today just as much as you don't, Princess. Now get dressed."

I do as I'm told, pulling on the sweats and hoodie. I was expecting them to be men's and massive on me, but it seems whoever he is actually went to the effort of finding me women's clothes.

The second he walks me back to the room I seem to be calling home, I regret my decision to get my hair wet, because the chill quickly surrounds me and a shiver runs down my spine.

"You won't be here long," he says but quickly slams the door closed before I get to ask what exactly he means by that, or how he could even know.

"Fuck's sake," I scream into the silence, although my mood quickly picks back up when I find a fresh tray of actual food waiting for me.

Dropping to my knees, I lift the sausage roll to my mouth and eat it as if it's the last thing I might ever taste.

By the time shouting from outside my door hits my ears, I'm resting back against the wall once more with my belly full, and the dull throb that's been assaulting my temples since I woke is starting to lessen.

Sitting forward, I try to make out what they're arguing about but it's too muffled.

Suddenly, footsteps thunder my way and the door flies open.

I gasp in shock, scrambling to my feet as the person standing before me glares at me.

"What do you want?" I snap, forcing as much strength into my tone as I can muster. I refuse to look weak. I refuse to cower when it's what most people do when being threatened with his wrath.

Luis Wolfe.

Lovell's most dangerous psychopath.

From some of the stories I've heard over the years—hell, even some of the things I've witnessed—it's safe to say that his psychotic nature even gives Theo a run for his money.

His cold, dead eyes assess me as I stand there with my head held high.

"What. Do. You. Want?" I seethe, my chest heaving and my fists curling at my sides.

There's movement behind him, but I don't move my eyes from his.

After all, I don't really give a fuck about his minions.

"Where's your mother?" His deep voice rumbles through the air as disbelief washes through me.

His brows lift when my only reaction is to start laughing.

"Are you fucking kidding?" I ask between my laughter. "All of this because you want my mother? Jesus, Luis. I really thought you had more important things to deal with."

"I do, but she's one of them. She has something I need."

I raise a brow in question.

"You're so fucking naïve, Ramsey," he spits out, looking me up and down.

"Is that right? And I think you'll find it's actually Ramsey-Cirillo. Do you realise the amount of shit you've landed yourself in with this stunt?"

His expression doesn't falter, but something flickers in his eyes.

If it were anyone else staring back at me, I'd say it was probably fear. No man alive can want the wrath of not only the Reapers but the Cirillo Family on them. But I'm pretty sure all I see staring back at me is excitement.

"I can't say that you don't have it coming. How you've lasted this long is beyond me."

"You have no idea what you're talking about, little girl."

"Do I not?" Folding my arms across my chest, I take a step toward him. "My mother might be weak, easily manipulated, willing to do your bidding. But make no mistake. I am not my mother, and I don't care who you are. I will not bend to your wishes.

"Right now, my mother is safe. Far, far away from scumbags like you," I spit out, looking him up and down as if he's nothing more than a piece of shit on my shoe.

He moves faster than I give him credit for, his fingers wrapping around my throat a beat before my back slams against the cold wall of my cell.

"Watch your fucking mouth, little girl," he spits in my face, his nose only a hair's width from mine.

I sneer at him, baring my teeth.

He might make others piss themselves with nothing more than a look. But I'm not everyone else.

I've had plenty of experience dancing with the devil, and Luis is just another power-hungry, big-headed prick who needs taking down a few pegs. Or sending directly to hell. Either works.

"Fuck you, Wolfe. I don't answer to you." My lip curls in disgust as his fingers tighten. He compresses my windpipe but even still, I hold his eyes, daring him to end it all right here.

I'd let it happen. My only regret would be not being able to witness the fallout when Dad and Cruz got their hands on him. Maybe even Theo too, if he doesn't totally hate me after the other night.

"Where. Is. Your. Mother?"

"Fuck. You," I force out.

A bang somewhere in the distance cuts off whatever his response was going to be.

"Boss, we need to move," someone shouts from outside the room. "Now."

Luis's eyes continue to hold mine despite the warning from one of his minions and yet another bang, which I'm starting to think is gunfire.

An inferno ignites in my belly and a smile curls at my lips.

"Go on, Wolfe. Run along back to your pack and let the big boys take over," I taunt, assuming what's about to happen.

"Wolfe," someone barks out, his voice a little more insistent this time.

He leans in, letting his whisky-laced breath wash over my face and making my stomach turn over.

"I will find her, and I will get what I want."

"I can't wait to see you try. I hope you've got your ducks in a row, Luis, because something tells me you're going to lose a few otherwise. And ones you care about." Using Archer as a threat when he's been nothing but a good friend and a half-decent lay over the years makes my chest ache, but desperate times and all that. Luis won't lose a second of sleep threatening people I care about, so why should I?

"Luis," someone barks as a loud bang makes the floor beneath me vibrate.

"Coming."

With one last threatening look in my direction, he bolts and disappears from the room, quickly followed by his little minions.

Luis Wolfe, you fucking dumb cunt.
You're going to die for this stunt.

6
_____

THEO

Seb and I drag the guy who was meant to be securing this place inside and release him with a thud, not bothering to look back at him as he continues to bleed out on the floor.

I'd have hoped that Luis would have had better guard dogs than this, but clearly, his little gang is about as weak as I always suspected it to be.

"She's not here," D booms from somewhere deeper in the house, making my heart drop.

After all the shit I got about chipping her in order to keep her safe, it seems that maybe I wasn't onto such a bad thing. Because no sooner had she run away from me and escaped my clutches, her dad and uncle took matters into their own hands to ensure her safety with things so up in the air with her mum and Ram.

But as much as it pisses me off, fuck am I glad they did.

"She has to be. It's where the tracker said she was," Link calls back. "Keep looking."

Marching down the hallway, I emerge in the

kitchen. Something immediately catches my eye in a bowl in the middle of the table.

"She's not here," I confirm, walking toward it and scooping the piece of jewellery up in my hand.

I had no idea she was wearing it, and damn if it didn't give me a shred of hope to cling to when Dawson explained what he, Cruz, and Link had done when they realised just how attached to it she was. She might not have been wearing it on her finger, but she hadn't immediately discarded it like I thought she might.

Letting Cruz, Seb, and Alex see what I've found, I slump down into one of the chairs.

"They're close by. There has to be something else here. They wouldn't be attempting to guard a fucking piece of jewellery, as nice as it is," Cruz adds when he catches a glimpse of the expression on my face.

"Cost more than you'll likely see in a lifetime," I mutter, much to his irritation.

"Shut the fuck up, both of you," Dawson snaps. "Link, get up a satellite view of this place. There has to be outbuildings. She's here somewhere. I know she is."

Curling my fingers around her ring, I send up a silent prayer to any deity who might be willing to listen that she's okay. Because if she's not then...

I blow out a long breath as the harsh reality of the situation slams into me.

If they've hurt her—really hurt her, no matter what the reason for it—it's all my fault.

I'm the one who was fucking about, playing games, keeping secrets, refusing to admit just how I felt about her.

All this time I should have been protecting her, and yet all I've done is push her toward danger. Forced her to run from and then run into a den full of fucking wolves.

My fists curl. Her ring digs into my skin as I think about Archer Wolfe and his phone call to tell me where my wife was.

Was the whole thing a setup?

Did they want her, but also want to hurt me too?

Is that why they forced that fucking acid on her?

I might not know Emmie as well as I probably should, but I know for a fact she'd never take any drugs, weed aside. I've heard the way she talks about her childhood, about her mum's addiction.

She wouldn't.

Even after everything I'd done.

Surely, she wouldn't.

Guilt continues to tug at me as Link lowers his tablet to the table.

We all wait in silence with our backs to the door as we stare at the screen, trusting Xander, Gunner, Toby, and Nico to secure the building and stop us getting ambushed while we try to figure this shit out.

"There." Link points to a dark patch in the trees.

"Let's go," D barks out, heading toward the front door before the image has even cleared enough to be able to take out a building. It could be anything.

Link hesitates for three seconds, his eyes locked on the screen, but the second he agrees, he slams it closed and marches right out behind Dawson, Cruz falling into step beside him, quickly followed by us.

"Get ready, boys," Cruz says as we head into the trees, ready to make our way to this building hopefully unnoticed. "We're about to put a dent in the Wolves' pack."

Pulling out the gun Cruz ensured we all had before we arrived from my waistband, I let my fingers flex around the handle, wishing it was mine.

It doesn't feel right, and I need everything to be fucking perfect right now if I stand any chance of fixing all this shit.

Blowing out a long breath, I push all my concerns aside.

I've been shooting with damn near perfect precision since I was a kid. Who gives a fuck whose gun it is? Who I'm protecting with it is more important.

Trust your instincts, Theodore.

Trust your training.

Dad's words ring out loud and clear in my head.

Moving faster, I step up beside Dawson and Cruz as a building begins to appear through the trees in the distance.

"They probably already know we're coming."

"So we're either expecting heavy fire, or they've already run like pussies," I suggest.

"I'd put money on the latter," Cruz mutters. "Wolfe loves his pretty face too much to risk getting it shot at."

"As long as they've not taken her with them," D adds.

"We'll get her, bro. Don't sweat it," Cruz says lightly, much to Dawson's irritation.

"Can you at least try to take this more seriously? We've not just lost her favourite teddy, this is my fucking daughter we're talking about."

"Take it seriously? Are you fucking shitting me, man? That girl means as much to me as she does to you. We're getting her back in one piece."

We fall silent as we come to a stop, still hidden by the trees and thick undergrowth.

The others step up behind us, but my eyes don't waver from the building, desperate to see some movement. To see her.

"Ready?" Dawson barks out.

"Let's go."

Both D and Cruz step forward, their bodies in perfect sync despite not having worked together in this capacity in years, maybe even ever, until recently.

I think back briefly to the day they turned up at my flat both covered in blood and wonder if they were as seamless with whoever they beat the shit out of that day.

Probably.

Twigs snap and old leaves rustle as we all emerge from the trees and spread out, ready to cover the entire building in the hope of stopping anyone from leaving.

Movement in one of the windows catches my eye a second later than Cruz's, and the pop of his shot echoes through the silence.

"If they didn't know we were here before, then they really do now. Let's go get our girl."

The second I get to a door, I lift my foot and slam it into the old, weathered wood.

Immediately, it swings open, revealing an old kitchen beyond.

The sound of gunfire fills my ears as doors slam and engines start in the distance.

"Motherfucker," someone grunts deeper in the building.

"Where is she?" Dawson's cold and terrifying voice reverberates from my right, and when I get to the doorway, I find him with a Wolf pinned against the wall, his arm pulled back at an angle which can only mean he's dislocated the fucker's shoulder.

Good. It's the least he deserves if he's got Emmie captive here somewhere.

"I said, where the fuck is she?" He booms when he doesn't get the response he was looking for.

The pussy screams like a girl when D pulls his arm farther back.

He must give Dawson the answer he wants because two seconds later, D drives his fist into the cunt's kidney and lets him drop to the floor like a sack of shit.

Stepping over the fuck as he groans and writhes on the floor, I take off after D.

More gunshots sound out, but I don't pay any attention to the fallout of what's happening around me. My focus is solely on one person. And I don't relax until Dawson darts to the left into a room and announces, "Emmie."

My feet move faster, racing in behind him.

I come to a grinding halt as I watch her jump into his arms. "You came," she cries.

"Of course we did, kiddo. Did you think we'd be anywhere else?"

She clings to him like he's her lifeline.

It hurts, really fucking hurts, as she tucks her face into his neck and allows him to hold her up.

"Take me home. Please," she begs, not pulling away even an inch.

She's not even noticed I'm standing here.

There's a part of me who wants to just walk up to her and announce my presence, allow her to acknowledge that I've been a part of this too. But there's also another part who just wants to back away and let her be with her dad. Let him be the person she needs right now.

And in the end, that's exactly what I do.

"Come on, let's head out," I say the second I find Alex and Seb standing at the front door.

They both immediately look over my shoulder as if Emmie is going to race after me.

"Where's Emmie? Is she okay?" Seb asks in a rush. I'm not surprised; the two of them have become closer since they discovered their connection.

"She's fine. D's got her. Come on, let's get out of their way."

"But—"

"Stella's going to be losing her shit. Call her and tell her everything is fine," I demand, taking off toward the main house where we left Alex's car.

She wanted to come with us, no surprise there, but the second Calli learned that something was up, she was blowing up Stella's phone, so she reluctantly agreed to go and keep her company while we dealt with everything. I can imagine her pacing back and forth as she waits for news.

"Are you sure you don't want to stay, make sure she gets home okay?" Alex asks, rushing to catch up with me.

"She's where she needs to be. Come on." I continue walking, and I'm about to turn a corner when I make the fucking mistake of looking back.

She's standing there with her dad's arm wrapped around her shoulder, her hands stuffed into the pocket of the hoodie she's wearing.

Her tired eyes find mine and I gasp at the pain within them.

What did they do to her? What has she endured in the past few hours while she's been captive here? Why did they want her in the first place?

"Theo?" Alex calls, having not seen what's stopped me.

Seb has though, because he's stopped with his phone to his ear and is staring right at Emmie as well.

"Go to her," I tell him. "Then come catch up with me later."

He looks back at me and then at his cousin again.

His face twists as he tries to decide who needs him more, but I don't allow him any longer to debate it.

With one final look at Emmie, I rip my eyes away and continue forward.

"Go," I bark when Alex doesn't immediately start to move once more, and although my body screams at me to do so, I never look back. I can't, because if I lay my eyes on her again, I won't be able to do the right thing and walk away.

7
———

EMMIE

My grip on my dad's waist tightens as I watch Theo disappear around the corner without looking back.

He left.

All the air rushes from my lungs as that thought hits me.

He came all this way, helped Dad and Cruz get to me, and shot and killed multiple Wolves, if the bodies littering the building as we made our way out were anything to go by.

Why would he just walk away?

Because he walked in on you getting off with another guy grinding on top of you, maybe?

"Are you okay?" Dad asks quietly, his grip on my waist the only thing holding me up right now.

"You're here. Of course I am." Stepping in front of him, I bury my face in his solid chest and breathe in his manly scent.

I'm safe.

Kicking myself for making such stupid, reckless

decisions, I vow to start being smarter.

There's too much shit going on around me to put myself—everyone I love— at risk like I did on Monday night.

"Come on, kiddo. Let's get you home." He drops a kiss to the top of my head before grasping my shoulders and pulling me from his body.

"We all good here?" he shouts back, and when I peer around his body, I find Cruz and Xander standing in the doorway to the building.

"All good, bro. Fancy leaving the Wolves a little present?" Cruz asks, a wicked smile tugging at his lips.

"You know it," Dad confirms, pushing me in the direction we watched Alex and Theo walk only minutes ago.

"Hey, cous," Seb says, stepping up beside me, his concerned eyes searching mine. I have no idea what he's looking for, but he clearly doesn't find it, because even after long seconds, his expression doesn't relax at all.

"Is... um..." I hesitate, both desperate to ask the question on the tip of my tongue but equally terrified to discover the answer. "Is he okay?" I ask, my eyes shooting in the direction Theo vanished.

"Uh... honestly, I have no idea," Seb confesses with a wince, pushing his fingers into his hair and pulling it back, exposing a splattering of blood covering his brow.

"Shit, are you okay?"

He rolls his eyes dramatically. "Obviously. None of those motherfuckers had a chance with me."

"Your ego really is something else," I mutter as footsteps pound behind us.

"Ready?" Cruz asks, stepping out of the building

with Link right behind him, a wicked smile playing on both of their lips.

"What are they doing?" I ask, not directing the question at anyone specifically.

"No idea," Seb mutters at the same time Link says, "Just wait, I think you're going to like it."

Dad keeps moving us backward, and the others join us, standing in a line.

"Theo and Alex are gonna be pissed they missed this," Nico says, rubbing his hands together in excitement.

My lips part to once again ask what's happening when a loud explosion before us makes the ground beneath my feet shake.

"Was that— Holy fuck," I gasp as the building I was locked inside not so long ago goes up in a fireball. "Wow," I breathe, watching as the burning hot flames lick up into the sky, the heat from them burning my skin. "That's—"

"Beautiful," Cruz sighs, sounding much like I imagine a father might when he lays eyes on his firstborn, not a house fire. But whatever. I guess it comes as no surprise that my uncle is... different.

"Just a shame that motherfucker Wolfe isn't inside."

"Or Ram," Dad mutters.

A million and one questions about all of this dance on the tip of my tongue, but I force my lips to stay shut. There's going to be plenty of time to analyse all of this once we're in the safety of Dad's house. Now is not the time.

"Right. Now, we can leave," Cruz says happily, scrubbing his hand on top of my head. "Come on,

Hellcat." He winks at me, but my heart skips a beat and my steps falter at his use of that nickname.

Pain slices through my heart that Theo walked away.

I'm not sure what I was really expecting, but the second I saw him standing out here and realised that he was a part of this... hell, that he survived that crash... All I wanted was for him to pull me into his arms and tell me that everything was going to be okay. That he forgave me for walking away from him at school, for getting down and dirty with Dax, for letting him place that fucking tab on my tongue and allowing myself get swept away with the craziness he brought into my life in the worst fucking way.

"We've got you, kiddo. Everything's going to be okay."

Sucking in a deep breath, I pull on my big girl panties and force my mask onto my face.

I'm better than this. Stronger than this.

Luis Wolfe. Theo Cirillo. My own fucking grandfather. None of them can touch me.

I will win against all of them.

There is no other option.

———

"Oh my God," someone squeals the second Dad pushes the front door open.

I look up to find three women running toward me.

Dad presses his hand to the base of my spine and pushes me forward, right into their clutches.

Arms surround me as the sweet scents of their

perfumes fill my nose, wiping away that of the leather, smoke and destruction that's emanated from my rescuers all the way home.

"I'm so glad you're okay," Calli breathes in my ear.

"I sincerely hope they let you shoot someone," Stella adds, making me snort a laugh.

"Sadly not. I left that to them. You should have come."

Stella pulls back from our embrace and holds my eyes.

"Someone had to look after Calli," she quips.

"Hey," Calli snaps out, smacking her around the head. "I was fine."

"You were freaking out."

"Our friend had been abducted. I was allowed to freak out."

"We need to up your training," Stella teases.

"All right, enough bickering," Piper says, her hard expression at odds with the lightness she forces into her tone. "What do you need, Em?"

"A bath," I say, stretching out my aching back. "And then sleep. And food."

"We've got you covered," Calli says, not giving Piper a chance to move and rushing toward the kitchen.

"Come on," Stella says, lacing her arm through mine and pulling me toward the stairs.

"You okay, kiddo?" Dad's voice pierces the air when we're halfway up the stairs.

"I've got everything I could need," I tell him with a smile, although my heart aches knowing that it's not the truth. Someone is missing. And if I'm being honest with myself, he's the only one I want beside me right now as I try to put myself back together.

"Go grab what you need, I'll get the bath running," Stella says the second we hit the second floor.

I push through into my bedroom with a lingering hope that I might find him in here. I have no idea if I even left the window open, allowing him entry, but my fickle heart still hopes.

It's pointless, because I soon discover that my window is locked up tight and my room is exactly as I left it the morning before. A fucking disaster zone.

A smile twitches at my lips, knowing how much he'd hate it if he did appear. It's way more of a mess than he could deal with.

Memories of driving him to insanity in the short time we lived together fill my mind, and for some bizarre reason, longing to go back to that tugs at me.

There was something weirdly enjoyable knowing just how much I was affecting him, how deep I was burying myself under his skin.

"I found some bubbles in the cupboard. I like to think they belong to your dad," Stella jokes. "All those muscles, the ink, and the bubbles," she muses.

Reaching for my pillow, I launch it across the room at her in the doorway.

"There's something wrong with you," I hiss as a shudder rips through my body at the image she just painted so vividly for me. Bitch.

"Sorry, would you rather I put another body in your head?" She wiggles her brows. "I bet he'd look hella hot surrounded by innocent fluffy bubbles." She bites down on her bottom lip as if she's imagining it, and I can't help following suit.

Yeah, that's a visual I'm gonna need one day.

"Okay, enough," I snap out, dragging my head from the gutter.

I gather up a clean pair of knickers and pyjamas and march past Stella and into the bathroom, dumping the lot onto the floor before peeling the clothes that guy gave me from my body.

"Burn these," I say, holding them out to Stella who I know is standing behind me. Her concerned stare makes the skin on my back tingle with awareness.

I might not want it, but I also can't deny that it feels nice, comforting.

"Sure." She takes a step away, but I don't let her get very far.

"Later. Come sit with me."

She hovers until I've stepped in the quickly filling bath and have mostly vanished in the mass of bubbles before she joins me and closes the door.

She hesitates for a beat, looking between me and the floor before she shocks the shit out of me and starts pulling her clothes off.

"What the hell are you doing?" I gasp.

"Shut up and spin around," she demands, and not two seconds later does the water rise around me as she joins me. "Tip your head back."

I follow orders and let her tip warm, soothing water over my head before she grabs my shampoo and sets about washing the stench of that place off me.

Neither of us says a word. They're not necessary. I feel it all though, deep down to my soul. Her support, her love, her need to look after me and make sure I come out of this in one piece.

It's not until she's rinsed the conditioner out of my

dark lengths that she tells me to spin back around once more. And the moment our eyes connect, red-hot tears fill mine.

'I love you,' I mouth, needing her to know how much I appreciate everything she just did for me. How much her support means to me.

She reaches for my hand and squeezes tightly.

"Talk to me, Em. What's going on in that pretty little head of yours."

Laying back, I rest my head on the bath and close my eyes, allowing the warmth to soothe me as well as banish the chill that's still in my bones.

"He just walked away, Stel. I have no idea what they did to find me, to get me out of there safely, but the second I walked out, he turned his back and left."

Pain lashes at my insides as I replay the scene in my head.

He looked wrecked. His skin was pale, and there was a massive gash on the side of his head, dried blood still clinging to it.

Was that from the crash, or had something else happened that I have no idea about?

"What happened after you got suspended yesterday?" Stella asks, taking me right back to the beginning of this mess.

"After I let him screw me in an empty classroom and walked out on him, you mean?"

She clears her throat, and I don't need to look to know she's fighting a smile.

"Empty classroom, damn. Why haven't Seb and I done that yet?"

"Focus," I joke.

"Sorry, sorry. It's just... that's hot."

I scoff, unable to deny that it was exactly that.

"I told him we were done and I left." When she stays quiet, I force myself to continue, reliving all my mistakes. "I went to Lovell. I just... I needed to get away. I needed space. Somewhere I could think and try to get my head around my mess of a life.

"A couple of old friends bunked off school and found me in the park we all used to hang out in. It was Misha's birthday. They had alcohol and weed, and before long we were at a Wolves party.

"One thing led to another, and I found myself out the back with one of the guys."

"Em," Stella breathes, and I cringe.

"I know, I know. But his attention, having his hands on me... it all felt too good. I just wanted to lose myself, and he was offering that to me."

"You don't have to explain that, Em. I get it. I really, really do."

"He offered me acid. I swear to fucking God, I've never had anything other than weed before, and I always said I wouldn't, but..." I blow out a long, regretful sigh. "He stood there offering me oblivion, and I was so fucking broken, Stel. I so desperately needed it. So I took it."

I pause, the weight of my stupid decision threatening to push me right under the water.

"Things with Dax—a guy from my past, a Wolf—got a little out of hand. I was tripping and I thought he was Theo so I let go. But then the door flew open and there was Theo with a gun in his hand and a murderous expression on his face.

"Theo shot him. Clipped me," I add, nodding to my

shoulder. It's kinda scabbed over since it happened, but there's no way she hasn't seen it.

"You need that looking at."

"I know," I agree, looking at the angry wound. "Theo was taking me to Alex's mum to get me cleaned up when we were run off the road."

"By the Wolves?"

"That was who was holding me, but Dad and Cruz keep talking about Pops like he's involved. I wouldn't be surprised," I sigh, sinking deeper under the water.

"But didn't they... I dunno, like... get rid of him?"

"Fuck knows what they did with him," I mutter as a soft knock sounds out on the door.

"It's just me," Calli says, inviting herself in. "And I've got hot chocolate with cream and marshmallows. Whoa, we having a tub party?" she asks in amusement when she finds us both submerged.

"My hero," I breathe, eyeing the mug happily.

"Just... letting Emmie get it all off her chest."

"Mind if I stay, too?" she asks, holding my eyes as I take the mug from her.

"Sure. The more the merrier."

"So..."

"Theo shot her," Stella says helpfully.

"What?" Calli gasps, her entire body going rigid as she lowers her arse to the closed toilet beside us.

"It's not like it sounds," I mutter after taking a sip of the chocolatey goodness she gifted me with.

"He shot the guy who'd just made me come."

"Oh, because that makes it sound better," she scoffs.

"It was his shoulder. He should be fine, I think."

"You think? Calli asks, looking concerned for someone she's never met.

"Cal, could you do me a favour?"

"Of course," she agrees. "Anything."

"Could you message Theo? Just find out if he's okay."

Her whole face softens at my request.

"Yeah. Yeah, of course," she says, rushing to pull her phone from her jeans pocket. "But... don't you think you should do it yourself?"

"Something tells me he wouldn't respond even if I did," I confess, trying to keep down the lump that threatens to crawl up my throat.

Both of them look at me with sympathetic expressions.

"I deserve it. I've hurt him just as much as he has me."

"I'm not sure that's true, Em," Stella says sadly.

I think back to the look on his face as he stood staring at me with Dax. Right up until that moment, I thought everything was a lie.

But even while I was tripping, I saw the second of hurt, of pain that flickered through his eyes as he watched me fall apart under the hands of another man.

He cares. In that moment, it was blatantly obvious.

But then his anger, his training, his dark, depraved self resurfaced and took matters into his own hands.

I'm not prepared for the sob that rips from my throat as I continue to run those few moments through my mind.

"Shit," Calli hisses, rushing to my side, and she takes the mug from my grasp, slipping her hand into mine instead. The three of us connected, both of them doing their very best to stop me from drowning.

"I'm sure he's fine, Em. Theo is made of steel. This will barely cause a dent," she says confidently, but it does little to eradicate that image of his devastation as he watched me fall.

"Y-yeah, I'm sure you're right," I force out.

"I know he's a prick," Calli says after a few silent minutes where only my ragged breathing can be heard. "But he does care about you, Em."

"We're a disaster," I blurt out.

"So are Stella and Seb, but it's not stopped them."

"Hey," Stella argues but quickly starts laughing in agreement.

They both squeeze my hand in support.

"I really thought you'd be telling me to run as fast as I could."

Calli's eyes hold mine, sadness filling them. "We can't help who we fall for, Em. You just need to decide if he's worth it."

"I think there are bigger issues right now than whether Theo is worthy of me."

She nods. "All of this will blow over."

"Blow over. I've got three of the most powerful criminal organisations fighting around me. How is that ever going to blow over?"

A sad smile tugs at her lips. "The losers will die, the winners will reign supreme. It's how it works."

"So the Wolves are fucked then, is that what you're saying?" I can't help feeling for Archer, Dax, and the other friends I had who are connected to that world.

I wouldn't wish this war on them.

Well, most of them.

"If they deserve it."

"I think today might point toward the fact that they do."

"Some of them. Not everyone is a bad egg, Em. You just need to find the rotten ones and eradicate them."

"You're sounding more like a mafia princess every day, Cal."

She just shrugs. "It's either that or I stay as naïve as they've tried to keep me and go through life not really understanding."

"You've made the right choice."

She sits back on her heels, her eyes flicking over my face. "So, are you going to scoot up and let me join you two or what?"

"Girly three-way in the bath. Oh, if only the boys could see us now," Stella quips, making me laugh in a way I never thought I would again only a few hours ago.

8

THEO

"You can go," I snap over my shoulder as I march deeper into my flat, leaving Alex watching my retreating back. "I don't need babysitting."

"That's not—I'm not—fuck," he hisses, following me into the living room. "What do you need?"

"What do I need?" I bark out, turning to him and stepping right into his space.

He doesn't back down, not that I really expected him to. This is Alex, and he's a dumb motherfucker at times.

"What I fucking need is for you to leave. I need to talk to my dad, and I need some fucking sleep."

"Liar," he states, his eyes holding mine steady, just begging me to take a swipe at him.

"Excuse me?" I ask, my brows damn near hitting my hairline.

"You don't need any of those fucking things. What you need is her."

He steps so close to me, taunting me, until our noses are almost touching.

"Go on. Lie to me again. Tell me it's not her."

"You need to get out of my fucking face, Deimos," I seethe.

"Or wha—" His question is cut off as all the air rushes from his lungs when my fist collides with his ribs. "Cunt," he barks out, recovering quickly and coming at me.

With my lack of sleep and the lingering injuries last night left me with, I'm not exactly in top form, and he has me on the floor embarrassingly fast.

My back slams against the wood beneath me, and I struggle to catch my breath.

"Okay, okay," I concede, holding my hands up in defeat.

"Gonna admit it yet?" he asks, sitting back on his arse and wiping a drop of blood that's trickling down his chin.

"Fuck off am I admitting anything. Prick."

"Just call her."

My response is nothing more than a grunt as I force my body to comply and get to my feet, marching straight toward my kitchen and swiping a bottle of vodka from the cupboard.

"See yourself out, yeah?"

He doesn't say a word as I make my way down to my room and slam the door behind me.

Twisting the cap off the bottle, I launch it across the room with a roar, although the pathetic *ting* it makes when it collides with the window does little to settle me.

Lifting the bottle to my lips, I chug the contents

until the burn becomes too much and the alcohol begins to warm my belly.

Fuck, I need it.

Anything to get the images of what those cunts might have done to my girl while they had her locked up in that cold fucking cell out of my head.

My blood oozes fury and the desire to go and slit some fucking throats for even considering taking something that belongs to me.

My busted knuckles burn as I shove my hand into my pocket and pull out my phone.

Scrolling through my contacts, I come to a stop on Archer fucking Wolfe.

My thumb hovers over his number, my need for an answer burning through me and forcing any rational thinking right out of my head.

Think with your head, Son. Always. Never your heart. And never with anger.

Keep. Your. Fucking. Head.

Enemies will smell your weakness. The chink in your armour.

Dad's voice is louder in my head than it usually is.

"FUCK," I roar, desperate to drown it out, but also knowing that I need it. I need that little devil on my shoulder to stop me from doing something stupid. Something that could get me killed, or worse... her.

Scrolling away from Archer, I hit call on the person I should be talking to right now.

"Son," Dad greets the second he picks up the phone. It's not usual for him to answer on my first call so he must be aware that something's going on. "I had your car collected. There's another on its way to you."

"Uh… thanks," I say, not expecting those words to come down the line. "What the hell is going on?"

"We're working on it."

"Okay, well any chance you could hurry up? I want Luis Wolfe's location. I owe him a bullet for this."

"Theodore, don't do anything stupid. Remember all the things I've sai—"

"I know, Dad. I am thinking with my head. But they fucking took her. They took her from me."

"We'll get to the bottom of it. I'll let you know once we've dug something up."

The line goes dead, and I only just stop myself from launching my phone across the room.

He didn't even ask if I was okay. Not that I'm fucking surprised. My safety has never really been that high up on his list. As long as I'm breathing and able to work, that's all he cares about.

Chugging down more of the vodka, I throw my phone onto my bedside table and strip out of my clothes in desperate need of a fucking shower.

I stand under the spray, jets hitting my body at all angles and massaging my aching muscles from being thrown around in my car as we tumbled off the road.

The plaster that Gianna covered the stitches on my head with quickly gets soaked through and begins peeling from my skin. I know I shouldn't be getting it wet, but fuck it. I'm sure there are worse things I could be doing right now.

Reaching for my shower gel inside the hidden panel on the wall, I stare at the products I bought for Emmie that are still here.

Wrapping my fingers around one of the bottles, I

flip the lid and lift it to my nose, breathing the scent in like a fucking pussy.

The palm of my free hand slams down on the tiles beside me in frustration.

My fingers curl around nothing as the ache in my chest that hasn't eased since I turned my back on her and walked away earlier only gets stronger.

My need to know she's okay, the ache I feel to pull her into my arms and tell her that I'll never let anyone touch her again burns through me.

I hang my head low, feeling utterly helpless.

If she's in her room right now, would her window be open for me?

Did watching me walk away hurt her as much as it did me?

Slamming the bottle back onto the shelf, I force those questions from my head.

She was partying with someone else. If I didn't turn up when I did, there's a very good fucking chance things would have gone further than they did.

The thought of her writhing with another guy, letting some other fucker inside her body, makes the beast inside me surge forward faster than I've ever experienced before.

Is she going to go running back to him? Does she care that I shot the cunt?

My breathing is ragged as I scrub at my skin until every inch of me is red raw.

Despite the pain that makes every single one of my movements hard work, I tug on some sweats and a t-shirt the second I'm in my bedroom and head for the gym.

It's that or I'm going to find myself in Lovell, gunning for a fight with a Wolf or two.

My phone lit up every few minutes while I was in the gym, but I ignored every single message and missed call.

There was only one person I wanted to talk to, and I had a feeling that her name was never going to flash up on my screen.

I just turn the lights out after climbing into bed, every single muscle in my body screaming in pain, when my phone illuminates the room once more.

Lifting it up, I glance at the screen, expecting it to be another message from Seb. I almost drop the thing when I discover I'm wrong.

Very wrong.

Just seeing her name there once more makes all the air rush from my lungs.

She hasn't turned this phone on since I took it from her, preferring to ignore all the messages and voicemails I left her after she disappeared.

Quickly unlocking it, I open her message, not giving a fuck that it'll show as read almost immediately. I'm over pretending that I'm not sitting here thinking about her.

Hellcat: Theo?

My heart pounds as I stare at those four little letters.

It's just my name. It means nothing. She could be

about to say anything, but they still give me a little hope.

At least I know she's okay.

Theo: Yeah.

I feel like a fucking preteen talking to a girl for the first time. It's pathetic. But that's what she does to me. It's what she reduces me to. She always has. I just always fought it, hoping that I could push past it. Put her behind me. Forget about her.

A laugh falls from my lips as I think about how naïve I was back then.

I had no clue of the kind of power she had over me.

Hell, I still don't truly know the depth of it, but I'm starting to think it's pretty fucking deep.

The dots keep bouncing, making me wonder if she's writing a fucking essay. So when the message does finally pop up, my eyes widen in shock at its simplicity.

Hellcat: I'm sorry.

"Shit," I breathe, my phone continuing to shake in my grip as the weight of those two words presses down on my shoulders.

I sit there for so long, staring, that the screen goes dark.

What the hell do I say to that?

How could I even begin to put into a message how I've felt these past few weeks?

Theo: Me too, babe. Me too.

I cringe when I read the words back. But what can I say?

I've told so many lies, hurt her in too many ways. Nothing I can tell her now is going to make her forgive me, allow her to forget everything that's gone before.

Does it make me a pussy not to even try? Not to fight?

Maybe.

But for once in my goddamn life, I'm going to do the right thing.

Emmie isn't some kind of pet, a belonging I can just keep to myself no matter how badly I might want her.

I can't force her to want me. Or at least to admit to herself that she wants me, because I know she does.

I feel it every time we connect. Whenever we're close.

She's mine. I just need to think about showing her in a different way from what I'm used to.

Locking her up in my castle certainly didn't work.

Fucking stupid fairy tales Larissa and Rhea used to force me to watch.

Sliding down the bed, I let my body sink into my memory foam mattress and sigh. The only thing that would be better right now would be if she were here beside me. Hell, even across the hall locked in my guest room would be better.

I stare up at my ceiling, assuming that now she's said what she needed to say, she'll ghost me once again.

It's what I deserve.

But then my phone lights up the room again and a little hope flickers in my veins.

Telling myself it'll just be the guys and that I'm

setting myself up for disappointment, I look at the screen.

"Holy shit."

Hellcat: Are you okay?

Honestly, no. I'm really fucking not. But the last thing I need is her pity.

Theo: Are you? Did they hurt you?

Hellcat: Nothing I couldn't handle.

The fact that she doesn't just say no makes that frustration and fury I've been fighting to keep down stir once more.

I'd put money on Archer and his little crew partying in their stupid fucking warehouse in Lovell, and I'm sure I could make my point well enough to get some answers out of them about Luis's whereabouts.

Or I could stay here and see if I can keep Emmie talking to feed my addiction.

Rolling onto my side, the knowledge that my tablet is in my drawer right beside me makes my fingers twist to reach for it so I can see her.

But something stops me.

For once, I don't want to invade her privacy.

If she's willing to talk, I want this to be real, true. Honest.

Theo: Did they tell you why they did it?

Hellcat: Luis just wanted to know where my mum was. Seems a little extreme.

Theo: Do you think she's told you everything?

Hellcat: No idea. Although I'm starting to think not.

Couldn't agree with you more there, babe.

Theo: Maybe you should try to talk to her. See what you can find out.

Hellcat: I'm not doing anything because you tell me to.

As I read the words, I hear her voice in my ear and my cock stirs at her defiance.

Theo: I love that tone on you. Makes me hard as steel.

Hellcat: Theo.

Theo: Fucking love it when you beg, too.

When she doesn't start typing, I put our conversation back on track, ignoring my need to push my hand inside my boxers.

Theo: I wasn't telling you to do anything,

Hellcat. It was just a suggestion. You deserve the truth.

It takes her a while to respond—so long that I start trying to come up with something to force her back into this conversation with me. I'm not ready to let her go yet. Thankfully, it's not necessary, because she does eventually reply. Although her words make my heart ache for her.

Hellcat: She's been lying to me my entire life. I don't expect her to change her ways now.

9

EMMIE

I roll over, pulling the warm covers with me, but I startle awake when my arm hits something cold.

Undiluted fear flows through my veins, my brain putting me back in that prison cell despite the warmth that surrounds me.

"Oh my God," I hiss, silently chastising myself for being so pathetic.

You're safe. You're home.

Grabbing my phone, the culprit for my rude awakening, I find a stream of messages from Theo and I'm instantly reminded of our conversation.

For hours I told myself that it was enough that Calli had reached out for me and told me that he was okay.

But in the end, my concern, plus my guilt over the whole situation got the better of me, and I turned on my old phone, my eyes widening at the sheer number of messages and voicemails he'd left me when I ran from the New Year's party.

I didn't read them.

Okay, that's a lie.

I only read the last few that were visible on my screen when I opened our previous conversation.

My heart thundered in my chest and my hand shook as Theo's voice rang out loud and clear in my head as I read his words.

'You're mine, Emmie. You can run, you can hide, but eventually, I will find you, and I will show you exactly where you belong.'

It was a threat, or at least I think it should have been, but nothing about his words scared me. I wasn't sure if that was because what I'd been through in the previous twenty-four hours was way more terrifying than anything Theodore Cirillo could do to me, or if I was just missing the thrill.

Our short time together in the classroom at Knight's Ridge feels like it was a million years ago now. And after watching him walk away from me, giving me the same treatment that I gave him multiple times before, I can't help but secretly crave him.

I always have wanted what I can't have.

Opening the chat, I read through the messages I missed.

His Lordship: What are your plans for the week?

His Lordship: Did you remember you hate me?

His Lordship: I'll take that as yes. That or you're too busy getting yourself off as you

imagine me lying here in my bed with my cock begging for you…

All the air rushes from my lungs as I re-read that message.

He's lying.

He has to be lying. Right?

I bite down on my bottom lip as I picture him in the middle of his black bedroom, his muscular body stretched out on the giant bed and his fingers wrapped around his length.

Heat surges through me, liquid lust filling my veins and a throb I really don't need to be distracted by starting up in my clit.

His Lordship: I'm not getting myself off. I want your hand, not mine. I want your body, not the cold sheets surrounding me. I want your wicked, filthy mouth telling me that I'm not good enough, that I don't deserve you.

My heart races as I take in every bit of his vulnerability within those words.

His Lordship: Everything you've said about me is true. But you're changing me. You have changed me. I want to be better. For you. Only for you. Always for you. My wife.

My eyes are so wide I swear they're about to pop out.

I kick the covers off me as my body burns up and disbelief washes through me.

I can't believe he's actually acknowledging these things about himself.

His Lordship: I'm hoping you've fallen asleep and that you're not just ignoring me as I bleed out through the phone. Although, I can't really blame you if you're reading all of this and cackling an evil laugh as you plan the best way to use it against me. If you are then do it. I'm sure Seb would help if you need it. But if you're asleep and not scheming up my epic fall from grace, then I hope you sleep well and dream of all the wicked things you want me to do to you. Sweet dreams, Hellcat. x

"Wow," I breathe.

I'm halfway through reading that message back, assuming I must have imagined the whole thing, when a soft knock sounds out from my door.

"Em?" Dad's voice rings out.

"Yeah, I'm awake," I reply, regretfully locking my phone and dropping it back to the bed.

Scooting up, I sit with my back against the headboard as he lets himself in.

"Hey, how are you feeling?" he asks, his brows pinching in concern.

"Better, seeing as you have coffee," I say, my eyes following the mug as it moves toward me.

He passes it over and I immediately wrap both of

my hands around it and lift it to my nose, breathing in the rich scent as he lowers himself to the edge of my bed.

"How are you doing?" he asks again after I've had a sip that I instantly regret when it burns a layer of skin off my tongue.

"I'm okay," I say, but the pain in my voice makes my words sound less than convincing.

"Emmie, you don't need to pretend with me." He wraps his giant inked hand around my leg and squeezes in support. I hold his eyes as emotion and exhaustion, despite just having woken up, swamp me.

"Y-yeah, I know," I force out through the lump in my throat as tears burn red hot at the backs of my eyes. "It's just... it's easier to pretend right now, you know?

His shoulders drop in defeat as he takes me in. "Shit, Em. I'm so fucking sorry."

Tears finally fill my eyes as I take in the wrecked expression on my dad's face.

In this moment, it's clear to see that he's shouldering the blame for this entire situation.

"Dad, no," I say, sitting forward, placing my mug on the side and wrapping my arms around his shoulders and squeezing him tight. "None of this is your fault."

"Em—"

"You're wrong," I assure him. "None of this is on us."

His body shudders against mine, making my chest ache.

My dad is the best man I know. I hate the fact that he's hurting because of my stupid decisions.

"I told you it was safe, that the Wolves weren't a

threat. If I hadn't told you that, you wouldn't have ended up in the middle of them."

"I trust you, Dad. If you say they weren't a threat, then I believe you genuinely didn't think they were. They lied to you, and there's nothing we can do about that."

"I should have been more cautious. I shouldn't have taken Luis goddamn Wolfe's word when he told me he had no interest in you."

"He doesn't. Not really."

Dad pulls back from our embrace and looks at me inquisitively.

We didn't talk last night. After I disappeared up here with Stella and Calli, he mostly stayed downstairs. Piper told me he was too angry after everything and was debriefing Cruz and the guys.

I got it. I didn't really feel like rehashing it all either, despite the fact that I needed someone, something. The exact reason why I reached for my phone and messaged Theo.

I needed that connection to someone to remind myself that I was safe, that it was over.

"You told me on the way home that he wanted your mum," Dad says softly. "But did he say anything else?"

I shake my head. "No. He just wanted to know where she was. Do you think..." Dad squeezes my leg again when I pause. "Do you think she's lied to us about her involvement in all of this?" I finally ask, terrified of the answer.

I believed her when she explained to me both in the hospital after her overdose and in that house in the Cotswolds what happened with Damien. How the Wolves had tricked her into believing they could help her make a quick buck off the back of the Cirillo Family.

I believed she was an innocent, desperate drug addict being played by men who were more powerful than I wanted to think about.

I believed her when she assured me that the only reason I've found myself tied to Theo is that she wanted me protected. That she wanted me away from the Wolves.

She looked so sincere when she held my hand and relayed it to all of us in that house. Her pain was palpable. Her fear for what she thought both Damien and Luis would do to her when they found her was too chilling to ignore.

So what are we missing?

Was she never trying to protect me at all?

Were my initial thoughts correct? Did she sell me? Am I a bigger part of this fucked-up mess than she wants to admit to?

"Yes," Dad states regretfully.

That one single word carves another deep hole in my already tattered heart.

Why do I always give her the benefit of the doubt? Why do I always believe her? So what, she carried me for nine months? So what, she was the one who gave me life? Not when it's been one full of pain, heartache, hunger, and neglect.

"There's more than she's telling us. She might not know everything, but I'm convinced she knows something that will help us put all the pieces together."

"This is a mess," I groan, falling back and tilting my head to the ceiling.

"You're telling me, kiddo. But we'll sort it. You

might not want to hear it, or accept it, but you've got some of the city's more powerful men standing right beside you. Cruz, Damien, Theo, *me*. We're not going to let anything happen to you, Em.

"Think of yourself as powerful, huh?" I tease.

"I may have been out of the game for a few years, but it's in my blood. Just like it is yours." He winks. "So, did you want to tell me why you broke some rich girl's nose at school Monday morning?" he asks, desperately trying to fight the smirk that wants to pull at his lips.

"Other than because she deserved it?"

"She was the one who spiked your drink?"

"Yeah, for that and the fact that she's a raging bitch."

"Like the last one you made bleed?"

"They're friends. They can have matching war wounds."

He doesn't comment, and any amusement that was on his face vanishes in the blink of an eye, making my stomach twist with nerves.

I might not give a flying fuck what most people in this world think of me, but my dad is a different story.

He's my hero, always has been and always will be. I want him to be proud of me, and I desperately want to be the daughter he deserves.

"You've been suspended for a week, Em. What was our agreement when you started at that school?" His brow quirks, and I see the disappointment swirling in his dark eyes. It makes me feel about an inch tall.

"I promised I'd keep my head down and behave," I mutter like a naughty kid who's just been caught stealing the sweeties out of the tin. "Please, don't take my bike, Dad. Please," I beg.

If I lose that, my freedom, my way to escape when things get too much—although never to Lovell again—then I'll lose my fucking mind.

"Emmie, I—"

"Things are so out of control," I try to argue. "When I started school, I was just the girl from the wrong side of town everyone looked down on. But now…" I blow out a breath as my reality comes back to me. "I'm half MC, half Cirillo, with a fucking husband, and I've just been abducted, after being held captive by said husband. You can't actually expect me to be holding it all together right now."

"Em, you're doing a way better job than most, I assure you." A sad smile tugs at my lips, although my heart is still in my throat at the thought of him taking my baby away. "I'm not taking your bike, Em. I'm pretty sure all of this has been punishment enough. But…" he quickly adds, "you're not going to spend this week moping about. You get today, and today only to do what you need to do. Tomorrow, I want you either here doing the work your teachers have set you, or you're at work showing Mickey just what you're made of."

"Really?" I ask lightly.

"Yeah, really. And as for today, Cruz is downstairs. He really wants to see you."

I nod, reaching for my mug of cooled coffee.

"Okay, I'll freshen up and come down."

"We're gonna get through this, kiddo. Just be honest with me, yeah? I don't care how bad it is, how scared you might be to get it off your chest. Nothing, and I literally mean nothing, can be as bad as having Theo turn up on my doorstep looking like he'd just walked out of a war zone and tell me that you're gone."

My lips part as I try to picture it, my heart shattering for the broken boy I know hides behind Theo's impenetrable exterior.

"He did?" I ask, unable to keep the question inside.

"Em," Dad sighs, his eyes softening as he looks at me. "There are many, many things I could say about that boy and the family he belongs to, but... there's no point. I've seen the way he looks at you. I saw the pure, undiluted fear in his eyes yesterday as he stood before me, thinking that something had happened to you.

"I've been that boy. And I was about the same age as you when I handed myself over to Piper, knowing that it could only end one way but also knowing there wasn't a damn thing I could do about it. She owned me back then and she still does now.

"Sometimes, it's not worth fighting. Sometimes you just need to let go and grab life by the balls. Not his balls though," he adds quickly. "I could happily go through life thinking you've never seen let alone touched a pair."

"Dad," I laugh, both moved and amused by his little speech.

"I know, I know. You've been on the pill for years. I know you've experienced things already that I never want to know about."

"You were young once too," I remind him.

"I remember it well. But let me tell you..." He leans in as if he's about to whisper the world's secrets in my ear. "It's way more fun with someone you care about, someone who would take a bullet for you."

I gasp, and I'm about to chastise him for talking about things I also don't need to know about when he glances at my shoulder. I reluctantly allowed Stella to clean and bandage it up last night after my bath.

"Dax is alive, right?" I finally ask the question that's been burning within me since I woke up in Theo's car with that acid making my head spin.

"I'm sure he's fine," Dad assures me. "Theo said it was just a shoulder wound."

"And you trust him?"

"With that, yeah."

"With me?"

Dad pushes from my bed and stalks toward my door.

I start to think he's not going to answer me when he looks over his shoulder.

"Like I said, it's always more fun with someone who cares enough to take a bullet for you."

I'm about to tell him that Theo hasn't taken one for me. Not like Seb did for Stella. But I conclude that it's just a figure of speech and nod, knowing that Theo has done plenty over the past few weeks to prove his loyalty. And clearly, it's worked with my father. Something I never thought I'd ever see.

"I swear to fucking God though, if he so much as waves a gun in your direction again, he's going to be looking down the barrel of mine, and it may just be the last thing he sees." With that ominous threat hanging in the air, Dad lets himself out of my bedroom, leaving me sitting there with my jaw on the floor.

The second I've recovered, I reach for my phone and finally tap out a reply to the messages that went unread last night.

Emmie: You were right… I fell asleep. I hope

you slept well, you looked like you needed it. How is your head?

I wait for a few minutes, but when it doesn't show as read, I finish my coffee and drag my aching arse out of bed.

10

THEO

The second I woke up and found that Emmie had replied, I shot one straight back.

I'd slept harder and longer than I ever remember doing, and I actually felt almost normal—until I rolled out of bed and my muscles twisted and pulled, reminding me of everything I'd been through to get here.

I figured it was a minor price to pay if she was going to continue talking to me.

Although, I started to question that when I emerged from the shower to find that not only had my message not been replied to, but it hadn't even been read.

So maybe I was jumping the gun, thinking something could actually come out of all of this. She was probably just exhausted and delusional and didn't really know what she was doing.

But then she wouldn't have replied this morning, dickhead.

Feeling like a fucking headcase letting myself go crazy over a girl, I dragged on a pair of sweats and headed to the kitchen, taking both my phone and tablet with me, telling myself that just checking in on her wouldn't be such a bad thing.

I fell onto the sofa with a steaming mug of coffee in my hand and opened my tablet. Logging into the app I had hidden, I discovered her room was empty.

And that's the way it stayed. All. Fucking. Day.

I spent the day doing fuck all and just waiting for Emmie to appear or even to reply. But I got nothing.

In fact, I had no idea the world still existed outside of my flat until my buzzer went off later that evening.

I knew it was going to be one of the guys. It was the perfect time for them to have finished training and to get home.

The only one of us who's not moved into the building yet is Alex. If I'd been paying attention to anything outside of my own drama recently, I might know why he's dragging his heels about it.

I'd have thought he'd have been the first one here, seeing as he practically lived with me in my coach house. He never seemed all that keen on going home, so I'm surprised he wants to now.

Pushing from the sofa, I stalk toward my door and open it without bothering to look at the screen. It was one of four people.

Realistically, probably one of three.

I didn't think Toby would have come to check on me. He's got enough of his own shit going on right now to worry about mine.

"All right," I mutter when I find Seb's blank expression staring back at me.

He doesn't say a word as I pull the door wider and invite him in.

I know he's pissed at me. He's made that more than clear since I confessed to knowing that he and Emmie were cousins.

"Good day at school?" I ask, pulling the fridge open and grabbing two beers, throwing one at him.

"You heard what your dad's doing?"

"Hopefully finding and torturing Luis fucking Wolfe."

"Pretty sure that's on his list after yesterday. But no."

"Are you going to tell me or am I meant to guess? Because I gotta tell you, where my dad is concerned, it could be fucking anything."

"He's organised for Jonas—the non-mafia, loving father version—to have a fucking funeral."

My eyes widen.

"But he's not dead. Is he?" I ask. The last I knew he was still sitting in a puddle of his own piss in a cell for Toby to play with whenever he felt like it.

Honestly, I didn't think Toby would be down for torture, but that motherfucker really has helped him to embrace his inner monster, because he's so fucking hungry for it. As he should be after the way Jonas treated both him, Maria, and Stella.

"No, he's not. Your dad's faked his death to give his other family closure. Apparently he 'died' before Christmas."

I scrub my hand down my face and rub at my rough jaw. "Jesus fucking Christ. Why does he think that's a good idea?"

"No clue. Toby is fucking pissed."

"I can imagine. When is it happening?"

"Next week."

I blow out a breath and fall back on the sofa, trying to imagine just how Toby is feeling right now.

That fucking cunt doesn't deserve a funeral or for anyone to mourn his passing.

The only place he should be going right now is hell for what he put his real family through.

"I think your dad is just trying to make things easier for his other family."

"Why the fuck are they his problem?"

Seb shrugs. "Fuck knows. They're not, and maybe he's trying to keep it that way."

"I swear to God, if anyone other than Toby and Maria gets even a penny of that fucker's money, I'll have something to say about it. They deserve to bleed that cunt dry after what he put them through."

"Bro, you won't hear me arguing," he says before taking a pull on his beer.

Silence descends around us, and it quickly turns uncomfortable as the elephant in the room becomes more and more obvious.

"Have you spoken to her?"

He shakes his head. "No, but Stella and Calli went over there after school. I'm sure I'll get a full report soon."

"I need to know what's going on," I confess. "If someone doesn't find something out soon, I'm going to be shooting up fucking Lovell trying to find that cunt."

"I'll be right behind you, man. It's something to do with Cora."

A growl rips from my throat. Emmie might have told me over message last night, but hearing it hits harder somehow.

"That's what Emmie told D when he found her yesterday."

"Motherfucker. After everything that's happened? She must have a fucking death wish if she's been lying to all of us."

D and Cruz were pretty tight-lipped about it all, but I'm pretty sure they know more than they're letting on.

"Where the fuck is Ram in all of this?"

Seb shrugs. "Your guess is as good as mine. From what I've heard from Mickey's, he's not been seen in a while."

"You think he's run?" I ask. I've heard the same gossip from the gym, and I've seen the same suspicion on his members' faces.

"He's got half the fucking club after him for what he did to Emmie. I wouldn't be surprised. He has to know that we're right behind him after the Joker stunt too."

"This is all going to blow up around us, isn't it?"

"Hey, it's been a while since we've all had an all-out war."

"And we could all fucking well do without one."

Seb sits back, draining his beer and letting it rest on the cushion, probably knowing that the condensation is rolling down the side of the bottle and is about to leave a damp ring on the fabric.

Arsehole.

"I'm sorry about all that shit. About keeping her from you."

His eyes find mine. He's pissed, I can see that on every inch of him, but he also understands.

Hell, he's the only one who comes close to having any idea how I feel right now.

"I know. I get it, T. I really do. You want to protect her. But you can't always have it your way. I know that must be a tough pill to swallow."

"You make me sound like a right entitled brat," I scoff, and Seb's brow lifts as if to say 'yeah, and?'. "Fuck. That wasn't what it was about. Well, not entirely."

"We'll be fine, man. Don't sweat it. I just want to make sure all our girls are safe."

"I wish she was still here."

"So you could keep her to yourself."

"So I can protect her. No one can get her here. Can we say the same about D's house?" I ask, knowing for a fact that we can't, because I've let myself into her room more times than I can count.

"You trying to tell me you've not got tabs on that place?" Seb asks with a knowing smirk playing on his lips.

Mine part to respond, to lie, but I quickly swallow down the words.

"You're so fucking predictable at times, bro. She got any idea you watch her?"

"Of fucking course not. You think I'd still be able to if she knew?"

"She's going to flip her lid when she finds out."

"You gonna tell her?"

He pauses for a moment, thinking over his options.

"No. I want her safe. And you need to take a fucking chill pill, so if you get your rocks off watching her then I guess we're all winning."

"Maybe I should allow her the same privilege so she can see me getting my rocks off."

"Bro, I don't want to know about your kinky shit with my cousin."

"Because I was just begging to know all yours with Stella?" I ask incredulously.

"You loved that shit and you know it. I saw how many tubs of Vaseline you got through after she moved in."

"Fuck you, man," I spit out, but whatever Seb's comeback was going to be is cut off when my tablet lights up on the table with an alert from my app telling me that the camera has been activated. "I guess that's the girls. I wonder how much they talk about us when we're not there," I say, partly as a joke. Although, I can't deny that I'm pretty damn curious.

Seb stares at the screen as if he's actually considering it.

"Bro, I'm joking. I don't invade her privacy that badly. I just like to watch her get herself off before she goes to sleep."

"You're fucked up," Seb barks out, standing from the sofa and marching toward the kitchen for another beer.

"Takes one to know one," I call out. "Order food while you're up."

"So you can rub one out while you hog the girls? No fucking chance."

"I'm not watching. Look." I wait for him to turn around before I make a show of turning my tablet off.

I can reactivate my stalker mode later.

Alex miraculously shows his face ten minutes before the pizzas arrive, and he demolishes almost half of what Seb ordered, much to his irritation.

"You guys ready for the weekend?"

"The weekend?" I ask.

"Jesus Christ, man. Get your head out of your fucking arse."

"Or Emmie's pussy," Seb scoffs.

"Chance would be a fine thing," I mutter.

"Ugh, you two have had too much action," Alex mutters.

"Us two?" I ask. "We all know it's this motherfucker that has so much sex he should be worried about wearing it out."

"Never gonna happen, man. My girl takes too good care of it."

"Prick," Alex hisses under his breath.

"When was the last time you got laid, Deimos?"

Alex's teeth grind, giving us both the answer. "Fuck knows, but I do know the next time I'm getting my dick wet," he announces with a grin.

"Why? You already booked her?"

"Fuck you. I don't need to pay. That's Nico's thing."

"So..." I prompt.

"This weekend," he says, his brows wiggling as if I should know what the fuck is happening. "Oxford?" he adds, glaring at me and waiting for the penny to drop.

"Fuck," I hiss. "That's this weekend."

"Bro, where is your fucking head right now? This is the weekend we've been fucking waiting for. We're gonna obliterate those All Hallows fucks and reign supreme over their pussy."

His face drops when I don't immediately start jumping up and down with excitement.

"Oh no," he warns. "Don't even think about coming up with some dumb-arse excuse to get out of this. We've been waiting for this for fucking years. It's our weekend, man."

I stare at him. One of my two best friends. One of only a handful of people I would pretty much do anything for, and I can literally feel myself being ripped in two, right down the fucking middle.

"Come on, we've dreamed about this since the day Coach gave us our places on the fucking team. This is what this year is all about."

Shoving down my uncertainty, I plaster a smile on my face and give him the words he's desperate for.

"Mate, I'm not going to fucking bail on Oxford. We're going to go and smash those stuck-up motherfuckers."

"But?" he pushes.

"Fuck." I slump back on the sofa. "What about Emmie? We can't all just leave town with all this shit going on."

"She can come."

"Yes," Seb hisses, his eyes lighting up in a way I've become all too used to since living with him and his walking sex doll. "Pack those Johnnys, boys."

"U-uh," Alex stutters. "Fucking hell. We were meant to embark on this weekend single and ready to take on the world."

"Don't you worry, my girl is more than prepared for world domination. Pretty sure his shorty will be right there beside her too."

"She won't come," I say confidently. "Emmie doesn't want to be anywhere near me." She won't even read my goddamn message right now.

"Pfft. Give Stella some credit. Emmie will be there. And if you're really lucky, then you'll get an up close and personal experience instead of creeping on her through a screen," Seb teases, making me groan.

"Uh... what have I missed?"

"Nothing new. Just Theo being a twisted, voyeuristic fuck."

"Oh yeah, that's old news. You creeping on Em now?"

"You fucking know he is."

"Bet she looks banging, fucking herself silly every night while calling out my name."

"You motherfucking—" Seb grabs both my upper arms before I make contact with the smarmy cunt.

Alex stares at me with a victorious smile splitting his face in two.

"I hope the skank you pick up at the weekend has herpes," I hiss, much to Alex's amusement.

"You two are so fucking whipped. Thank fuck I'll have Nico and Toby as wingmen."

"Oh wait, now God's gift to women needs the support of wingmen?" Seb asks, dragging me back to the sofa before shoving me down into the cushions none too gently.

"Fucking dicks. All this pussy is going to your heads."

Alex gets up and storms across the room, flipping us off over his shoulder.

"Jealousy isn't a good look on you, bro," Seb shouts after him.

11

EMMIE

The second a female voice floats down from the front door Dad just got up to open, excited tingles erupt in my belly.

I love both my dad and uncle dearly, but if I have to endure one more programme watching a couple of greasy dudes restoring old cars, I'm legit going to scream.

"How's our girl doing?" Stella asks, getting closer with every word.

"Pain in the arse, like usual," he mutters lightly.

"Same can be said for you, old man," I shout back, making Cruz laugh.

I stand the moment Stella emerges around the corner, followed by Calli and then my dad.

They both say hi to Cruz before focusing on me.

"We brought coffee and doughnuts."

"Hell, yes," Cruz barks out.

"For Emmie," Stella quips. "Sorry, VP." She winks cheekily.

"Go hang out with your friends, Em," Dad says,

dropping down on the other end of the sofa again and hitting play on his boring-arse TV show.

"I don't need telling twice. Laters, losers," I shoot over my shoulder as I head for the stairs.

Footsteps behind me confirm they're both following instead of continuing to stand and drool over my dad and Cruz.

Ew.

"So they seem to be getting on better," Stella says as she closes my bedroom door behind them both.

"Yeah, they seem to be bonding nicely over my disastrous life."

"They just needed a common cause to fight for," Calli suggests.

"Maybe." Although I can't deny that whatever Cruz put in that letter he asked me to deliver to Dad before his wedding seemed to have some impact.

I didn't ask about it. I figured it was none of my business, but I did see Cruz's name light up Dad's phone while we were in that cabin, so I could only assume the letter had broken the ice. I was glad. From the stories I've heard from both sides, they were close growing up despite the years and differences between them. It was only after Piper turned Dad's life upside down and he walked away from the club, leaving Cruz next in line to take over, something he's always been bitter about.

"Whatever it is, it's nice to see them getting on."

"You think it'll last?" Stella asks, opening the box of doughnuts and filling my room with the mouthwatering scent of sweet goodness.

"I hope so," I say, practically diving for the box and

grabbing what I hope is the salted caramel one from the selection.

Stella's frustrated groan tells me that I'm right.

"You snooze you lose, Princess," I mumble around a mouthful of soft fluffy dough. "Oh my God, this is so fucking good." My cheeks heat at just how desperate my voice sounds.

"Jesus, Em. Should we leave you alone with that thing?" Calli jokes.

Laughter sounds out around my room and I can't help but smile. I always wondered what it would be like to have friends like these two.

The reality is way better than I could ever have imagined.

Or it was until Stella opens her mouth again.

"You heard from Theo?"

I swallow my mouthful with a groan as the memories from our late-night conversation come back to me.

"She has," Calli announces. "Look at her cheeks. She's blushing."

"I am not," I sulk, not that they believe a word of it. They can see the heat on my face as much as I can feel it.

Both of their brows rise, silently demanding I spill the beans.

"We messaged a bit last night."

"And?" Calli urges, her romantic heart running away from her.

"And nothing. I just wanted to make sure he was okay. Apologise, I guess."

"What did he say?"

"He... uh... did the same thing."

"He apologised too?"

"Yep," I confirm, grabbing my takeout coffee cup and having a sip.

"So... are things... okay between you now?"

"You mean, am I about to move back into my marital home and live happily ever after?" I ask Calli sarcastically.

"Uh..." To her credit, she does look a little embarrassed.

"No, things aren't okay. But there's now a higher chance I won't kill him with my bare hands the next time I have to see him."

"Well, that's progress right there," Stella jokes, something mischievous flashing in her eyes.

"What?" I ask, knowing that look all too well. It's the one she gets before she convinces us to cause trouble with her.

"We're going away this weekend."

"Stel," Calli warns, but Stella waves her off.

"It'll be good for her," Stella argues. "We've got a suite at this insane spa hotel."

"And you think dropping in a spa will help convince me? Do you even know me?"

"I'm not suggesting you have to use it, I'm just saying. It's fancy as shit, and it's out of the city, away from all this bullshit. It'll do you good."

"Why?"

"Why will it do you good?" Stella asks, a frown forming on her brow.

"No, why are we going? Why this weekend?"

Stella hesitates, but Calli refuses to cover up the real reason and blurts it all out.

"The guys have this huge football match against a

rival school in Oxford. It's this huge annual thing that's a kind of rite of passage for the year thirteen boys."

"No," I state firmly. "I'm not going to some school football weekend. Just... no."

"Come on, Em. Just because they'll be there, it doesn't mean we have to hang out with them."

"There is no way on this Earth you'll abandon Seb all weekend, and we all know it."

"I would for you," Stella admits.

"Bullshit. You're too addicted to his cock."

She gets this faraway look in her eyes as if she's imagining bouncing up and down on it. "It is pretty magical."

"Fucking hell," I groan. "Want my advice, Cal?" I ask, not giving her a chance to respond before following it up with, "Stay a fucking virgin. It's way less stress."

Her cheeks heat in embarrassment and she looks down at her hands.

"Or we take our girl out this weekend and find her a hot one-night stand to banish the V-card for good," Stella suggests with her brows wiggling in excitement.

"Even if I wanted to, I doubt Dad would let me," I say, hoping it's my way out of this.

Any other time, I'd be more than up for a wild weekend with my girls. Hell, even the guys. But after everything, I'm more than happy to hide in my room.

"Let me work on your dad," Stella says with a wink, making a show of wiggling her tits as if they're going to convince him.

"You're a fucking nightmare," Calli mutters. "He's not going to fall for that."

"We'll see. I could really do with a glass of water. Anyone else?" she asks, climbing from the bed.

"Please try not to embarrass my dad too much. He's old, his heart might not be able to take it."

Stella salutes me before slipping from the room, leaving me and Calli falling about laughing.

"Tell me that she's not actually going to attempt to flirt your dad into allowing you out this weekend."

"Cal, I really, really want to say that she's not going to. But this is Stella. And," I add, "not many men say no to her."

"Seb never stood a chance."

"Girl, I'm just surprised she didn't wrap them all around her little finger and end up with a harem full of mafia princes."

Calli's lips part to argue, but she doesn't have one, because she knows I'm right.

"So Oxford," Dad says the second I pull out a chair at the dining room table after Piper called up to tell me that dinner was ready.

Stella and Calli left about thirty minutes ago after handing me a stack of homework they helpfully volunteered to deliver to me.

"Don't," I sigh. "I've already told them I'm not going." Reaching for the glass of water waiting for me, I take a sip as the scent of whatever Piper has been cooking fills my nose and makes my stomach growl, despite the two doughnuts I stuffed not long ago.

When he doesn't say anything, I lift my eyes from the rim of the glass to find him staring at me.

"What?" I ask, sensing he's got something he wants to say about it. "What did Stella do when she came down to talk about it?" I wince, imagining all the twisted ways she could have tried to convince him in the ten minutes she was down here.

A smirk pulls at his lips and I slump down in my chair.

"On second thoughts, don't tell me. If I know how badly she embarrassed herself then I might never let her in here again."

"She was fine, kiddo. She didn't embarrass herself, or me." I should probably feel a little relief, but honestly, my stomach is still knotted over this whole weekend situation.

"Oxford is a big thing for the sixth formers," Piper chips in helpfully. "A rite of passage kind of thing."

"Lucky for you I'm not the kind of girl who worries about that kind of stuff then."

Silence ripples around the room. Aside from the sizzling of the frying pan in the kitchen, the only thing I can hear for a few seconds is my own heartbeat.

Then Dad's firm voice shatters the peace.

"You should go."

"W-what?" I blurt out, shocked to my core that he's even suggesting this. "That's crazy. *You're* crazy."

I'm still amazed he's not threatened to lock me up in the house for forever and a day after what I've done. This should be the last thing on his mind right now.

"Getting out of town for a couple of days might be just what you need."

I study him, narrowing my eyes in suspicion. "Why?" I ask, feeling like I'm missing something.

"Because a few days of fun with your friends will help you forget all this shit."

"Theo will be there," I point out.

"Which is why I know you'll be safe. I trust Theo, Seb, and the others. They won't let anything happen to you, Calli or Stella."

My eyes continue to narrow in suspicion.

"And Cruz will send a bodyguard just in case."

"Or I could just stay here under your watchful eye."

"Yeah, you could." Piper walks over and lowers a plate before me. The sight of the perfectly cooked steak, homemade chips and side salad makes my mouth water. "I'll be working all weekend. Piper is going out both Friday and Saturday night, and all your friends will be gone."

I shrug. Being alone has never bothered me before.

"I'm sure I'll cope."

"Okay, well. It's up to you. I just wanted you to know that if you wanted to, you could."

I smile at him, realising that he's just trying to do anything he can to make all this better. "Thank you," I say, stabbing my fork into a chip and pushing it into my mouth. "Any updates on Luis or anything?"

"Nothing for you to worry about, kiddo."

I suck in a breath, ready to argue with him. But I quickly figure out that he's probably right. I don't want to be any deeper in the Reapers, the Wolves, or the Cirillo Family business than I already am.

"I trust you."

"I trust you too."

Piper squeezes my shoulder in support as she passes me once more before putting her plate down and slipping into her seat.

"I'll think about it."

Thankfully, the conversation moves onto what some kid I've never heard of did at school today, and just like that, any talk of the weekend, or thankfully anything to do with my life right now is banished.

"I've told Mickey I'm going to spend the next two days at the gym. I'm gonna head up to get some work done."

"I get your need to fight, Em. I really do. But don't let your schoolwork suffer."

"I won't, I promise." I drop a kiss on Dad's cheek before grabbing a can of Fanta from the fridge and leaving them to their night.

"We're here if you need anything," Piper says softly.

"I know," I say, stopping at the door to look back at them. "Thank you, for both being so... cool about all this."

"What else did you expect, kiddo? We *are* cool," Dad jokes.

"Yeah, you keep telling yourself that, old man."

Just like I have all day, I ignore my phone sitting face down on the bedside table as I set myself up with my laptop on my thighs and the stack of paper and textbooks Stella and Calli brought for me.

The need to know if he's replied burns through me. But it's a temptation I don't need.

I know just how easy it would be to lose myself in a conversation with him and not get any of this done.

Stuffing down my need to close everything up and distract myself with deviant thoughts about a certain mafia prince who just so happens to be my husband, I focus on the task at hand. I figure the faster I can get this done, the sooner I can move on to the art project my teacher has set and allow myself to drift off into fantasy land.

A fantasy land where I'll be dreaming about all the things I could do to his body—or rather, all the things he could do to mine.

"For fuck's sake, Emmie," I mutter to myself as my head goes straight into the gutter.

With a sigh, I find the right page in the textbook and get to work, my eyes flicking to my phone every few minutes.

———

By some fucking miracle, I make it just over four hours before I can't ignore my phone anymore.

I've got messages from Seb, Stella, Calli, Cruz, Xander, and even Dad—probably testing to see if I'm actually working or just playing on my phone. But I ignore all of them and open his.

To my surprise, there's only one. But it's enough to get my blood pumping.

His Lordship: Did you dream of me?

Heat surges through me, knowing that I don't need to be asleep to be dreaming about him.

As if he's been waiting for me to read it, the dots start bouncing.

His Lordship: Did you have a good day? Seb's just left. He's drunk, Stella's in for a good night.

I can't help but laugh at his aubergine and peach emoji. It's so unlike him, or the him he allows everyone else to see. Somehow I've been granted permission to the other side of him. He's not just a brutal killer, a force to be reckoned with, but he's sweet, funny, caring, in his own unique way.

Emmie: Spent most of the day watching shitty car renovation shows with Dad and Cruz. Not exactly my idea of fun, although, I must admit, a couple of the mechanics were easy watching.

His Lordship: Funny, I thought you preferred a guy in a sharp suit with a filthy mouth to dirty clothes and greasy fingers.

A smile twitches at my lips.

Emmie: I guess it all depends on my mood. I wasn't really in the mood for prim and proper, more dark and dirty.

My cheeks burn, knowing that I shouldn't be flirting with him, taunting him. But I figure I've been unable to hold myself back all this time. He'd probably find it weird if I were any other way.

His Lordship: I think you're more than aware that an expensive suit doesn't always mean boring and gentle.

"Fuuuck," I groan, my thighs rubbing together as some of the time we've spent together flickers through my mind.

Emmie: Is Seb the only one who's drunk?

His Lordship: Maybe, maybe not...

His teasing makes me think it's probably the latter.

Emmie: Careful, Master Cirillo. Dropping your inhibitions might lead you to all sorts of trouble.

His Lordship: What if I'm ready to throw them all out of the window?

My heart continues to race as everything south of my waist clenches in desire.

Emmie: Just how far are you willing to throw them? Give me something to work with.

12

THEO

My eyes are locked on my tablet as she stares down at her phone, her bottom lip taking the brunt of her desire as she waits for my response.

With my grip on my phone tightening, I force myself to get off the bed and drag my eyes away from her.

She's got her dark hair piled on top of her head, and she's wearing an oversized vest that hangs low enough at the front to give me the perfect tease of what I know she's hiding beneath. But it also shows off the bandage on her shoulder, ensuring the guilt that I'm still feeling over my reaction Monday night continues to swirl around my gut, even with the amount of vodka Seb and I consumed after Alex left, filling my veins.

Coming to a stop in front of my floor-to-ceiling mirrored wardrobe doors, I adjust the waistband of my boxers just so. When I'm happy, I open the camera on my phone and rest my other forearm against the glass.

With my head dipped low, I stare at the camera,

imagining I'm looking right into her heated eyes as she begs for me to fuck her.

Snapping a picture, I shoot it off before even checking it. If I look, I'll pick out a million and one ways I could make it better, and that's not what this is about.

Be real, Theo. Show her who you really are. Insecurities and all.

She deserves it.

It shows as read straight away, and I rush back over to the bed so I can see her reaction.

"Holy shit," she breathes, her eyes widening, the movement of her chest increasing the longer she stares.

"What are you going to do now then, Hellcat?"

"This is a really fucking bad idea," she mutters to herself, pushing a loose strand of hair back behind her ear, her eyes still not wavering from the screen in front of her.

Unable to resist, I start typing.

Theo: Did I render you speechless, babe?

Hellcat: …

I burst out laughing when a string of drooling emojis follow.

Theo: Do I get a treat in return?

Hellcat: Not sure what I'm wearing right now comes anywhere close to matching up to that. It's gone straight in my wank bank.

My cock jerks the second I read those words, my mind instantly conjuring up an image of her hand pushed into her lace underwear as she rubs one out to that photo of me.

Fuck, yeah. Give me a live show of that, babe.

Theo: You're stunning no matter what you're wearing. Try me.

I watch as she flips the covers back and bark out a laugh. She's wearing the tiniest sleep shorts that I'm sure would cut perfectly across her arse if she were to stand up and turn around for me. But it's not those that amuse me, it's the massive hot pink fluffy socks on her feet that I wasn't expecting.

And it's those I get a photo of a few seconds later.

Theo: HOT AS FUCK but any chance at something more than your feet?

Hellcat: Theo, Theo, Theo. That's not how this works. A photo for a photo.

The smile that plays on her lips as she types makes something inside me light up like a fucking Christmas tree.

I fucking love that smile.

Reaching up, I rub the pad of my thumb along my bottom lip as I study her. Fuck, I wish I was there with her, staring into her eyes as she waited to see what I was going to do next.

Shifting position, I push my hand into my boxers,

grasping my aching cock and angling my phone just so. It doesn't show anything. I don't want to go from zero to sixty quite that fast, but there's no mistaking just how fucking hard I am for her.

Once again, I hit send without scrutinising the image, and watch the screen.

Her smile only widens as she takes in the photo, and I can't help but laugh as she blatantly zooms in.

Oh hell, yeah. My dirty girl is desperate for more.

Theo: See what you do to me. You don't even have to be in the room. I fucking burn for you, Hellcat.

She bites down on her bottom lip, a salacious smile on her full, delectable lips.

Shaking her head, she lowers her phone and tips her face to the ceiling.

I can imagine her giving herself a good talking to. Trying to convince herself not to get carried away.

"Come on, Hellcat. Listen to your body, not your head. Show me how much you want me," I beg, as if she can hear me.

The thought of turning the two-way audio on and doing just that races through my head.

One day soon that's going to happen.

I'm going to sit here and watch her follow my every demand.

My grip on my dick tightens, and a growl rumbles deep in my throat.

She moves, slipping down the bed, her vest hitching up over her toned stomach and giving me more inches to lust over before she copies my move and pushes her hand inside her shorts.

"Damn, babe. You're fucking killing me and you have no idea."

A small gasp of pleasure spills from her lips as she touches herself.

"I bet you're fucking dripping for me. Have you ruined your knickers just thinking of me, Hellcat?"

She snaps a picture and sends it. My phone vibrates in my hand, but I can't rip my eyes away from the screen. She's writing something to go along with her photo, but her other hand slowly moves beneath the fabric, ensuring her lips remain parted, her back arches, and her hips roll.

My phone buzzes and I can't resist the temptation to see what she's written.

Hellcat: Until next time. Good night, Theo.

My hand drops as a moan rips from the tablet's speakers and I forget all about that final message as I watch her.

"Fuck, Hellcat," I breathe, taking her in as she works her body into a frenzy. I'm not even pissed she's doing it without me, because she looks so fucking beautiful.

Releasing her phone, her hand slips under her vest, palming her breast and pinching her nipple as my cock begins to weep for her.

"Come for me, babe. Show me how hot you are for me."

Not five seconds later does she give me exactly what I need.

"Theo," she cries, her hips lifting from the mattress. "Theo, yes. Yes. Fuck."

And fuck if I don't come in my pants like a fucking twelve-year-old watching his first porno.

"I'm gonna spend the day at Mickey's," Emmie talks into her phone as she sits at her dressing table, doing her makeup the next morning.

I can't tell who she's talking to. Stella probably.

I don't really give a crap, so long as I get to watch her like this.

She's enthralling when she's totally relaxed and her well-constructed walls are down.

Do I feel like a cunt invading her privacy like this when I told myself that I was going to do the right thing? Nah, not really.

Right now, I know she's safe. And even better than that, I know her plans for the day. Things couldn't really be any more perfect.

Well, I guess they could. I could be sitting here, listening to her telling whoever is on the phone that she's going to forgive me. She could be explaining how awesome I am and how hot those photos were last night, and how she can't wait to see how hard I get for her in real life.

Keep dreaming, Cirillo.

It's going to take a bit more than a few dirty photos to make Emmie change her mind about any of this.

Reaching over, I pull my top drawer open and rummage inside for the box I know is in there without taking my eyes from the screen.

Pulling out the velvet box, I flip the lid and pluck her ring from the centre.

The tracker Link put inside it has been deactivated and removed.

A heavy sigh passes my lips as I finally look at it.

My heart sits heavy in my chest as I move it back and forth, allowing the red diamond to catch the light.

It looks all kinds of lonely, not on her body.

This piece of jewellery was made for her.

It's her to a T. It's beautiful, dark, mysterious, edgy, dangerous. And one of a fucking kind.

Somehow, I need to find a way to get it back to her. It belongs to her, even if she's not wearing it on her finger as my wife.

Pain pierces my chest at the thought of her walking away from this.

Dad has assured me that our marriage came with a pretty iron-tight prenup that even the best lawyer in the country is going to struggle to get out of.

But I won't hold her to it. I can't.

Not in the ways I've tried in the past, anyway.

Forcing her hand didn't work. All she did was push back harder.

I've got to remind her of all the good stuff, of all the reasons we're like fire when we connect. Why she fucking consumes my every thought, brings me to my goddamn knees, and lights an inferno inside me... all without even being in the same part of the city.

Grabbing my phone, I shoot her a message.

Theo: Good morning, beautiful. I hope you dreamed of me.

A smile twitches at my lips and my stomach knots in excitement when she looks at her phone that lights up on her dresser.

Her smile starts slow, but it soon increases as she reads my words, her own conversation coming to a grinding halt mid-conversation.

My chest swells, my own smile spreading across my face, knowing I can render her useless with just a few words.

I might have spent my life trying to overpower men bigger, older, and better than me, but I've never felt more powerful in my entire life, knowing I have this effect over her.

"Oh... uh... y-yeah. I'm still here," Emmie says, picking up her phone and reading it again. "Yeah okay. Sure. I'll talk to you later. Have a good day. Throat punch him for me, yeah?"

I can't help but bark out a laugh at the image her request conjures up.

She laughs too at whatever is said in return before hanging up and pulling her AirPods from her ears and discarding them on her dresser.

She walks across the room with her phone in her hand, I assume trying to come up with something to send back.

Finally, she starts typing, laughing like a lunatic as she does.

Hellcat: Morning. Sorry, can't say I remember you featuring in any of my nighttime fantasies. Please try harder next time.

My smile widens. "Such a filthy liar, Hellcat."

Theo: I'll work on my modelling skills. Give you something you're never going to be able to get out of your head.

She lifts her finger to her lips, chewing on her nail as she scrolls up in our chat, much to my delight.

My cock jerks, knowing that she's standing there lusting after me, remembering just how I feel moving inside her.

The temptation to message again, telling her that I know exactly what she's thinking, is strong, but I rein myself in because I'm not ready for her to know this little secret yet. I'm not ready to lose this connection to her, because I know she'll sever it the second she discovers the truth.

Eventually, she pulls her head out of the gutter and begins typing.

Hellcat: I'll await the results of this with bated breath. Have a good day at school, Theodore. Try not to get into any trouble.

Theo: I'll do my best, babe. But I can't make any promises. I'm feeling especially deviant today…

Hellcat: Okay, well… try not to kill anyone then.

Theo: Hopefully that's a promise I can keep. For today at least.

Her lips part in shock at my words, but really, what else did she expect? She's more than aware of what I'm capable of, of the things I've done in my past.

The dots start bouncing and I wait for her response, but it never comes. She obviously deletes whatever she types and instead throws her phone down on her bed as she walks toward her drawers and starts selecting what she's going to wear today.

The robe that was covering her falls to the floor, and I'm gifted with the most incredible sight of her naked body.

"Fuck, I miss you," I breathe, shamelessly getting closer to the screen like a fucking junkie needing his next hit.

My plans for the day were already pretty solid after hearing what she was going to be doing, but seeing all of her, and combining that with the need burning through my muscles to stand in front of her, to see her reactions to my words in person, is too much to deny.

I wait until she's dressed, and then I reluctantly shut the app down and get ready for school.

13

___

EMMIE

The second I walked into Mickey's, I felt like I'd come home. It was strange, but I welcomed it.

There were more than a few Reapers here working out, and knowing they were keeping an eye on me ensured I didn't look to the door in a panic every time it opened.

Mickey had me doing everything, from organising both the reception and his desk to sorting out his god-awful filing situation on the computer, and replying to some emails that he couldn't be bothered to deal with, on his behalf.

It's almost time for my lunch break, and I'm placing an order for cleaning supplies when the main door opens once more.

I don't immediately look up, needing to finish this first, but the second a violent shiver races down my spine, my eyes fly up as icy claws of fear wrap around me.

They wouldn't come for you here.

They wouldn't.

All the air rushes from my lungs when I lock eyes on the person who has just walked in.

"Theo," I breathe, my eyes feasting on him as longing surges through me.

The last memory I have of him is him walking away after they rescued me, and that hurts more than I'm willing to admit.

He marches right up to the reception desk I'm sitting behind, his face set with determination and his eyes dark with challenge.

Jumping to my feet so that I'm not at such a height disadvantage when he gets to me, I hold his stare steady despite every muscle in my body screaming at me to run.

I already know that he has the power to disarm me, to catch me up in his net and lure me into his web.

"Shouldn't you be at school trying not to kill someone?" I sass.

"Yeah, I should." His deep, raspy voice washes over me, making my skin erupt in goosebumps.

Fuck, I've missed that voice and the things it does to me.

My hate and lust for this psychotic man collide with such force it makes my head spin as I just stare at him as if he might disappear if I were to blink.

"But I suddenly fancied jumping in a ring and sparring with someone."

Something twinkles in his eyes and my stomach somersaults, half excited, half livid that Stella opened her big mouth and told him where I was.

"You knew I was here," I state. There's no point in asking, I already know the truth.

He shrugs, attempting to look innocent.

I quirk a brow. "Don't even try to pull that shit with me, Cirillo," I snap, annoyed with myself that he's pulled me in with no more than a handful of words.

"Oh come on, you love it," he says, resting his forearms on the counter and leaning closer.

His addictive, manly scent hits my nose, and I silently curse him out as my mouth waters and my body begs to get closer.

I'm hit with the realisation that this is probably how Mum has felt her entire life about drugs and alcohol. I guess things could be worse. I could be addicted to crack, not a hot as fuck boy with the power to shatter my battered and broken heart all over again.

"I'm busy, I don't have time for this—"

"Lunch break, Shorty," Mickey none-too-helpfully calls from his office.

I suck in a sharp breath as an accomplished smile appears on Theo's lips.

"Come spar with me and I'll buy you lunch."

My heart thumps against my ribs at the possibility of getting up close and personal to him, to feel his hands on me.

"I don't need you to buy me lunch, Theodore."

His eyes darken to two dangerous pools of green at my use of his full name.

"I know you don't. But I want to."

Folding my arms over my chest, I glare at him.

"Why would I want to be anywhere near you, let alone eat with you?" I hiss.

"Because, Hellcat." Pure, unfiltered arrogance appears on his face, and it makes my fists curl with my need to wipe it clean off. "You miss me."

"No, I'm pretty sure I just hate you."

Holding my eyes, he rounds the desk.

I swear to God my heart pounds in time with every step he takes.

My skin burns and tingles rush over me, knowing that we're currently the objects of almost every guy's attention in this entire gym.

He steps right into my space, allowing his heat to seep into my body.

Damn him. Damn him to hell.

He knows exactly what he's doing.

"So..." He tilts his head to the side. "Prove it. Get in the ring with me, Hellcat. Show me what you've got."

My teeth grind as I stare at him.

"If I beat you, will you leave?"

His chuckle fills the air, and the sound goes straight to my clit.

"If you win, I'll do whatever you want me to, babe," he offers, his eyes darkening.

"Anything?"

"Anything," he confirms.

"Fine," I say, stepping around him, escaping the confines of the reception area and keeping my back to him.

Curling my fingers in the bottom of my Mickey's Gym hoodie, I peel it up my body, letting every other guy in here get a look at me first.

A frustrated growl sounds out from behind me, and I can't help but smile. That is until his warmth covers my back and his breath tickles the shell of my ear.

"You're playing a very dangerous game right now, Hellcat." His fingers gently brush up my hip and over my waist, sending a tsunami of desire through me.

Straightening my spine, I hold my head high, my eyes locked on the empty ring before me.

"I have no idea what you're talking about, Cirillo. Ready to get your arse handed to you by a girl?"

His laughter makes heat pool between my thighs, but I don't let it consume me. Instead, I force my legs into action and march toward the ring, knowing as sure as the sky is blue that his eyes are locked on my arse in my leggings.

I can't really say I blame him, mind you. I chose this set this morning for a reason.

I needed the confidence boost that came with the way this outfit made my body look. I'm just glad it's not going to waste.

Spinning around, I gift him a look at my front.

"Holy—" he breathes as his eyes zero in on my rack. I get it, my cleavage is killer in this.

"You a pussy, Cirillo?"

His eyes lift to mine and I swallow thickly, trying not to allow the look of pure desire on his face to affect me.

"Worried the MC princess is better than the mafia prince?"

He takes a step forward, closing the space between us, but I quickly take one back.

"Worried? Never. I think we both know who's going to win this," he says arrogantly, continuing to move closer.

He sheds his own hoodie and I instantly realise that he's playing me just as much as I am him when he doesn't stop there and drags his t-shirt off as well.

"Fuck, Theo," I gasp, taking in the bruising that

didn't look half as bad in that photo last night. "You shouldn't be—"

My words are cut off when my back collides with the ring and he steps right into my space.

"Don't let my bruises put you off, babe. I can still have you beneath me in seconds. I'd put money on you begging my name too."

My chest heaves, my breasts brushing against him with every breath I take.

"You're delusional." It's meant to be a vicious comeback, but honestly, it sounds more like I'm well on my way to that begging he wants.

"You could call me worse," he quips, leaning closer and pressing the length of his body against mine. My eyes drop to his lips, thinking that he's about to try and kiss me, but he throws me for a loop—which amuses him greatly—when he says. "In you go then."

It takes a couple of seconds for my brain to catch up with what's happening around me, but when I finally rip my eyes from Theo, I find he's holding the rope up for me so I can slip into the ring.

"T-thanks," I mutter, much to his amusement as I turn my back on him once more.

A growl rumbles from him when I bend over and climb in, but I don't react as I look at the pair of gloves Gunner's holding out for me. He's suspiciously been here, keeping an eye on me all day.

If the situation were any different, I might be annoyed that Cruz has blatantly sent him to watch over me, but mostly, I'm just grateful. It's nice to be surrounded by people who care after the dickheads Mum brought in and out of my life over the years.

"Give him hell, Shorty."

"You got it, G. But I don't need those. I want it to hurt."

"Brutal. I love it."

He throws the gloves down and grabs some tape instead while I roll my eyes.

"We don't want to bust up these pretty hands," he says softly, and I reluctantly allow him to wrap me up.

When I turn back around, Theo is staring at me with a smirk and a twinkle in his eye that makes butterflies flutter in my belly.

"Bring it, Cirillo."

He shakes his head at me.

"Confidence is so fucking sexy on you, Hellcat."

"Watching you writhe in pain will be even better."

He's still laughing at me when I surge forward, planting my fist right in the centre of the bruise that's covering his ribs.

Is it a low blow? Probably. I don't really give a fuck.

All the air rushes from his lungs as he bends over. The arrogant look on his face morphed into one of shock.

"Oh sorry, did you want me to pretend I was fighting a girl?"

His smirk returns, and faster than I anticipated, he lunges for me.

My back collides with the sprung floor with a thud, but I don't let it stop me.

Using every ounce of strength I have and every bit of skill these guys have taught me, I manage to break free of his hold and get a solid knee to his stomach, making him fall to the side to catch his breath as I jump to my feet.

"You got this, Shorty," Gunner says, his phone

raised, recording our fight.

"Really?" I ask.

"What? Cruz is gonna wanna see this."

Waving him off, I turn back to my opponent.

His eyes are almost black, although as he lifts his hand to push his hair from his brow, I wonder if it's his burning need to win or just pure undiluted desire as he stares at me.

"Let's go, Pretty Boy."

"Pretty?" he scoffs. "A pretty boy would go easy, let you win. I have zero intentions of doing either."

This time, I'm ready when he comes at me, and I block each of his attempts all while managing to get a few hits of my own in.

More and more guys crowd around the ring to watch as we duel, all of them calling my name in support and spurring me on.

"Come on, Shorty. Knock him on his pretentious arse," a familiar voice booms over the others.

Glancing over, I find Xander standing there with a wide, proud smile on his face.

'You got this,' he mouths, giving me the confidence boost I needed.

Theo is still drinking from the bottle of water someone gave him when I fly at him, knocking it from his hand and sending it spinning across the gym.

I lock down every single emotion other than the anger and hate he ignites in me, and I lay into him with everything I have.

My muscles scream, my lungs burn, but fuck, as the sweat starts to cover both of our bodies, I'm pretty sure I've never felt better.

"Umph," Theo grunts when I manage to swipe his

feet out from beneath him and he lands on his back so hard it sends a tremor through my body.

I don't give him even a second to recover though, jumping on top of him and wrestling him hopefully to victory.

"Come on, Shorty. You can do this," Xander screams as I pin Theo's hands to the mat above his head.

I stare down at him, our eyes locking as our chests heave.

Damn locks of hair that have escaped my band hang around my face, and sweat trickles down my spine as I wait for victory to be announced.

A smile twitches at his lips, and I can't help but grind my hips down on his when I feel him growing hard beneath me.

"Gotta say, Hellcat," he says between heaving breaths. "I'm impressed."

I scoff, not wanting any kind of praise from him.

"Five," someone shouts, finally beginning the countdown to my epic win. "Four."

"But," he says, his eyes darkening and his smirk growing wider.

"Two."

"Not that impressed."

A squeal rips from my lips as he flips us.

We switch positions, his grip on my wrists so tight I swear my bones rub together.

"You started celebrating too early, babe. Take this as a lesson. Never assume victory until it's called."

"I hate you," I seethe, trying to buck beneath him, but he's like a lead fucking weight pinning me into the mat.

"You sure, or do you just hate how much you want me?"

"Five," someone calls again as he lowers down, bringing our noses so close they almost touch.

"Arse. Hole."

"Aw, come on, Hellcat. We both know you can do better than that," he taunts.

"Fine, you self-righteous, self-absorbed, pretentious, arrogant arsehole. I hope karma fucks you up the arse with a cactus for this bullshit. Sideways."

"Fuck, It gets me all fired up when you tell me you love me," he breathes, his eyes locked on my lips.

"Two." I barely hear the countdown as electricity crackles between us.

"You must be gutted you lost, babe," he drawls. "Now you're not going to get anything you want."

"One."

A wide, smug smile lights up his face but he doesn't sit up. He doesn't move a fucking inch.

"Get off me, wanker."

But he does the fucking opposite despite my attempt to move him.

The tip of his tongue runs along the edge of my jaw, tasting me until his nose hits my ear.

"That's the thing though, Emmie." A shiver rips through me, hearing him growl my name. "You might be getting me hard as fuck with your sinful body and wicked words. But the only person who's going to be making me come any time soon is you."

Desire shoots through me like a lightning strike and my thighs clench, something I know he hasn't missed.

"Run out of Vaseline already, boss?" I quip.

A growl rumbles deep in his chest.

"And you can deny it all you like, but I know just how badly you want to make me fall apart for you right now. How much you want to give in and get on your knees before me."

"Fuck you," I hiss, my breathing only coming faster as the image he so vividly painted plays out in my mind.

"Nah, because you didn't win, so you're not calling the shots. I am."

A gasp rips from my lungs as he suddenly jumps up, allowing a rush of cold air to race over my burning skin.

"Aw, don't be a sore loser, babe. It was a good fight."

He grins down at me and holds his hand out to help me up.

Ignoring it, I push to my feet, my eyes lingering on the more than obvious boner he's sporting behind his shorts.

"There's only one loser here, Cirillo. And that's the one standing looking with a hard-on for a girl he can't have. I suggest you stop in the shop on the way home and buy yourself a new tub of lube, because you've got some long, lonely nights ahead of you."

"It's cute that you think I care that these arseholes know I want you. Hell, I bet most of them are hard for you right now too."

I scoff, keeping my eyes on him, not wanting to look at anyone else and have that statement confirmed.

He surges forward, his hot fingers wrapping around my throat as a gasp ripples through our spectators.

"Only difference is, I'll be the only one to witness you begging when you come to your senses and realise just how badly you need me."

"Wrong. I've got all I need in my top drawer. As you well know. And," I add for good measure, "I've got a box of brand new batteries ready for tonight."

"Now that is something I'd pay to see, Hellcat."

The thought of him standing on the other side of my window watching me makes my insides turn to molten lava.

"Maybe I'll leave my curtains open. Give you a good show."

His fingers tighten on my throat in warning, but his eyes burn with lust at the suggestion.

The seconds tick by as we stare at each other, the tension crackling so loud I'm sure everyone around us must be able to hear it.

One second I'm convinced he's about to slam his lips down on mine and make me forget my own goddamn name with his drugging kisses, and then the next, I'm stumbling back and colliding with the ropes as Xander drags Theo away from me and throws him into the opposite ones.

"Get the hell out of here," he growls in his face.

I'm unable to rip my eyes from them as they square up to each other.

"Xan," Gunner shouts from the sidelines.

Neither of them reacts to him. Hell, they don't even move.

"You fucking care about her at all, then you'll walk away right now."

Theo's jaw tics as he glares pure death at Xander.

But something in his words must break through, because after a couple more tense seconds, Theo's eyes dart to mine.

"Yeah," he says. "I won, so I get to choose what happens next."

My heart pounds, assuming that he's going to make some kind of asinine request. But after allowing his eyes to take a leisurely trip around my body, he takes a step back.

"I'll see you soon, Hellcat. Don't forget that promise you made me about the curtains." He winks before ducking under the rope, swiping his discarded hoodie and t-shirt from beside the reception desk and blowing out of the gym like he didn't just make the world shift beneath me.

———

I'm still cursing the prick out as I turn the shower off and grab a towel to wrap around my body, and another to wring the water out of my hair.

I should have beat him. I had him right there beneath me.

I thought— Ugh.

He was right, and I fucking hate it.

I thought I'd won too soon and I eased up.

Idiot, Emmie. Fucking idiot.

I pull on clean underwear and a fresh sports bra while rummaging in my locker for some deodorant.

A knock on the door startles me, and I chastise myself for being so on edge, thinking he's going to come back.

The need he stirred in me as he stared down into my eyes resurfaces, but I stuff that desire back inside the lockbox it belongs in.

"Shorty," a familiar voice calls out, and despite

knowing better, disappointment washes through me that he hasn't come back.

That he didn't realise he couldn't possibly leave after that and is about to storm in here, back me up against the lockers and take exactly what he threatened to out there on the mat while his boner rubbed deliciously against my clit.

"You decent?" he calls out again, throwing a bucket of ice-cold water over my little fantasy.

I look down at myself.

Not really. But I also don't give a shit.

"Yeah," I call out and the door clicks open.

"This just got delivered and I thought— Holy shit," he gasps the second he rounds the corner and gets a look at me.

He makes a show of slapping his hand over his eyes and turning around.

"Cirillo will castrate me for this," he mutters to himself. I'm not sure if I'm meant to hear it or not, but all it does is piss me off.

"What's wrong, X? Not seen a pair of fucking knickers before?" I hiss.

"Don't," he snaps.

A smirk tugs at my lips as he stays with his back to me.

"From what I've heard around the club, you're more than familiar with girls' underwear, or more specifically, taking it off them."

"Emmie," he growls.

"Oh for fuck's sake, Xan. You're being a baby." Pulling out a pair of leggings from my locker, I drag them up my legs.

Quite honestly, I can't see how it's all that different since they're skintight. But whatever.

"Okay, you can turn around."

Slowly he does as I say, and his eyes flash with heat when they find my body.

"Not much better, Shorty."

"You're a pain in my arse," I spit. "What have you got for me?" I ask, remembering he said something had been delivered.

He lifts the brown paper bag that's in his hand.

"No idea, but it smells insane."

My brows pinch as he comes closer.

"I didn't order anything."

"Well, it's got your name on it."

Our fingers brush as I take the bag from him, and it becomes instantly obvious to me that while I might think he's hot, he's not the one who sends tingles and desire shooting around my body from one innocent touch. That would be a certain mafia prince who just walked out on me, leaving me burning hot for him.

Wanker.

"The only person who's going to be making me come any time soon is you."

I squeeze my eyes closed tight as his words come back to me, desire hitting me with the force of a ten-ton truck.

"Are you okay?" Xander asks, and when I drag my eyes open once more, I find him staring at me with a mixture of concern and confusion.

"Yeah," I sigh. "I'm good. Thanks for this." My stomach growls loudly as the familiar scent of what's hiding inside hits me. "And you're right. It does smell incredible."

"I'll leave you to it," he says, taking a step back. "Good fight out there though, Ramsey. You really held your own."

"Nah," I mutter, shaking my head. "He went easy on me."

"Maybe. Maybe not. One thing's for sure though."

"Oh yeah, what's that?" I ask, my curiosity more than piqued.

"That poor fuck is going to be hard as nails all day. That was like foreplay to the extreme."

I laugh, but it's totally forced.

"He isn't the only one," I mutter under my breath.

"Uh... yeah... I'm gonna..." He thumbs over his shoulder and continues backing away.

I have no idea what he's expecting me to do, but he looks like a rabbit caught in headlights.

I don't look down at the bag in my hand until the door swings closed behind him.

Lifting it, my eyes find the label on the side.

Mrs. Cirillo.

"Motherfucker," I bark, knowing exactly who ordered me lunch.

Shoving my feet into my trainers, I wrap a hoodie around me and stick my phone into the pocket. Slamming my locker closed behind me, I march to the small staff room at the back of the gym.

Thankfully, it's empty.

My eyes land on the bin sitting on the floor in the corner, and my fingers tighten on the bag in my hands.

The need to throw it out and forget all about it in favour of the pot noodle I pinched from the kitchen before I left the house this morning is strong.

But then I get another waft of the garlicky, sweet scent, and my mouth waters.

"Damn you, Cirillo. Damn you to hell and back with your pretty face and fucking fantastic cock," I hiss to myself as I grab a fork and drop into one of the chairs with a huff.

Ripping the bag open, I find two of my favourite Chinese dishes staring back at me.

"Why? Why do you need to be so sweet?" I mutter, twisting my fork in the noodles before me, my stomach growling again in desperation.

My phone pings in my pocket and my heart jumps into my throat. I have no idea how I know it's him. But I know it is.

Ignoring him, I push the fork into my mouth and groan as the flavours hit my tongue.

I have to admit, it softens the blow of losing somewhat. Although, he did exactly what I would have demanded if I'd won anyway. So maybe I did win, in a roundabout way. I just wish he could have taken the memory of him pinning me to the mat with him.

With a growl of frustration, I stuff my free hand into my hoodie pocket and pull my phone out.

His Lordship: Eat up, babe. You're going to need your strength for your vibrating little friend later.

"Ugh, infuriating dick," I mutter, shovelling another forkful of food into my mouth.

His Lordship: Just remember how inferior it

will feel compared to the real thing.

Unable to stop myself, I start typing.

Emmie: Aw… you still hard and lonely?

I chuckle as I hit send and see it's read immediately.

Stabbing a piece of shredded beef, I pop it in my mouth, only for me to choke on it two seconds later when a photo appears on my screen, proving that my previous comment was bang on the money.

Emmie: Jerking off in the school toilets. That's desperate, Cirillo.

His Lordship: Would you rather I do it in class?

I'd rather you do it over me, but whatever.

I roll my eyes at myself.

You're nothing but a shameless slut, Emmie Ramsey.

I'm still trying to come up with a witty comeback that isn't my previous thought when the door slams open and heavy footsteps march into the room.

"Oh fuck," I squeak, trying to close that image down so fast that my phone tumbles from my hand and lands right at my visitor's feet. Screen. Side. Up. "Shit."

Reaching out, I snatch it up before letting my eyes roll up the giant body before me. I want to legitimately die with every inch I take in as realisation hits me.

"Hey, Cruz, how's it going?" I ask, not sounding like myself in any way.

"Emmie," he growls, a smirk twitching at the corner of his lips.

"The last ten seconds didn't happen, okay?" I say in a rush, pocketing my phone while wishing the ground would swallow me up.

If it were anyone else—okay, maybe not Dad—then I could probably play this off, but fuck. My uncle blatantly just saw Theo's dick pic on my phone.

"So," he says, pulling out the chair opposite me. "I hear you're having an exciting day."

My cheeks burn red hot as his eyes hold mine, amusement dancing within them.

"Gunner sent you the video then."

"Yeah. You killed it, Em."

"I lost."

"You almost beat Cirillo's arse. You didn't lose fuck all. You should be proud."

"It's all the training you guys have been giving me."

"Well, I'm glad it's paying off. Clearly, he enjoyed himself." Cruz winks.

"Don't," I snap, holding my hand up. "Just... no. No."

Silence falls around us and I squirm in my seat as his eyes burn into me.

I begin poking my food around the plastic container it was delivered in, hoping this awkwardness dissipates sometime soon.

"Your dad told me about Oxford."

"I'm not going. Why does everyone other than me think it's such a good fucking idea?" I snap.

"Maybe because it is."

14

EMMIE

Slipping back into my bedroom, I look around the room.

Everything is exactly as I left it. As it should be, seeing as I double-checked the window was shut when I first got back from Mickey's.

My afternoon was much less eventful than my morning, and I've still not decided if that's a good thing or not.

It dragged. And I can't help wondering if that's because I looked up every fucking time someone entered, hoping it was Theo.

It wasn't.

He was at school, then football training, and then... I don't know, probably out killing someone or something utterly fucked up.

My heart pounds and my temperature spikes as I move across the room wearing an oversized Reapers shirt. I long for Theo's shirt that I was forced to leave behind in his flat when I escaped. This is the closest I've got to that. It's not as soft, and it doesn't smell like him—

not that it actually did, because it had been through the wash enough to eradicate that. It was all in my head, but it was good enough for me.

My eyes lock on the darkness outside the window.

Is he out there?

Is he waiting?

My pulse thrums through my body and my skin tingles in anticipation.

I've spent all afternoon and evening trying to decide what to do about tonight.

Part of me wanted to ask Dad if I could go and have a sleepover with Calli and completely abandon him, should he actually turn up.

Surely he won't... will he?

I've not had my window open since we came home.

I hated sleeping being shut in those first few nights in the Cotswolds, but I had little choice. I was terrified he'd find me and come and throttle me in the dead of night. But thankfully, it got easier.

I ordered a fan for when I got home so now I might not have fresh air—as fresh as London air gets—but at least my room stays cool.

But there's nothing to say he hasn't been out there every night.

No, he's been home in his room when he's been messaging me. In his bed like he said, like the photos showed.

But even as I tell myself that, doubt creeps through me and my temperature soars at the thought of him watching me get off through a crack in the curtains, calling out his name as I come.

A smile twitches at my lips as I make my way over to the bed and throw the covers back.

This is wrong. So fucking wrong.

But hell if I'm backing out of this challenge.

Desire still tingles just beneath my skin from our fight earlier, and my clit pounds a steady rhythm with its need for some action.

Grabbing my phone, I find a message that came through an hour ago while I was downstairs hanging out with Piper.

His Lordship: Don't keep me waiting…

I suck in a sharp breath, my spine straightening with thoughts of being watched. Of him actually waiting.

If this were anyone else I was messaging, I'd say it was a joke. But this is Theo. The same guy who spent fuck knows how long sitting at the end of my bed and watching me sleep without my knowledge. I'd be naïve to think he wasn't deadly serious about this right now.

Emmie: I don't follow orders from dickheads.

His Lordship: No. You follow orders from me. There's a difference.

"Is there though?" I mutter, rolling my eyes to myself.

His Lordship: Did you just roll your eyes at me?

My mouth pops open in shock.

Emmie: Multiple times a day. Get over it.

His Lordship: Fucking love flirting with you.

Emmie: This isn't flirting, you twisted fuck.

His Lordship: Babe, I thought you knew me better than that…

I push myself back so I'm sitting against my headboard and shamelessly let my thighs fall open, testing to see if he's really watching me right now.

Dots start bouncing on my screen and my heart rate increases to a dangerous speed.

He is.

My eyes lift to the window, desperately searching the darkness for any sign of him. But with my lights on, all I get is my own reflection.

His Lordship: Did I ever tell you how fucking perfect your pussy is?

"Oh fuck," I breathe, my legs falling wider.

His Lordship: I dream about tasting it again.

His Lordship: About hearing you call my name when I curl my fingers deep inside you.

My breathing becomes ragged as I read his dirty words. Heat blooms between my legs, my cunt aching for me to touch it, to relieve the pressure building down there.

His Lordship: Do it, Emmie. Show me how bad you need it too.

I fight it, my fingers curling into a tight fist, my nails cutting into the soft skin of my palm.

His Lordship: I want to see your fingers glistening with arousal. I want to see how much you miss me.

My head spins as my eyes remain glued to the screen. The defiant part of me wants to refuse, wants me to pretend that I'm not totally into this right now. But even if he's not watching my every move, I'm not confident that I could pull off lying to him.

His Lordship: Take it off.

Startled by his command, I find the brain cells to reply.

Emmie: Take what off?

His Lordship: The man's shirt you're wearing that doesn't belong to me. Take. It. Off. Now.

Well, if there was any doubt that he was watching, I guess that well and truly obliterates it.

Wrapping my fingers around the bottom of the shirt, I tug it from beneath me and lift it up my stomach but stop before I expose my breasts.

Emmie: Why are you the only one who gets to see anything?

His Lordship: Because I won. Now take it off. Show me how hard your nipples are for me.

Emmie: I hate you.

His Lordship: Is that why your pussy is so slick for me. Hate?

"Yes," I hiss, assuming he can't actually hear me, but what the fuck ever.

Releasing my phone, I drag the shirt over my head and throw it at the window, laughing as it collides with the glass and falls to the floor.

His Lordship: I love your fire. Makes me so fucking hard.

"Show me," I moan, squeezing my breast and pinching my peaked nipple until a moan rumbles in the back of my throat.

My phone buzzes.

"Holy fu—" I sit bolt upright. "How'd you do that?" I ask, staring at the window.

His Lordship: Trust me, Hellcat.

Emmie: Never.

His Lordship: Lie back, prop your phone up so you can see it. You're going to need both of your hands.

"Oh God," I moan, doing exactly as I'm told, because, despite my better judgement, I'm fucking powerless but to follow his demands.

His Lordship: Just the devil, babe. Don't be mistaken by my looks.

"Conceited dick," I half snap, half moan as I take the lead and cup both of my heavy breasts in my palms.

His Lordship: Pinch your nipples. Hard. Imagine it's my teeth.

"Theo," I cry, my back arching off the bed as I follow orders.

His Lordship: So. Fucking. Beautiful.

His Lordship: I'm aching for you, babe. Fucking aching.

"Touch yourself. I want to imagine your hand wrapped around your cock," I moan.

His Lordship: Can't do that, babe. Remember what I said earlier. Only you.

"You're not actually serious?"

His Lordship: Deadly.

His Lordship: I need you.

His Lordship: I want you.

His Lordship: I'm fucking dying for you.

His Lordship: Touch yourself, Hellcat. Show me how you play that pretty pussy.

I'm a moaning, writhing, desperate ball of lust as my hand slides down my belly.

"Yes," I hiss when my fingers connect with my swollen clit.

His Lordship: You fucking undo me Emmie Cirillo.

"Theo," I cry, letting my other hand join the party and pushing two fingers deep into my pussy.

I don't care whether he's doing it or not, the second my eyes slam shut, I picture him with his hand wrapped around his cock, his muscles pulled tight as he works himself almost violently in his need to be here with me.

"Yes, yes," I chant as my release surges forward thanks to my imagination.

My phone continues to buzz but I don't look. I can't peel my eyes open to see what he's saying as I race toward the breakpoint I've been desperate for all day.

"Oh God. Yes. Theo. THEO," I scream, probably way too loudly with my stepmum downstairs, but fuck it. I needed this. I needed this so fucking badly.

Utterly spent, my body sinks into the mattress as my heart pounds, my muscles twitch and endorphins on top of endorphins fill my blood.

Fuck. I needed that.

I might have got myself off last night while I was talking to him. But knowing he was watching took the experience to a whole new level. A twisted and deviant level I didn't know I needed but now totally crave.

My phone continues to buzz somewhere beside me, but it takes me longer than I'm sure is really necessary to finally move to find it.

When I light it up, I discover I've got the longest stream of the filthiest messages I've ever read in my life as Theo explained to me in vivid detail just how watching me made him feel.

His words ignite another inferno inside me and I quickly find myself rubbing my thighs together in an attempt to squash another wave of desire taking over me.

Wrong. So wrong.

But it's his final message that gives me pause and throws cold water over my out-of-control libido.

His Lordship: I need you, babe. So fucking bad. Tell me you're coming this weekend. I know Stella's invited you.

"Shit," I hiss, shifting on the bed so I can pull the sheets over my rapidly cooling body.

The longer I lie there staring at that message, the more my skin burns with his stare despite the covers hiding me from him.

He wants an answer. He deserves an answer. But I don't have one.

I shouldn't go, I know that. I should stand my ground, let them all go and do their thing. It would be safer for me to stay here, to lock myself in my room and forget all about them having fun.

So why is it that the thought of letting them go without me sends a shooting pain through my chest?

I finally have friends. The kind I've always wanted. I shouldn't squander this chance to be normal.

Fuck the crazy psychopaths who seem to be after me. They shouldn't have me cowering and hiding in my fucking bedroom like a pussy.

But even as I think it, a rush of fear that still lingers from being locked up in that cell—even if it was for only a short time—races through me.

Unable to answer his demand but not willing to just ghost him after everything that just happened, I start tapping out a reply.

Emmie: Good night, Theo. Sleep well. x

Immediately, I put my phone on aeroplane mode

and breathe out a sigh of relief before throwing the covers off and rushing toward the window. I keep my eyes down, not wanting to risk seeing him out there, if he actually is, as I tug the curtains closed.

I hoped that I might feel some kind of relief cutting myself off from him, from the outside world, but as I walk across the room, ignoring the old Reapers shirt I was wearing and pulling out a pair of my own pyjamas, the only thing I can focus on is the tight knot of anxiety sitting heavy in my belly.

I stop, resting my palms on my dresser, and take a few deep breaths.

I was meant to walk away. To sever whatever this thing was between us. To stand firm in my quest to prove that Theo, his father, my grandfather are all fucking certifiable for this whole situation.

I don't care that Theo was as blindsided with it as I was. He accepted it and followed Daddy's orders. He lied, used me, played me, tormented me.

All because of her and her stupid fucking decisions and life choices.

"Argh," I scream into the silence of my room.

Why am I so drawn to those who are bad for me?

Why do I keep going back time and time again no matter how much they hurt me?

What is wrong with me?

With my heart in tatters and my body still weak from my earth-shattering release, I clean up and get ready for bed.

My phone taunts me, but I don't turn it back on.

I can't.

My fragile state won't cope with whatever he might have said back to my final message.

Instead, I just lie there in the dark, running the events of the past few weeks through my mind.

Moving here. Starting over at Knight's Ridge. It was meant to be a fresh start. The beginning of a new future, one that might even include some success, unlike the one I was destined to live if I stayed in Lovell. But... I let out a sigh. Yet here I am tangled up in the middle of three gangs, none of which I really want anything to do with.

I toss and turn, but I never manage to drift off, and I'm still awake when Dad finishes his shift at the studio sometime after midnight.

He often stops and knocks, but normally I only answer if I'm still awake working or watching TV. If I'm curled up in bed, I usually pretend I'm asleep.

But not tonight.

Tonight, something forces me to call out to him.

Pushing the door open, he pokes his head around the door.

"Hey, kiddo. You doing okay?" he asks, slipping inside.

"Yeah, can't sleep."

"I'd have thought you'd be exhausted after all that exercise earlier," he quips.

Groaning, I shove my face into my pillow.

"Cruz sent it to you?"

"Yeah, he's pretty proud of his bad-arse niece. Gotta say, I am too. You killed it in that ring, kiddo."

I shrug, risking a look at him. "I lost."

"Against a boy who's been training since he could first walk and must be double your body weight. You held your own like a pro, and you should be proud."

"Meh," I mutter, flipping onto my back. "What's that?" I ask, noticing a parcel in his hand.

"No idea. Found it at the front door. It's got your name on it," he says, holding it out to me.

My brow wrinkles as I stare at it.

"Not expecting anything then?" he jokes.

"N-no, I wasn't," I mutter, taking in the black wrapping paper it's covered in.

That in itself should have been a clue, but I can't claim that I'm really firing on all cylinders at this moment in time, so when a very familiar shirt falls from the wrapping, I gasp in shock.

I stare down at it with my heart in my throat and tears burning the backs of my eyes.

My shirt. I mean... Theo's shirt.

My heart is like a runaway train in my chest as I think about him dropping it off.

Why didn't he knock? Why didn't he try to convince me to let him in?

"Knocks a guy on his arse and still gets gifts. You've got him wrapped right around your little finger, huh?" Dad says lightly, studying my over-the-top reaction to a stupid t-shirt.

"I-I—" I stutter but give up trying to even start explaining how I feel.

"Life's complicated, Emmie. Love is even worse. Take your time to figure all this out. You don't need to make rash decisions. We have time to work out a way to get you out of all of this, if that's what you want?"

"And if I don't?" I ask, feeling weird even hearing the question fall from my lips.

"That's for you to decide, kiddo. This is your life,

your future. All I can do is advise you the best I can, but only you know what's truly in your heart."

I stare at my dad, tears balancing dangerously on my lashes. "Who are you and what did Piper do to my hard-arse father?"

"Em," he breathes, dropping down on the edge of my bed and taking my cheeks in his hands. "I loved Piper more than life when I was not much older than you. Things might not have worked out for us back then, but I never forgot or let go of that feeling. And no one else would ever have filled the hole she left behind.

"I guess... What I'm trying to say is that I get it. People might say you're too young to understand, to feel as strongly as adults do, but I know all of that is bullshit. I fell in love young, and I know just how real, how raw, how painful that can be."

When my tears finally drop, Dad swipes them away with his thumbs.

"Trust your heart, Emmie. No one else's opinion on this matters. Not mine, or Damien's, or your friends. Only the two of you know what it's really like, and only the two of you can decide where it goes from here.

"You want to walk away, I'll be right by your side and find you the best lawyer in the country to get you out of this. You want to stay, see what can come of it, well then, I'll be right here too."

The sob that rips from my throat is anything but attractive, but his words cut me open in the best possible way.

To have his unwavering support means more to me than I could ever begin to explain.

"I might think he's an entitled prick," Dad mutters, making me laugh. "But I've seen the way he looks at you. He cares, Em. Really fucking cares." His lips part to say more, but he decides against it. "I can't ask for any more than that for my little girl."

He pulls me into his arms and holds me once again as I cry, my tears soaking his shirt through.

I have no clue how long we sit there, but when he finally pulls back and presses a kiss to my head, exhaustion hits me.

"Get some sleep kiddo. You've got some big decisions to make. Starting with tomorrow."

With another kiss, he stands and leaves me alone with just a little bit of Theo.

Gathering the shirt in my hands, I bring it to my nose and breathe him in deep.

I knew the second it fell in my lap and his scent hit me that he's been wearing this. He's been wearing it so he could give it back, knowing it would smell like him. If only he understood just how much that meant to me.

15

THEO

"This is fucking bullshit," I bark, slamming my hand down on the steering wheel of the replacement Maserati Dad managed to sort me out with while I decide what to do about the wreck I left on the side of the road at the beginning of the week.

How the fuck that was only four days ago, fuck only knows.

The pain might have mostly subsided, even after sparring with Emmie yesterday, but the bruises linger.

The car is fine. Nice even. But it's not mine. And that makes it all kinds of wrong.

The seat isn't right despite playing with its positioning for days. The mirror doesn't sit right. The speakers don't quite cut it.

"Chill the fuck out, man. We're almost there," Seb says lightly from the passenger seat while Alex mumbles around a mouthful of fucking crisps in the back.

My grip on the wheel tightens as I think about all

the fucking crumbs he's currently pushing into the fabric around him.

It might not be my car, but that doesn't mean I want it to be covered in his shit.

"Is that really fucking necessary?" I snap, glaring at him in the mirror.

"What?" he mumbles. "I'm hungry."

We're still thirty minutes out from All Hallows, the school we're playing tonight's match at.

The school bus, and Nico and Toby, left almost forty-five minutes before us at the beginning of lunch, but someone, the one currently giving me the stink eye in the mirror, was busy banging some fucking slut in the humanities bathrooms and made us fucking late. Now, we're stuck in Oxford traffic and risking missing kick-off.

"I swear to fuck, if we miss this I'm going to beat your arse into next week," I warn.

"Pfft," Alex scoffs, waving me off with his greasy fingers. "I've seen you fighting this week. There's only one of us who'll be on their arse." He lifts a brow at me in amusement as Seb grunts, making me look forward to realise the traffic has moved and I haven't.

Thanks to the fucking Reapers, that video went around Knight's Ridge like wildfire, and when I turned up at school this morning, anyone who was brave enough had something to say about the fact that I almost had my arse handed to me by my wife.

The thought of them all watching her lay into me with that skintight outfit she was wearing and the angry, sexy look in her eyes made me damn right murderous, and it's amazing that I managed to make it through to lunchtime only giving some stupid motherfucker in my economics class a black eye.

"Enough," Seb snaps. "Just focus on the game. You can bicker like a couple of old women later. We want to beat these motherfuckers."

"And we will. If we ever fucking get there," I hiss.

"You need to get laid," Alex helpfully adds from the back, having swallowed his mouthful of food.

"Bro, shut the fuck up," Seb barks, also shooting him a death glare.

"What? It's true. He's a miserable motherfucker when he's not seeing any action. You need to go and grovel your arse off to your wife and see if she'll suck your—"

I slam my foot down on the brake so hard, I'm amazed the car behind doesn't plough straight into the back of us.

"Don't fucking talk about her like that," I boom, my voice bouncing around the confines of the car, making it sound even more brutal. "She's my fucking wife, not some whore you fuck in the bathroom."

"Jeez, man. Sorry," Alex mutters insincerely. "Didn't realise it was such a touchy subject."

"Then I suggest you get your fucking head out of your fucking arse and pay attention." I glare at him, about two seconds from kicking him the fuck out of the car when the person behind slams their hand down on the horn.

"Watch your fucking mouth about my girl," I hiss, turning back around to move forward again.

"I'm hardly going to disrespect her seriously. She's my fucking friend, dickwad," Alex mutters.

I'm about to turn back around to finally kick him out when Seb's hand lands on my shoulder.

"She'll come around, man. Just fucking breathe, yeah?"

Sucking in a deep breath, I turn back to the traffic and roll my shoulders, hoping to relieve some of the tension that's locking my body up tight.

"Just focus on beating these arseholes. Enjoy the weekend. Give her some space and then start again Monday. Everything might be different by then."

"Yeah, she might have run away again. Or worse," I say quietly, so only he can hear me.

"She won't. She'll be there waiting for you," he assures me.

"I can't believe she's not coming," Alex says, bravely poking his head between our seats.

My grip on the wheel tightens once more to stop me from planting my elbow in his face and breaking his nose. It's mostly only the thought of all the blood that stops me from doing it.

"I thought she'd want to come and hang with the girls at least."

Silence ripples through the car as thankfully, the road opens up before us, allowing me to put my foot down and get to All Hallows' stadium in the nick of time.

The three of us barrel into the locker rooms while Coach is giving everyone else a pep talk. If looks could kill, the one he gives us as we crash through everyone to get changed would put us six feet under in a heartbeat.

"I know there's an unhealthy rivalry between us and them," Coach continues, "but I do not expect any foul play on the field. Do you hear me?" he booms before a quiet round of agreement ripples through the team. "If I catch any of you doing things you shouldn't be, you'll be benched for the rest of your Knight's Ridge career. Got it?"

"Got it, sir," I shout, spurring the others on to agree with a little more seriousness.

After a little more encouragement, he finally lets us out and we jog down the tunnel toward All Hallows' more than impressive stadium.

I hate to admit it, but it makes ours look like a cheap copy.

The crowd goes wild as we emerge. The majority of our sixth form bailed on school at the first opportunity this afternoon to be here for this duel, although we're still well outnumbered by the home crowd who boo us with aggression.

"Thompson," I spit, my lip curling back in disgust as I approach their captain.

His eyes hold mine as his teeth grind.

The last time I saw him, he was running away from Emmie like a pussy after his dumb-arse cousin had spiked her drink. Something I'm going to ensure he doesn't forget any time soon.

Although, I quickly learn that he's got his own agenda when he opens his mouth.

"How is Emmie? I'm looking forward to seeing her again," he taunts. "We can trade stories about putting you on your arse."

I suck in a deep breath through my nose as my fingers twitch, desperate to curl into fists ready to fly toward his face like I should have done that night.

"Aw, not embarrassed are you, Cirillo? It doesn't

make you any less of a man if your girl can put you down, much. I bet Daddy is mortified."

"Shut the fuck up," I growl, taking a step toward him.

I might be taller than him, but he's got a few pounds on me and I really don't fancy my chances right now.

"So where is she?" he asks, looking over my shoulder to search the crowd.

"She's not here, so you can stop hunting. The thought of seeing you again put her off."

A smirk curls at his lips.

"Sure. So it's got nothing to do with trying to get away from *you* then?"

My lips part to come back at him, but Coach shouts from the sideline and someone throws the ball at my head. Alex probably, from the smug-as-fuck look on his face when I glance over.

"We fucking playing this game or what?" he barks.

"Yeah, we are," I mutter, turning back to Thompson. "And we're going to fucking ruin you."

"Would like to see you try, Cirillo. When I find where you're hiding your girl, I'll make sure the only one she's celebrating with tonight is me."

My shoulders square as I take a step toward him, but a hand clamps down on my shoulder, pulling me back.

"Focus," Seb snaps in my ear. "I'm not playing the rest of the fucking season without you, man."

"You got it," I agree, turning to take up my position, ready for the whistle.

***

The game is fucking hard, and it's not helped by Thompson's intimidation tactics. More than once he almost taunts me into the fucking fight he's gunning for. But I refuse to give into him, to allow him the satisfaction of watching Coach end my Knight's Ridge football career early.

Football has pretty much been the only thing I've ever had for myself. Everything else in my life is dictated by my father, by the Family. And I fucking need it. I need it almost as much as I need her.

My eyes find the Knight's Ridge supporters once more as we wait for All Hallows to throw the ball in.

I've already found Stella and Calli right at the front, both wearing their Knight's Ridge shirts and shouting and screaming for us. Hell, I've even spotted Teagan, Sloane, and Lylah cheering us on. But I never find her.

Each time I look up, a little bit more of the hope I was secretly holding onto that she might come to support us, not just me but Seb and the others as well, withers and dies.

Maybe she really doesn't care.

Maybe everything the past few days was just her getting me out of her system and she really stands by her parting words to me on Monday. That she really believes there's nothing to be salvaged between us.

I'd really hoped after last night that things were turning a corner. The way she reacted to me despite me being miles away in the warmth of my own bedroom, I really thought it might just be the start of a new us.

Well, it seems the joke is on me because she's not here.

"You might as well stop looking, Cirillo. We both

know your girl is waiting in our locker rooms, ready to suck me off after we beat your arses out here."

"Fuck you," I hiss, walking away from him, refusing to allow him to ruin this entire experience for me.

"Nah, I'm much more of a pussy guy. I'd totally let you watch though as I slowly pushed my co—"

I'm on him before he even realises, my fingers curling in his shirt as I hold him in place, our noses almost touching, our heaving breaths mingling between us.

"Cirillo," Coach barks behind me as I try to convince myself not to take this fucker to the floor.

"Go on," he taunts. "You'll make my night so much sweeter."

My eyes hold his, but then some movement over his shoulder drags my attention away from the fuck in front of me.

All the air rushes from my lungs the second my eyes land on her.

She's here.

She came.

Releasing Thompson, I shove him away from me, the force of it making him stumble, but to my disappointment, he doesn't fall on his arse.

Looking back up, I find her again standing with her leather jacket wrapped around herself as if she's freezing, standing out here watching us.

The need to run over and wrap my arms around her, to warm her up and take her away from everyone here so it can just be the two of us burns through me.

But then she leans to the side and an arm wraps around her shoulders, tugging her into his body.

"Motherfucker," I spit.

16

EMMIE

Emmie

The doorbell rings through the empty house as I scramble to shove everything I might need for a night away into my bag.

"Coming," I bellow, although I'm pretty sure he won't hear it.

My phone starts ringing and I snatch it up from the bed where I abandoned it.

"I'm coming, I'm coming."

"Overshare much," he mutters in jest.

"Fuck off, idiot." Shoving my finger into the screen to end the call, I finish up before throwing my bag over my shoulder and leaving my room.

My stomach is in knots as I descend the stairs.

You're doing the right thing, the little voice in my head says.

But it does little to make me relax.

He might have said he wanted me there, but he never responded to my crass good night message, and we haven't spoken since.

He could have changed his mind very quickly once the high of that night lessened. He probably regretted every message he sent that showed me a little bit more of the soul he hides from everyone else.

"You okay?" Xander asks the second I open the door for him. "You look like you're about to puke."

"I might," I admit.

He rocks on his feet, looking all kinds of out of his comfort zone.

"You... uh... don't have to go, not if you don't want to. We could just hang here instead," he offers sweetly.

"I appreciate that, but I promised you a night away," I say, silently convincing myself to do this.

Just walk in there and face him like everything is normal.

"This isn't about me, Shorty. I'm happy wherever." He shrugs and my lips pull into a smile.

"You're a good friend, X."

"Meh," he mutters, taking my bag from me while I pull my boots on and grab my jacket. "It's cold out, you might want more than—"

"Really, *Mum*?" I tease.

He rolls his eyes at me and stalks toward his bike.

Excitement begins to trickle through my veins as I look at his beast of a machine.

Oh hell yeah, this part of the trip is something I can totally get on board with.

Zipping my leather jacket right up, I grab my helmet from the side and head out.

"Your carriage awaits, Princess."

"And you're sure I can't drive?" I ask.

"Don't push your luck, Shorty. I've already signed my life away to Cruz in order to do this."

"Shut up, you idiot." I smack his shoulder lightly.

"I'm serious. No going over fifty. No more than three drinks. No drugs. The only male to touch you is Cirillo. No—"

"He said that?" I hiss, trying to ignore the way my stomach tightens at the mere mention of my husband.

"Yep. Don't be thinking I'm here for the fun, Shorty. I've got more rules than I can remember."

"Well, you'd better be a good boy, then, Xanny."

"Really?" he asks, his lips twitching in amusement.

"Really."

Climbing on the back of his bike behind him, I wrap my thighs around his arse and my arms around his waist.

"Wait. I'm allowed to do this, right?" I ask, squeezing him tighter.

He doesn't answer for a beat and I'm about to let up on my teasing, but his hand covers mine reassuringly.

"Falling off the back of my bike would probably break more than a few rules. Hold on tight, Princess. I'm about to rock your world."

"At no more than fifty?" I mock.

"Yeah, we'll see."

"Woohoo," I squeal when he revs the engine and guns it down the street in the exact way I'm sure Cruz told him not to ride with me on the back.

"**O**h my God, I fucking love you," I squeal, my face aching from smiling like a complete maniac all the way here.

Take it steady he did not, and I loved every hair-raising second of it.

"Don't let someone else hear you say that," he mutters, pulling his helmet off and ruffling his hair into the messy style it usually sits in.

"Cirillo can kiss my arse," I announce happily, bouncing on the balls of my feet as the adrenaline from the ride continues to flood my veins.

"I bet he'd fucking love to, Shorty."

I flip him off over my shoulder and head toward the stadium, which is fucking insane for a school building. If I thought Knight's Ridge was over the top, then clearly I've seen nothing, because All Hallows is beyond ridiculous.

I feel like I'm about to walk into the Etihad for a premier league game—if I were at all into football of course—not a school football match.

"This wasn't quite what I was expecting."

"Oh, so you didn't go to a school like this?" I ask, faux shock evident in my tone.

"Nah, I'm more at home in the middle of Lovell, Shorty."

"You and me both. I'll take the poverty and depravity any day over this show of privilege and wealth."

"Let's go and surround ourselves with the pricks, shall we?" He wraps his arm around my shoulder, and together we walk toward the entrance.

Despite our hair-raising ride here, the game has

already started. Actually, it's coming toward the end. I was insistent that if I was doing this, then I wasn't spending an entire ninety minutes, or however long it is with half-time, standing, freezing my tits off and watching some—albeit hot—guys run around chasing a ball. Well, that was the story I fed everyone. Mostly, I just didn't want Theo to read too much into me being here, because I've still not convinced myself that I'm even doing the right thing.

We're directed toward the Knight's Ridge supporters and we find ourselves seats at the end of a row.

I spot both Stella and Calli right at the front of the crowd and laugh to myself as Stella screams bloody murder, despite openly admitting she knows nothing about soccer—her words, not mine—as the game plays out in front of us.

Unable to keep my eyes from the pitch any longer, I scan the bodies running around on it, picking out the copper and black coloured kits our players are in until I find the one I'm looking for.

I still the second I find him, my eyes running down the length of his body. His hair is soaked through with sweat, his shirt clinging to his muscular torso, and he has mud smeared pretty much everywhere.

He looks the complete opposite of the put-together prince I'm used to, and fuck if this side of him doesn't make something flutter with excitement inside me.

A fantasy of him taking me exactly like that in the locker rooms hits me out of nowhere, the intensity of the lust that floods my system enough to make my head spin.

The image of him pushing me up against the tiles,

his filthy hands running all over me and dirtying me up right along with him plays out in my mind as vividly as if I were watching it on a plasma fucking screen.

"Emmie," a voice snaps, dragging me from my wicked thoughts.

Blinking to clear the image, I look up to find Xander watching me with a smirk.

"I don't want to know where your mind just went, do I?"

Shaking my head, mostly to clear the lingering images but also to answer his question, I take the hand he holds out for me and let him pull me into my seat.

"You've got it bad, Shorty."

"I've no idea what you're talking about," I hiss, my eyes tracking Theo across the pitch.

The minutes drag on as the adrenaline from the journey and seeing him for the first time begins to fade and the cold Xander warned me about, starts to creep in.

A shiver rips through me at the same time Theo turns on one of the All Hallows players. I've paid them —or the rest of our team, to be fair—zero attention since I arrived, and it's not until Theo squares up to this guy that recognition hits me.

"Holy shit," I breathe, making Xander look up from his phone—clearly not a football fan either.

"What?"

"That guy. The one Theo is about to floor. That's Ben, he was the guy Theo thought spiked me at a party."

"Oh shit."

"Yeah, shit. But it wasn't him. It was his jealous bitch of a cousin. Ben was nothing but nice that night."

Theo grasps Ben's shirt and holds his eyes in warning. Even from this distance, I can feel the tension, the hate between them.

I stand without realising I do it as I silently beg Theo not to do something he's going to regret.

Another shiver rushes through me and my teeth chatter.

"Told you it was fucking cold, Shorty," Xander mutters, innocently wrapping his arm around my shoulders and pulling me into his body—but he does it at exactly the wrong moment because no sooner does he lift his arm than Theo's eyes collide with mine.

For a heartbeat, all I see is relief and happiness that he's found me, and it makes my heart sing that he really does want me here. But then I'm pulled closer into Xander's side and both those expressions make way for unfiltered hate.

He shoves Ben away from him, turning his whole focus on me.

I try pushing from Xander, but the irritating fuck is having none of it and holds me tighter.

Dropping his lips to my ear, he mutters. "We're not doing anything wrong, Shorty. If he wants to be a fuckwit, then that's on him."

"B-but—"

"But nothing. He needs to deal with his own shit. Meanwhile, you're fucking freezing your tits off. And I'm pretty sure he'd prefer them to stay on your body."

Without realising it, a smile creeps onto my lips and I teasingly slap him in the stomach.

I don't realise just how massive a mistake that is until I look back at Theo's murderous eyes.

He says something, but I'm too lost in my panic that

he's going to come running up the fucking stands and kill Xander with his bare hands.

Thankfully, Seb and Alex notice what's going on and both walk over, dragging Theo backward and spinning him around to sever our connection.

"Well, I think it's safe to say he's noticed you," Xander quips.

"This was a bad idea."

He shakes his head, continuing to hold me. While I might want to break free for Theo's sake, I stay right where I am, because Xander is like a freaking radiator and I need the warmth.

"Try telling me that later when you two are hate fucking so hard you can't remember your own name."

"Xan," I gasp in shock, but all he does is chuckle.

"Oh come off it, Em. The tension between you two is fucking unbearable even for me. There's no way you're not getting out of this trip without a handful of screaming orgasms at his hands, and you know it." He leans in again right as the referee blows the whistle for some reason, and Theo turns back our way. Fucking typical. "It's why we're here, Shorty."

A bolt of fear and desire crackles through me in the split second our eyes connect.

"You brought me here to hook up?" I ask in disbelief, talking to Xander but looking at Theo.

"I sure didn't come here for the game," he scoffs. "And who knows, maybe I'll even find myself a little rich girl to play with tonight."

When Theo is forced to look away from me again, I let out the breath I didn't realise I was holding.

"We should go," I mutter.

"And miss him killing every motherfucker on that

pitch, wishing it were me? Nah, let's stay for the entertainment."

"There's something fucking wrong with you."

"Takes one to know one."

My lips part to argue, but I soon discover I don't have any kind of comeback because, yeah, I'm as fucked up as the best of them.

"You came," Stella screams once the game is over and we're all piling out into the car park.

"It would seem that way," I mutter as I get jostled from behind and my heart jumps into my throat, thinking that it could be Theo.

"Why aren't you more excited? You just watched your husband slaughter All Hallows in front of your very eyes," Calli damn near squeals.

She's not wrong. According to the crowd around us, something changed after we arrived because suddenly All Hallows couldn't keep up, and in the final fifteen minutes of the game, the score went from a boring nil – nil to three – nil to the visitors faster than anyone could believe, thanks to Theo's right foot.

The thought of it being because of me, of being the one that really lit a fire under Theo's arse and spurred him on makes me all warm and fuzzy inside. Not that I'm going to admit that.

"Did you see the way he was looking at you, girl? You're in for a good night." Stella winks.

"I think we're going to head home. This was a bad idea."

Xander nudges me with his shoulder in disapproval, but I can't help the gut-twisting feeling that I've made a massive mistake.

"Don't you fucking dare," Stella warns me. "We're going to the hotel to get ready then everyone is meeting in a bar called The Cellar, or something." She waves it off. "And, I brought you the perfect outfit."

"Tell me it's not pink," I demand, not realising that I'm totally conceding to her plans.

"Yes, girl. This is going to be the best night ever. And no, it's not pink."

"Fuck it. Let's go," I sigh.

"Follow us, yeah?" she says to Xander. "I got you a room just in case."

"Stella," I warn.

"What? I was hopeful." She winks, sharing a conspiratorial look with Xander.

"Seriously. You two were in on this?" I sulk, stalking off toward Xander's bike.

"You're cute when you're pissed, Shorty," Xander points out with a smirk.

"I'm never fucking cute. And if you want to return to London with your balls still attached, you won't call me it again."

"You need to get laid. Sooner rather than later."

"So do you with the number of times you've brought sex up tonight."

"I'm a guy. I always need to get laid, Shorty."

"Fucking men. Fucking pain in the arse, horny douchebags," I mutter, much to his amusement, as I pull my helmet on. "Get on then," I hiss at him when he just stands there watching me.

His eyes lift to something behind me and a wicked smirk appears on his lips.

"Sure thing, Princess."

I wait for him to throw his leg over before doing the same and snuggling into his warm body once more.

It's not until he's backed out of his space that I realise what, or who, caught his attention. Standing like a fucking statue in front of the players' entrance where there's a crowd of supporters, including Stella and Calli, is Theo. And he's staring right at us.

His eyes lock on mine through my visor and a tremor races through me for all the promises of things to come that linger in his dark green depths.

A chuckle rumbles in Xander's chest as we pass and I slap him once more.

Sometime soon, he's going to really regret poking the bear.

17

THEO

"**D**rink this, you miserable motherfucker," Alex barks, slamming both a glass and a bottle of vodka down on the table in front of me.

Dad ensured that the entire top floor of this hotel was booked for us this weekend. We've got one suite, Toby and Nico another, and the girls have the other.

The girls and... *him?*

My blood boils as I think about him touching her, comforting her, having her coiled around his body like a fucking snake as they rode off together.

Ignoring the glass, I reach for the bottle.

"Bro, you won us the fucking game. You're meant to be on top of the fucking world right now," Seb points out.

I am. Well, a part of me is.

Seeing her standing there in the crowd ignited something inside me I've never really experienced before. The strength of my need to make her proud of me, to impress her, to prove to her that I'm not just some privileged fuck-up who likes to watch her get off like a creep, was quite frankly, disturbing. But it pushed me forward. And thank fuck it did, because we were heading toward having to walk off that pitch at ninety minutes with a fucking nil – nil draw. Not fucking good enough.

I'd rather lose fairly than have a fucking goalless draw.

Seeing the look on Ben's face when he failed to stop me from putting the ball in the back of their net for the third time in less than ten minutes was fucking beautiful. Almost as beautiful as my girl standing in the crowd with a wide smile on her face.

I have no idea if she knew she had even reacted to my success, but her smile meant fucking everything to me. Her presence, despite her bodyguard, meant everything to me.

"I'm ecstatic about that," I tell them both.

"Well," Alex mutters, "did you want to tell your face?"

I flip him off and take another shot from the bottle.

"Whose fucking idea was it that we couldn't see the girls until we leave for The Cellar?" Seb sulks. "I could really fucking do with a victory blow job right about now."

"Mine. Asshole. It was my fucking idea to stop you both abandoning me for pussy," Alex pipes up happily.

"Like you do every fucking time we go out?" I ask. "All it takes is a girl to glance in your general direction and you're in front of her panting like a bitch in heat."

"I am not. And anyway, you're just jealous because I get more girls than you."

"Jealous. Yeah. That must be fucking it. Did you

manage to get rid of the crabs the last skank gave you?" I ask, my voice deadly serious.

"Once," Alex spits. "It happened once. Can you fucking leave it in the past now?"

"Un-fucking-likely," Seb offers, swigging from his own bottle while Alex mutters in irritation.

"Just think, if you didn't ban the girls, you could be having silent one-on-one time with your right hand at this very moment."

"You know," Alex says, standing up sharply as if something just bit his arse, "you two are such killjoys now you're pussy-whipped. I'm gonna go find Nico and Tobes. At least they still know how to have fun."

"Ouch," Seb says, covering his heart as if Alex's words actually hurt him. "One day you'll meet a girl who turns you to the dark side, man. And I'm fucking here for it."

"Whatever," he mutters, swiping his bottle from the table and pulling a baggie of weed from his pocket. "Time to go and celebrate, motherfuckers." He stalks to the door before turning back to me. "Calli's still single, right? Maybe it's time to pop that baby's cherry."

My fingers curl around the sofa cushions beneath me at the thought of Calli being corrupted by a brute like him.

"Stay the fuck away from my cousin, Deimos," I growl. "She's not kept her V-card this long just to hand it over to a fucking dog like you."

"Yeah... we'll see. I bet her virgin pussy tastes so fucking good."

I swipe the glass from the table—not willing to sacrifice the vodka—and launch it at his head.

He sees it coming, though, and ducks through the

door, letting it shatter against the wood, shards of glass raining down on the stained oak floor.

"Really?" Seb hisses. "Was that necessary?"

"Imagine if it was Demi," I spit. It's a low blow, bringing up his dead little sister, but fuck. I've got Calli in the same box as my little sisters, so I know he would have too if life had turned out differently.

"Fair point. You're an arsehole for bringing it up though." He shrugs, swallowing down shot after shot.

"You can break his rules now if you really wanna get your dick sucked so bad."

He stares at me, lowering the bottle slowly.

"And you don't?"

My lips part to agree, but I quickly remember one massive difference between us.

"You've got a girl who'll drop to her knees without so much as blinking. Mine is more likely to bite it off if I get her down there."

He snorts a laugh. "You might have a point, but I'm pretty sure she's as desperate for it as you are."

I shrug, images of her writhing on her bed, moaning my name the last night playing out in my mind and making my dick twitch.

"You need to shower first. You might deserve a victory blow job for your win, but no one wants that sweaty thing in their mouth."

"Fuck you, man. It's like fucking roses down there."

Seb lifts a brow at me.

"Whatever," I mutter.

We all showered after the game, but I didn't do anywhere near a good enough job to go out and hopefully end up in bed with a naked Emmie.

Pushing from the sofa with my bottle in hand, I pad

toward the room I was left with after Seb and Alex both claimed theirs first, and swing the door closed behind me, cutting off Seb's smug laugh.

I'm hardly surprised to hear the main door to the hotel suite slam shut not two seconds later.

"Fucking sex addict," I mutter to myself, placing my bottle on the bedside table, I shed my sweats and shirt. But instead of marching straight toward the shower, I fall back on the bed as I try to get my head on straight.

She's here. She came. And this is meant to be the best fucking weekend of the year.

So why do I have an irritating sinking feeling in my belly like something is going to go very, very wrong?

Because you refuse to believe anything good can happen to you at this point.

Blowing out a breath, I shove my fingers into my hair and pull until pain shoots down my spine. That and the lingering images of Emmie last night makes all the blood in my body head south.

Could tonight be the night I'm able to get her back where she belongs?

18

EMMIE

The cocktails Stella has been making for us since we got back to the hotel have helped settle some of my unease as the four of us sit around shooting the shit.

Apparently, Alex banned any boy/girl mixing until we're due to leave in a couple of hours to head to the bar. Something I can't say I'm all that bothered about because it gives me a little more time to figure out how I'm going to play it when I finally come face to face with Theo. That, and I can only hope that his anger has lessened a little the next time he has to look at Xander.

I tried to convince him to head home when we got back here, but he stood firm, telling me that his babysitting gig didn't end until we were all back safely on London soil.

I rolled my eyes hard at that, but I didn't argue. Things are so fucked up right now that I can't deny it settles something inside me, knowing that I've got him there looking out for me—for us.

He turns his focus on Calli as she asks him

something about the club while I watch Stella shake another cocktail concoction she's made up.

"So where's this outfit you've got for me?" I ask, wondering why she's not already presented it to me.

"Waiting."

"Waiting for what?" I ask nervously.

As if he were summoned, the hotel room door opens and Seb pokes his head inside.

"Evening ladies, looking good," he says happily, although his eyes don't stray from Stella.

"Ugh," I complain teasingly. "I thought we were free of cocks for a few hours."

"Nice, cous. Really fucking nice," he mutters, beelining for his girl. "And to think, I come bearing gifts for my favourite cousin."

My lips part to tell him that I'm his only cousin, but the reality is, I have no idea if I am. We haven't sat down to have that kind of conversation yet, and quite frankly I've not got enough head space to deal with the potential outcome of it.

I'm happy living in ignorant bliss right now that Seb and his sisters are my only new relatives.

"Gifts?" I ask, hoping he's got something exciting up his sleeve.

Pulling his arm from behind his back, he reveals a tablet.

"Uh..." I start, confused as fuck.

He ignores me as he leans down, pins Stella to the sofa with his hand around her throat and slams his lips down on her.

"If your gift was watching you two fuck right in front of me, then I think I'll pass. Neanderthal," I scoff, pushing from the sofa after draining my cocktail. I'm going to need more to put up with their antics.

By the time he releases her, leaving them both out of breath and clearly in need of more, I've made another very strong drink.

"Nah, we'll save that for later. Hopefully, you'll be too distracted by then to pay any attention to us."

"Hmm... We'll see," I mutter, taking a sip of my drink and wincing at just how potent it is.

If I didn't already have a buzz going from Stella's bartending skills, then I will after this.

"Come on," he says, snatching up my hand and dragging me toward the bedrooms.

"This one," I say, pointing to my room, assuming it's where he's heading. Although fuck knows why. "What's going on?" I ask when he swings the door open and steps inside as if he owns the place.

"Like I said, I've got a gift. I really think you're going to love it."

"Jury's still out on that."

"No faith," he mutters, dropping down onto the bed and resting the tablet on his thighs. "No fucking faith."

"So..." I prompt, getting irritated with his teasing.

"Come sit," he says, tapping the space on the bed beside him. "So..." he starts. "Theo and I don't have any secrets, and I know him better than I do myself most of the time."

My cheeks burn as I think about the things we've been up to recently.

"I know he's been watching you."

"Sneaking in through my open window and being a creep, you mean?"

"Originally, yeah. But I know you've shut him out."

"Okay... I don't really know where this is going," I say, a frown marring my brow.

"Don't shoot the messenger, okay? And I organised something in retaliation."

"Retaliation," I mutter. "That's something I could get on board with."

"See, this is how I know we share the same blood, Shorty."

"Keep talking."

"Theo's a control freak, I'm sure you've figured that out by now. He likes... being in control and knowing what's happening. He's also fucking obsessive. But I've never seen him as bad with anything as he is with you, Em. He's so fucking gone for you, it's laughable."

I stare at him with my brow raised.

"Yeah, okay, I'm totally whipped too, whatever. Anyway, his watching you extends beyond sneaking into your bedroom. Ever feel like you've always got his eyes on you?"

It takes longer for the penny to drop than it really should.

Memories of him responding to my questions and demands last night slam into me.

"Motherfucker," I bark, shooting up from the end of my bed. "He's been fucking watching me. How?" I demand, turning on Seb.

"He's got cameras in your room."

"H-he... He... Fuck, Seb. Do you realise how fucked up that is?"

"Yeah, and just a little bit hot. What have you been showing him, Emmie?"

"Oh my God," I drop my head into my hands,

thinking of the last few nights, getting myself off with his name as a plea on my lips. "Oh my God."

Seb laughs, the fucking dickhead. "Yeah, his balls are bluer than fucking Papa Smurf's right now. Anyway, I thought a little payback was in order."

I stare at him as he brings the tablet to life, opens an app, and spins it toward me.

The image of Theo laid out almost naked on a bed appears on the screen.

"Oh my God," I breathe, my eyes glued to his insane body.

"You're welcome."

"You bugged his fucking room?"

"Yeah. I'd have done it in his flat if I could have figured out a way to get in there without being caught."

My mouth opens and closes to respond, but I'm too distracted by Theo.

The way he's lying there. He looks totally defeated.

He should be buzzing. He just won that match for his team. Yet he's lying there like it could be the worst day of his life. Although, there is more than a small bulge in his boxers. I mean, I know he's big. But he's definitely rocking at least a semi down there right now. Maybe it's not the worst day of his life after all.

I wonder what he's thinking about...

"So... that's my gift. The truth, and a little revenge. We good?" Seb asks, standing from my bed and stalking toward me.

"Um... I... uh..."

Wrapping his hand around the back of my head, he drops the sweetest kiss to my hairline.

"Give him hell, cous. I love him like a brother, but he can be a fucking cock sometimes."

"Oh don't worry. I'm all for some fun and games."

He chuckles as he walks to the door.

"We've got two hours before we need to leave. No excuses."

"Yeah, yeah," I mutter, not lifting my eyes from the screen as ideas begin formulating in my mind.

Seb slips from the room and I barely hear the door close as I tug my boots off and crawl onto the bed, pulling my phone from my pocket.

I open our conversation and pause, trying to come up with the perfect first message.

Emmie: I can't stop thinking about last night...

The second I lower my phone, I turn the volume up on the tablet and damn near squeal in delight when he hears his phone buzz. He rolls over, gifting me the delicious sight of his muscles pulling and stretching as he leans over the side of the bed and pulls it from his pocket.

The second he sees my name, his entire face lights up. It's mesmerising, and damn it if it doesn't make some of my anger over this situation begin to ebb away.

I have no idea what he might have seen over the past... fuck knows how long. But I'm not ashamed of anything I do. Yes, it's a massive invasion of privacy, but getting this opportunity to retaliate makes it somewhat better.

His eyes widen when he reads my message, his lips pulling up into a smile.

"Damn," he mutters, pushing his fingers into his hair to brush it off his face.

He starts typing and I pick up my phone again, desperate to see what he's going to come back with.

His Lordship: Is that why you're here? Hoping for a repeat?

"Something like that," I mutter to myself but quickly panic that he might be able to hear me. But when he doesn't move or react, I soon realise he has no idea.

Seb, you cheeky fucking bastard.

Emmie: Did you get off? Or are you staying true to your word?

His Lordship: I don't joke about orgasms, Hellcat.

He's still staring at the screen as his hand skates down his abs, cupping himself over the fabric of his boxers.

His Lordship: I'm fucking aching for you.

Emmie: Oh yeah?

His Lordship: You have no fucking idea.

Emmie: Show me.

Butterflies flutter in my belly as I send my demand.

Scooting back against the headboard, I rest the tablet on my thighs as he smirks at his phone.

Not two seconds later does he tuck his thumbs into the waistband of his boxers, pushing them down his hips and releasing his now fully hard cock.

My teeth sink into my bottom lip and a groan of desire rumbles deep in my chest as I stare at him.

Who knew the devil could be so beautiful?

My heart begins to run away with itself when he wraps his hand around his length and strokes it once.

Forcing my eyes from his cock, I look at his face.

His jaw is clenched tight, the muscles down his neck straining as he holds himself back.

My breathing becomes ragged as I watch him snap a photo of his dick and hit send.

My phone buzzes with the image, but I don't look at it for a few seconds. I'm too enthralled with all of him.

After watching him write a message, I look down, taking in the image before I get to read the comment.

His Lordship: I'm always hard for you, Hellcat. ALWAYS. Now all I need is you.

My eyes float back to him as if we're two magnets drawn together at all times.

He's still got his hand around his dick, but he's not moving it. He's not doing anything but staring at his screen in hope.

His Lordship: The guys have left. You know you wanna be here in person right now.

Fucking right I do.

His Lordship: Don't you want to feel my cock buried so deep in your pussy you have no idea where you end and I begin?

"Yes."

His Lordship: I know you're lying if you say no. I heard you calling my name last night, babe.

Emmie: And I want you calling mine now.

His Lordship: I told you, babe. Only for you.

Emmie: It is for me. I'm asking for it.

His hand still doesn't move, but my need to break his resolve is stronger than his restraint. I know it is.

Emmie: I want to know I've brought you to your knees without even being there.

His Lordship: You do. Every. Fucking. Day.

Unable to stop myself, I climb from the bed.

I've got a fire burning beneath my skin from watching him, and my blood is running at boiling point, but it's not enough.

Storming through to the living room, I find Seb's

arse first where he's got Stella pinned beneath him on the sofa.

"Room key," I demand.

"Yes, girl," he sings after pulling his lips from my girl.

"Nah, I ain't touching him. Just proving a point."

Seb stuffs his hand into his pocket and reveals his key.

"First door on the right."

"Thanks." I pluck it from his fingers and leave them to it.

I stop outside their door and send my next message.

Emmie: Show me. I want to see you calling my name.

He stares at the screen for a beat as I tap the key to the wireless pad and silently slip into their suite.

It takes a couple of seconds, but he sits bolt upright as realisation hits him.

Emmie: You're not playing the game, Theodore.

Emmie: Show. Me.

Sucking in a breath, I swing his bedroom door open, revealing the man himself with his boxers around his thighs, his cock in his hand and a shocked-as-fuck look on his face.

"Busted, creep," I say, resting my hip against the

door frame as I run my eyes down the length of him. "Now. Show. Me."

"Holy shit," he breathes. "You were watching me?"

His chest rises and falls rapidly as we stare at each other, the air between us crackling so loud I'm sure the rest of the hotel guests are able to hear it.

A wicked smile curls at my lips.

"Payback is a bitch, Cirillo. You sneaky fucking bastard."

His head falls back as he barks out a laugh, not giving two single shits about the fact that he's been caught.

"How long?" I ask.

"How long what?"

"How long have you been watching me for?"

"Ages, babe. Although I must admit, to start with, it was just to watch you sleep the nights I couldn't get there," he confesses as easily as if we're discussing the weather.

"So when did you start using it to watch me getting off?"

His eyes flash with heat, telling me just how much he's been enjoying it.

"Since you came back." Thankfully, he has the decency to look a little ashamed this time. "But I swear, I haven't been listening to you with the girls, or your dad or anything."

"So it was just to satisfy your sick and twisted mind that I still wanted you."

"I already know you still want me, Hellcat."

He shifts as if he's about to get up.

"Don't move," I bark. "Hand over that control, Cirillo. Right now, it's mine."

His teeth grind so hard I wouldn't be surprised if they just turned to dust.

"And what do you want from me, babe?" He tilts his head to the side, and damn it if the look on him doesn't make me want him that much more.

"I've already told you. I want to watch you come apart just like you've been watching me. But you're too fucking stubborn."

"I told you, babe. I'm only coming for you."

"So come for me. I'm standing right here."

Unable to resist any longer, his hand moves, stroking up the length of his monster cock.

A deep groan rumbles in the back of his throat, sending a wave of heat rushing through me. But I lock it down.

This isn't about me. It's about him.

Lifting the screen, I hit the little red record button I spotted earlier and wait a beat to make sure it's capturing this moment for me. Something tells me that I'm going to be able to make use of it many, many times in the near future.

"Hellcat," he growls.

"Theodore," I state, lifting a brow at him. "Don't keep your wife waiting."

"Fuck, babe," he groans, falling back onto one elbow, and I really can't complain because the definition of his abs from the move is fucking insane.

Hugging the tablet to my belly, I tuck my phone into my pocket and lift my finger to my mouth, biting down on it as he starts to stroke himself faster.

"I'm not gonna last," he warns.

"At least you've done more than two pumps," I tease. "Pretty sure a video of that would really ruin your rep after getting your arse kicked in the ring yesterday."

The way his teeth clench tells me that he's had some stick over it.

"Don't care," he grunts, his movements becoming more and more erratic.

"Nice try. We all know your reputation is everything. You want Daddy to approve. And getting your arse beat by a girl... I don't think the big bad mafia boss will be anywhere close to approving of that."

"I don't care about him, Hellcat. I don't care about anyone."

"Oh?" I ask, more than happy to push him as he gets closer to his release.

"The only one I care about is you. Always you. Only fucking you."

I gasp at the sincerity in both his eyes and his voice as he says those words.

But it's not enough to put a halt to my plans.

"Stop," I boom, pushing from the doorway and placing the tablet down before marching to the bed and looming over him, resting my palms on either side of his waist.

His chest heaves, his eyes are blown, and his skin is covered in a sheen of sweat. Sweat that makes my mouth water as I think about licking it from his tense muscles.

His breaths race out, fanning over my face, allowing me to smell the alcohol on it.

"Get dressed, Theo. We're all going out to party."

"W-what?" he stutters, clearly thrown for a loop in his haze of lust.

"You heard me. And don't you dare finish that off. You need me to do it, remember?"

I push from his bed, ready to make my escape, but he comes to his senses enough to capture my wrist, hauling me back.

His hungry eyes burn into mine as I stare down at him sitting on the bed.

"Let. Go," I hiss, tugging my arm free from his grasp. "Consider this punishment for invading my privacy."

A smirk spreads across his face that makes my stomach clench.

"Aw, come on, babe. Admit just how hot it gets you, knowing that I was watching... listening to you when you cried out my name, wishing I was the one with my fingers buried inside you."

"Not the point," I spit, unable to deny the truth.

"Maybe not. But it's fucking hot."

"I'll see you later," I shoot over my shoulder, grabbing the tablet and fleeing from his room before he can do anything to convince me otherwise. Something tells me it wouldn't take all that much if he wanted to.

I storm back through into our suite and throw Seb's room key at him.

"Your best friend is a prick," I spit, my anger—and desire—over this whole situation having exploded in the short walk back here.

"No happy ending from that visit then?" Seb asks with a grin.

"You fucking—" I fly at him, jabbing him in the ribs while he holds his hands up in surrender.

"I think I should probably go make sure she's not strung Theo up by his balls, Princess."

The second Stella agrees, he bolts for the door.

"Pussy," I call after him, and he leaves us with only the sound of his laughter lingering behind him.

"Dickheads. All of them," I mutter, folding my arms over my chest and falling down on the sofa in frustration.

19

EMMIE

"**I** am not fucking wearing that," I screech as Calli holds the monstrosity in front of me. "I'm sorry, no. I played along with your little Pink Ladies joke at Halloween. But this... Nah. You're fucking insane."

Stella laughs, but the determination on her face tells me that I'm not getting out of this quite so easily. "The only one who will be going insane is your husband, especially after you just left him ready to explode." She snorts another laugh, holding her hand up to high-five me. "Fuck, I love you, Em," she slurs, already more than drunk.

I clearly am not, considering I'm seeing the... *dress?* that Calli is holding up through very sober eyes.

"Oh come on, I made them specially."

I rear back a little. "Wait," I say, snatching the fabric out of her hands to study it. "You made these?"

"Yeah," she whispers, a blush creeping onto her cheeks. "I've been experimenting with stuff since

Halloween while you two have been busy with Seb and Theo."

"Shit, Cal," Stella breathes, suddenly sounding very sober.

"It's fine. You've got stuff going on, I get it. I didn't say that to make you both feel guilty. I've been enjoying it. Other than gym and cheer, I've never really had anything for myself like this. It's nice."

"Damn it, Cal. You're pulling on my heartstrings," I admit, although still really not wanting to wear this damn dress thing.

"You want to drive him to the brink of insanity, then this is for sure the way to do it," Stella says again.

"Oh, and don't forget these." Calli throws something else at me, and my eyes widen when I realise what they are.

"You made matching knickers too?"

Calli laughs, a mischievous twinkle in her eye.

"So who are you intending on driving crazy with this tonight then, Cal?" I ask, lifting the third dress from the bed.

"No one. I made them for your benefit, mostly."

I turn her dress around and sigh in disappointment when I discover she's right.

"You totally should have put someone else's name on the back just to join my quest to torture Theo. Can you imagine if you put 'Deimos' on it or something?" I joke.

Her cheeks flame to the point at which I wonder if she's about to combust in front of us. "I am not walking around with that idiot's name on me," she spits.

"Whoa, okay. What the hell did Alex do to you, anyway?"

"Nothing. I just have no interest in belonging to any of them, thank you very much."

Stella looks at me over Calli's shoulders, her eyes widening in amusement, which makes me snort.

"What?" Calli demands.

"Nothing, Cal. I'm gonna go shower and put this on. I can't wait to see Seb's face. You're the best."

She smacks a kiss on Calli's cheek before disappearing.

"I may never forgive you for this."

"Yeah, you will. Probably sometime after midnight when I can hear you screaming Theo's name through the wall."

My lips part to rip her a new one and tell her that won't be happening. But let's be honest...

"We'll see," I mutter, snatching up the damn dress and stalking from the room.

"We will," she calls from behind me. "We sure will."

I leave Stella and Calli still curling their hair and march toward the living room, where I know there's plenty of alcohol that's going to help me walk out of here with my head held high.

I'm asking for trouble, wearing this. So much fucking trouble. But even knowing that, I can't stop myself.

His reaction is going to be worth it and then some.

Xander looks up from his phone and actually gives me a double take as his chin drops.

It would be funny if I weren't slowly dying of mortification inside.

"Whoa, Emmie. You look... Shit. How the fuck am I meant to keep you out of trouble wearing that?"

His eyes run up and down the length of me in shock.

I should probably tell him to stop, remind him that he friend-zoned me a long time ago, and that I'm a married woman. But his eyes find mine and he gathers himself back together.

I can't deny that his reaction does good things for my confidence, mind you.

I left my hair to air dry and then scrunched it with some wax to give it a messy look and added my standard black makeup before pulling on the... dress.

I must admit I was impressed when I looked in the mirror. But shit, I also feel like a fucking idiot.

I'm wearing the kind of outfit that Sloane and her bunch of bitches would wear to get the guys' attention. I feel like a sell-out. Exactly the kind of girl I never wanted to be. Even if I do look hot doing it.

"You're not meant to keep me out of trouble, X. Just keep me alive and in your sight at all times," I remind him.

"Me and every other guy tonight," he mutters.

"Wait, it gets better," I admit as he takes a swig of beer.

The second I turn around and lift my hair, the beer sprays out of his mouth, covering the coffee table in front of him

"I think you've probably just made my job easy. You're going to spend the night locked in a bedroom with the one man who's allowed to go near you. Easiest babysitting job ever."

Flipping him off, I march toward the liquor cabinet and pull out a bottle of vodka, sloshing a generous measure into one of the tumblers.

"We'll see."

"You left him with his balls about to explode, Em. He's gonna fucking blow the second he sees you."

"Can you make sure you record it if he does?" I ask seriously before knocking my shot back.

He's still laughing at me when I walk across the room, grab my leather jacket from the back of the chair I threw it on and stuff my feet into my boots. I might have conceded to the dress, but there's no way in hell they're getting me in a pair of heels too.

"Right, let's go," I announce.

Xander looks down toward the bedrooms. "I thought we were all—"

"You thought wrong. We've got an Uber waiting outside."

"Uh... right, okay." He jumps up, shoves his phone into his pocket and stalks over.

I take a minute to look him over. He's wearing a pair of dark black trousers and a fitted dark grey button-down shirt. His hair is styled, although still a total mess. He looks... "Hot."

"Huh?" he asks, clearly not quite hearing me.

"Um... I said you look hot."

He flashes me a knee-weakening smile. Although, it doesn't have the effect on me I'm sure it'll have on the rest of the female population. He might be hot, but my body is craving another.

One that's going to be waiting for me to climb into a

car with them shortly.

Not happening.

I'd rather keep him on his toes.

"Thanks, Shorty. Let's hope tonight is my lucky night, huh?"

"Make the most of that hotel room, X." I wink before pulling the door open and marching out with him hot on my heels.

Thankfully, we make it out of the hotel and into the Uber without walking straight into Theo or any of the guys.

He's going to be pissed, even more than I'm sure he already is after the state I left him in. Assuming he followed orders, that is.

My phone has been buzzing every couple of minutes since I left his room, but I've refused to even look.

I'm more than aware that his dirty words would hold the power to have me crawling back into his room, kneeling at his feet and promising to be a good girl.

But I refuse to even be tempted.

The second he finds me, I know it's going to go to shit, especially with the buzz of vodka tingling beneath my skin.

"Did you ever consider cutting out this waste of time and just showing up at his room wearing that?" Xander asks when the car pulls to a stop on a street lined with clubs and bars.

"Where would be the fun in that?"

He rolls his eyes at me before thanking our driver and climbing from the car. Not wanting to battle with the passing cars, I slide along to follow him.

Thankfully, we're early enough that there's not a

huge queue, and after showing the bored-looking bouncer my fake ID, we're allowed to head inside.

Following everyone else, we head down a spiral staircase, the space around us getting darker with each step we take and the music getting louder.

I'm really not a fan of dance music, but even I can't deny the heavy bass gets my pulse racing as we descend deeper underground.

The walls are lined with wood from old wine crates, and when we emerge into the main bar, our steps falter a little as we take in the walls that are made out of glass bottles of all colours. It's really quite something.

"This is different," Xander shouts in my ear as I spot more than a few of the kids from Knight's Ridge looking over at me.

"Yeah, I guess." Kind of feels like home from home right now, being judged by those arseholes. "I need a drink."

"You got it, Shorty."

Xander's fingers thread through mine and he drags me through the crowd and toward the bar, where he orders four Jäger bombs that we throw back almost the second the glass hits the counter.

"Ugh," I complain as I swallow the second. "That is rank."

I wipe my mouth with the back of my hand in the hope that it wipes the taste away as my belly begins to warm.

"Vodka and Coke. Double," Xander shouts at the barman. "And..." He runs his eyes over the bottles of whisky behind the bar and I turn my back on them, putting my attention to my surroundings.

We're on what seems to be a large platform running

around the edge of the room, because in the middle there's a barrier that I can only assume looks over another level. Seeing as no one is really dancing up here, I'm guessing that's the dance floor. Somewhere I have every intention of being at some point tonight with a certain guy's hands all over my body.

I bite down on my dark stained lip at the thought of him showing every motherfucker in this club just who I belong to.

It might not have been so long ago that I would have fought such a show of ownership. But now, after our time apart, after everything that's gone down between us…

I need it.

I crave it.

I miss him, damn it.

The second our glasses are empty, I stretch up on my tiptoes and shout in Xander's ear.

"Let's go dance."

He pulls back a little, looking me dead in the eyes.

"I don't think that's a very good idea. They're due any minute and I'd rather not end the night with a broken nose."

"Aw, Xanny," I say, resting my hands on his chest. "You can handle my husband, can't you?" I tease. "The big bad biker isn't really scared of the pretentious mafia prince?"

"I'm not scared of him, Shorty. I'd just really rather not get into it and have both of us spend the night in a cell. Not when he's going to spend the night inside you."

"You're wicked, Xanny." I wink. "Now, man up, and let's go. I need to move."

20

THEO

"Where is she?" I growl the second I join the others in the hotel foyer.

I'm angry. Really fucking angry.

Not at her for her little stunt with the camera. Or even Seb, who clearly set it up.

I'm fucking furious with myself for letting her walk out like she'd just won.

She had. We both knew that.

But fuck. I can't get the dark, hungry look in her eyes out of my head as she stared down at me.

I should have reached for her sooner, should have dragged her down on top of me and put an end to this fucking stupid game we're playing.

She came here this weekend.

For me.

And we're not fucking leaving until we've sorted this shit out.

My entire body aches, although nowhere more so than my cock.

The temptation to defy her was strong, so fucking

strong, as I stood in the shower with my solid dick bobbing between my legs and images of her in my mind.

But I didn't.

I didn't because I want to prove to her that I'm serious. That I'm not taking any of this as a joke. And most importantly, that I'm not lying to her.

"She... um... she went ahead with Xander," Stella says, briefly glancing at Seb in concern.

I get it, they've all witnessed me lose my shit over smaller stuff than this, especially when it comes to my one weakness in life.

Emmie Cirillo.

Just the thought of her surname, of knowing she belongs to me makes my cock twitch.

She's fucking mine. And by the end of the night, every motherfucker in this city is going to know about it. Including the girl herself who is trying so fucking hard to keep her walls up around me that I'm actually impressed.

But it all ends tonight.

"Let's go," I snap, pulling the passenger door open of one of the cars that's waiting for us.

Twisting back before I fall inside, I bark. "Seb, you and Stella are in the other car."

Seb smirks at me and I just flip him off. There's no way in hell I'm putting up with the pair of them dry humping, or worse, behind me right now.

"I ain't going with them," Alex snaps, darting toward the car I chose. "Come on, Baby C, I'll keep you warm."

She glares at him, her lip curling in disgust.

"Touch me and I'll make use of the knife Stella bought me for Christmas," she hisses.

"Ooh... Calli grew up," he mutters, his eyes lighting up.

"Careful, bro, or I'll be the one pulling my knife to cut off your balls."

"Chill, man. I'm kidding. Right, Baby C?"

She mutters something about him being a dog before stepping around him and climbing into the car.

"Burn, bro," I joke, as Nico and Toby finally emerge, both of them looking like they've already started their party. Nico nods at me as Toby damn near falls into the back of the car.

My brows pinch in concern. Ever since the truth came out about Jonas, he's been falling deeper and deeper into the darkness he harbours inside.

His attacks on the man who claimed to be his father all these years are getting more and more brutal, and I worry that one day, he's going to go too far and not be able to handle it.

"Fuck off. It's not like I was actually flirting," Alex scoffs, reminding me that we were in the middle of something.

"Good. I should fucking hope not," I snap before finally joining the driver and hearing Alex climb in a second later.

"Good to go?" the driver asks, before double-checking our destination and taking off.

The tension in the car is pretty thick, but with thoughts of Emmie flickering through my mind as we make our way closer to the bar, I push it aside and think about how I want my night to end.

It might have only been a few hours, but hearing

the final whistle on that game feels like a lifetime ago already.

I should be on cloud nine celebrating. But the importance of it all dulls in comparison to claiming my wife.

The silence in the car is shattered when Alex decides to get under Calli's skin once more.

"Who are you talking to?"

"No one," Calli hisses back, and I can't help but smile at her obvious distaste for Alex's manwhore ways. It certainly makes my life easier.

Hopefully, she'll find herself a decent guy to settle down with and cause neither me nor her brother any issues.

"Calli," he warns. I don't need to turn around to see the smirk on his face. "Are you talking to a boy?"

A smile curls at my lips as anger comes from her in waves.

"Fuck off, Alex," she spits.

The driver shoots me an amused glance before pulling to a stop outside the bar.

"Good timing," I say, pushing the door open and climbing out. "Come on, Baby C. I don't want to be cleaning up Deimos blood tonight," I say after holding her door open like the gentleman I'm most certainly not.

"He's a dick," she mutters, storming straight past me and toward the bouncer.

It's not until she's flounced through the door, having been let straight inside, that her dress catches my eyes.

Was she wearing a—

"Man, she is feisty tonight. She needs to ditch that V-card and let out some of that tension."

My fist collides with his stomach and he bends over, wheezing out a breath as I stand over him.

"She's right. You're a dick. Now let's go."

Gripping the back of his neck, I drag him forward.

The bouncer's eyes narrow on me, giving me a silent warning about my behaviour before letting us straight inside.

We might have only been sixteen last year, and we were meant to get back on the bus with all the other year twelves, but that didn't fucking happen. We might not have the reputation here as we do in our part of our home city, but we still managed to get inside this place and party with all of last year's year thirteens. Although it wasn't such a celebration, seeing as we lost. Not that any of us really gave a fuck. Some of last year's girls were downright filthy. It was a fucking epic night.

This place has a lot to live up to, and I can only hope that tonight blows it out of the water.

Pushing my hair back from my brow, I straighten my shirt as we descend the stairs.

"I need alcohol and a willing girl grinding up against me," Alex announces behind me.

"A-fucking-men to that," I mutter.

The second the club comes into view before us, I scan the crowd looking for her, but I come up empty.

I swear to God, if she's not here somewhere waiting for me, I'm going to fucking throttle her.

Reaching out, I rearrange myself once more, my semi still aching for her as Alex fights his way to the front of the bar.

With two shots of their most expensive vodka heading for my stomach, we take off on the search—

Alex for any willing girl he can get his hands on, and me for my fucking wife.

The second we approach the railing that reveals the dance floor below us, I see her.

My fists curl at my sides and my anger surges forward as I watch her dancing with Xander. His back is to me, cutting off my view of anything but the top of her head as she rests it back on his shoulder.

A growl rips from my throat a second before I take off, more than ready to rip his hands clean from his arms for touching something that belongs to me.

I make it two steps before a body blocks my way.

"Drinks," Nico shouts over the music, thrusting another vodka at me.

I stare at the glass as if it just personally offended me as my heart continues to race and blood rushes past my ears.

"What? It's the fancy shit you like."

Taking it from his fingers, I throw it back before shoving the glass into his chest and barrelling through both him and a wrecked-looking Toby. If someone doesn't have to carry him home tonight, I'll be fucking surprised.

More people get shoved aside as I make my way toward the stairs that lead down to the lower level.

By the time I manage to cut through the crowd to where they're dancing, my body is trembling with pent-up rage and need.

But the second I catch his eye, it explodes like an old bomb just waiting for the right moment to cause the most devastation.

The faces around me blur. The only thing I can see is the two of them. And when I manage to move around, my eyes zero in on where his hand is resting on the curve of her waist.

My chest heaves as I stand there frozen, staring, too overwhelmed with everything that's racing through my veins to act.

Xander's face dips as he whispers something to Emmie, but his eyes never leave mine, his smirk telling me just how much he's enjoying getting up close and personal with my girl.

His smile only grows as he turns her back to me, taunting me with her body. My foot lifts, more than ready to go and physically remove her from his touch, but before I get a chance to move, he lifts his hand to her hair.

She has to know I'm here. I feel her presence like a physical fucking force pressing down on my chest. And I know that she feels it too.

She's taunting me. Teasing me. Playing me.

But I am going to fucking win.

I will always win.

His fingers twist in her dark, wavy lengths before he gathers it all up and tucks it over her shoulder.

His brow lifts before he nods toward her.

Despite my anger, I follow his orders, and fuck am I glad I do.

Cirillo 07 is printed in copper right across the back of her black dress.

My chin drops in shock.

Lifting my hand, I push my hair back once more, rendered fucking useless by her very public display of ownership before I find Xander's eyes.

He winks, before releasing both her hair and her

body and taking a step back, basically handing her over to me.

Fuck... I... Fuck.

How the fuck can one five-foot-two woman render me so fucking useless.

Love makes you weak. Dad's words flicker through my mind.

But fuck him. Fuck him and his stupid ideals for what a perfect soldier, the heir for this Family should look like.

Emmie doesn't make me weak. She makes me stronger. So much fucking stronger.

She gives me something to fight for. A reason to keep going. A motive to be a better person.

"Fuck, you fucking slay me, Hellcat," I mutter to myself, finally surging forward.

She's just about to turn around when I get to her. My hands wrap around her hips and I pull her harshly back into my body, letting her feel exactly what her little stunt does to me.

"No other man should be touching you when you're wearing my name on your back, Hellcat," I growl in her ear, causing a violent shudder to rip through her entire body.

Resting her head back on my shoulder, her warm breath races over my neck as she shouts, "Maybe you should have got here sooner then, boss."

A chuckle falls from my lips before I turn to look her dead in the eyes.

"I really hope you don't have any plans for tonight, wife, because I'm not letting you out of my fucking sight." My hand skims up her body, over her toned stomach, brushing over her breast, making her gasp with need before it finds its home around her throat. "Mine," I growl in her ear.

"Less talk, more action," she teases. "I'd hate to start thinking you're not man enough to do the dirty in person."

I bark a laugh. "I think we're both more than aware that I'm man enough for anything, Hellcat."

She shrugs as if she doesn't believe me before suddenly dropping down my body.

A groan of desire rips from my throat as I catch sight of that damn near indecent football shirt that's wrapped around her sinful body.

If I die tonight, I'll go a very, very happy man. Blue balls and all.

21

EMMIE

Arching my back, I press my arse against his leg and stand back up seductively, my eyes catching with Stella and Seb's, who are dancing together only a few feet away.

Stella winks at me before I'm at full height once more, and his hands land on my hips, finally spinning me to face him.

I knew the second he saw me. The tremor of awareness that ripped through my body was like nothing I'd ever experienced. Then the closer he got, the more my body burned for him. The more my entire being ached for him.

The only regret I have was not seeing the look on his face when Xander moved my hair and revealed exactly who owns me by showing him the name and number stamped on the back of the football shirt-cum-dress I conceded to wear.

I might not have wanted to come out dressed up like Theodore Cirillo's number-one fan, but who the fuck am I kidding? I fucking am.

"Hey," I say, plastering an innocent smile on my face as I drape my arms over his shoulders.

The heat of his large hands burn me up from the inside out as his fingertips dig into my arse with enough pressure that it makes my clit throb.

"Hellcat," he growls. "You're playing a dangerous game." His eyes flick between my eyes and my lips.

"Oh yeah?" I ask, tilting my head to the side. "Why is that, Theodore?"

"Because you've just sealed your fate for good."

His lips slam down on mine and I swear to fucking God, my entire body screams with joy.

His grip on me tightens even more, dragging me forward so our bodies are touching as much as possible, his hard length pressed against my stomach as his tongue invades my mouth.

He kisses me like a starved man and I'm the only thing that can keep him alive. His movements, his possession is almost violent as his tongue licks deep into my mouth.

It utterly consumes me, but at the same time, it's nowhere near enough.

Everything around us ceases to exist, the music fades away, and the people vanish as we finally give into the bullshit surrounding us and just admit the truth.

This. Us.

It is happening.

It might be the worst idea in the world. We might be headed for disaster, but in that moment, I really don't give one single shit about what might happen after the kiss, after this night finishes. All I know is that I never want him to let me go.

Releasing my hip, his fingers tangle in my hair

before my head is ripped back and I mourn the loss of his lips... until they land on my jaw and he continues kissing as he works his way up to my ear.

"Say yes," he breathes in my ear.

"W-what?" I stutter, my head swimming in lust and unable to focus.

"Say yes," he demands again.

And despite my better judgement when it comes to this man, my lips part and I breathe, "Yes," because I know, no matter what, that he won't hurt me. And if he does, you can damn well bet that I've begged for it.

His hand finds mine and I'm pulled through the gyrating crowd.

One quick look over my shoulder and I find Stella laughing at me as she dances before Seb captures her lips and our connection ends.

Theo marches toward a set of double doors at the back, ignoring the short queue for the ladies' toilet, until he gets to a door at the end which has a sign that says 'Staff only' on it.

"Theo, we can't—"

A harsh tug on my arm cuts off my argument, and I quickly find myself pressed up against the door frame with his dark, hungry eyes boring down into mine.

"We have to," he chokes out, his head dipping so his lips brush mine once more. "Right fucking now."

The door beside me opens, and I'm pushed back into the darkness.

"Oh my God, this is insane," I gasp, the emergency lighting above us casting enough of a glow that I see him stalking toward me like a starving lion would his prey.

My heart thunders and my core throbs, knowing what's about to come.

"Theoooo," I squeal when he grips the backs of my legs and my feet leave the floor.

My heart jumps into my throat as I fly through the air, totally at his mercy.

My back collides with a solid surface, and my knickers are dragged down my legs before my thighs are pushed apart and his head drops down.

"Oh my God," I scream as his tongue collides with my sensitive, needy skin.

A satisfied growl rumbles deep in his chest, making the sensation of him licking at me that much more intense.

My head spins as he eats me like a starving man, and I realise that the desperation I saw in his eyes outside wasn't his need to come, but his need to make me his. And something tells me that if I were to call time on this the second I come, he'd reluctantly walk out of here without getting his but with the satisfaction that I got mine.

The thought makes my heart sing.

Threading my fingers through his hair, I try to drag him closer, desperately needing more as my orgasm begins to climb.

My skin burns, feeling like it's too small to fit my body as he drives me higher and higher.

The second he pushes two thick fingers inside of me, I'm teetering right on the edge of the cliff, more than ready to dive right off with him at my side.

"Come for me, Hellcat," he growls, curling his fingers in just the right place.

My toes curl, my back arches, and I scream out his name as my release slams into me.

It goes on and on, and when he finally pulls back,

his chin glistening under the minimal light from above with my release, aftershocks ripple through my body.

"Fuck, you're so beautiful, babe."

In contrast to his words, he fists the front of my dress and drags me from whatever counter he had laid me out on. He drags me into his body, his grip on my bare arse burning before my back slams against the door.

"Theo," I gasp when the burning heat of his cock strokes through my folds.

"Say yes, babe," he demands again, as if there was even the slightest chance I'd ever say no right now.

"Yes. Yes. Fuck me, boss."

His hips thrust forward at the same time he drops me down, and he fills me so fucking full that I feel him everywhere.

"Oh my God," I moan, my fingers digging into his shoulders as I fight to adjust to his size.

Fuck, I've missed this burn.

Latching onto the soft skin beneath my ear, he sucks until I'm crying out for him once more. My thighs clench as my heels dig into his arse, desperately needing him to move.

"You good?" he whispers, and my heart tumbles in my chest that even in this moment, the cruel, depraved monster before me actually thinks to check if I'm okay.

"Yes, yes," I chant, clawing at his shoulders, wishing there weren't as many clothes between us and that I could scratch his skin until I left my marks behind.

The second he circles his hips, all my thoughts fall from my head, every single bit of my focus going to what he's doing to me.

"Fucking missed you, Hellcat. Miss you so fucking much," he groans as if he's in physical pain.

"Theo, please. Fuck me like you own me."

I gasp when his hand wraps around my throat. He pulls his head back and stares so deep into my eyes I swear he's looking straight into my soul. "I fucking do own you, Emmie Cirillo."

I cry out as he thrusts into me, his fingers tightening on my throat.

He begins fucking me with a relentless rhythm. My body burns as an inferno blazes beneath my skin. His searing touch leaves intense tingles in its wake as sweat begins to gather at my hairline and trickle down my spine.

"Who owns you, Emmie?" he grunts, beginning to lose control, his movements becoming more and more erratic as he chases his release.

"You. You do."

"Who does?" he booms, clearly not happy with that answer.

"You do, Theo. You fucking own me."

Releasing my throat almost as quickly as he claimed it, his fingers find my clit.

"Holy shit," I hiss as he pinches me with the perfect pressure and I go flying off the cliff once more, but this time, he's right there with me. His cock jerks violently inside me as his lips slam down on mine, swallowing my cries as my body pulsates around me.

Our kiss slows as our heart rates return to normal, and I drown in everything about this guy holding me up, wishing that we were anywhere but in the middle of a packed club, fucking in a storage cupboard.

"We never should have left the hotel," I confess into his gentle kiss.

"At last," he says lightly. "Something we agree on."

I can't help but laugh, suddenly feeling lighter with some of the weight I've been carrying around lifted.

"I'm pretty sure we agree on more than just that."

"Oh yeah?" he asks, nuzzling my neck, licking at the sweat covering my skin. "Like what?"

"Like we're going to be doing that again tonight."

"More than once."

I groan, my body sagging in his hold.

"But right now, you're going to go and clean up, and then we're going to dance."

I pull my head to the side so I can look at him.

"You want to dance with me, boss?" I tease.

His hand cups my jaw, his thumb brushing over my swollen bottom lip.

"I want to feel my wife grinding all over me before I take her back to the hotel and make her do it all over again. Naked."

A shiver of need rushes through me.

I think about his words for a moment, making his lips twitch in amusement.

"Speak to her nicely and she might consider it."

"Is that right, Hellcat?" he asks, nudging my nose with the tip of his.

"Yeah. Mentioning just how many orgasms she might get out of the deal could help."

"Well lucky for her, she's going to get more than she can count," he promises, his eyes blazing with the challenge I just set.

"Big words, boss," I tease, feeling him hardening inside me again at the thought alone.

"You know I love a good challenge. I wouldn't be standing here right now if I didn't."

I swat his shoulder playfully. "Hey."

"Best win of my life, babe." Pulling out of me, he places me back on my feet before tucking himself away.

The second my knickers poking out of his pocket catch my eye, I reach out and steal them back.

"Hey, I wanted them for my collection."

"Trust me. You're going to want to see them on me later. Probably almost as much as you don't want me walking out there in this obscene dress without them on."

His eyes run down the length of me appreciatively before he nods.

"Something else we agree on." He steps forward, reaching under my ridiculously short dress and cupping my pussy. "This is mine," he growls, dipping into me, collecting up his cum and pushing it deeper. "And only mine."

"Yours," I agree.

"Whose idea was this dress? I need to buy them a drink. Or maybe a house or something," he jokes.

"Calli made them." His brows rise in surprise. "You like?"

"Like?" he asks, slipping a second finger inside me, making me hot for him all over again. "I fucking love it. I might burn the rest of your clothes and make you wear this all the time."

"So having your name and your ring isn't enough."

I realise my mistake the second the words fall from my lips, because I don't have his ring.

Not anymore.

And it fucking kills me that I lost something so precious.

"Theo, I—"

Ripping his fingers from inside me, he paints his fingertips across my bottom lip before pushing them into my mouth, leaving them there until I've licked them clean, tasting the two of us mixed together.

His pupils dilate once more as he studies my lips.

The second he pulls them free, I try again.

"Theo, I lost—"

But then his other hand lifts and something red catches the light above us.

"Oh my God," I breathe, not believing what I'm seeing.

"You want me, babe?" he asks, holding it between us.

I bite down on my bottom lip, not because I don't know the answer to that question, but because we're in a freaking nightclub storage room right now, and I've got his cum dripping down my thighs.

This really isn't the time for some big, heartfelt declaration.

He takes my hesitation for doubt and continues.

"I know that I'm fucked up. I know that this whole situation is fucked up. But I want it, Em. I want you. More than I've ever wanted anything. Ever."

"Theo," I breathe, but I'm quickly stopped when he presses two fingers to my lips.

"I'm not expecting everything to be forgotten. I don't want it to be. I deserve to be put through hell for how I've treated you. I don't expect you to move in with me or anything crazy. I just... I want you to say that something might be possible. You don't even have to wear this if you don't want to," he says, taking my hand and playing with the ring he's pushed onto my finger. "You don't have to use my name, you don't have to do any of the wife shit. We can forget about it. And maybe, just maybe, we can revisit it if you're still with me in a few years."

Everything in me sags at his words, at the sincerity behind them.

"Theo," I try again, reaching for him and cupping his jaw in my palm. "I don't want to forget it all. It might have been painful. But it's ours. It's a part of our story. And as fucked up as it is, I wouldn't change it. Well, maybe parts of it."

Pain flickers across his features, and I can't help wondering if he's thinking about the same things as me. But as much as I might want to know, now isn't the time.

"Let's just take it one step at a time, yeah? We've still got things to deal with and a lot of stuff to talk about." I quirk a brow just to let him know how serious I am about it. Because as much as I might want to embrace our past, we bloody well will be talking about it. All of it. Every lie, secret and brutal part of it. There is no way I'm letting him get away with any of it. But I'm fed up of fighting from a distance.

I want this.

I want him.

And it's time to embrace how we both really feel. It's been a long time coming.

"But right now, I've got your jizz running down my thighs, and I want to go out there, dance with my husband, celebrate his epic win, and hang out with our friends."

He crowds me, wrapping his hand around the back of my neck and pressing his brow to mine.

"I want to say I couldn't think of anything better, but that would be a lie."

"Come on, boss. Let's go and show everyone how it's done."

I take his hand in mine and pull him toward the door.

We get more than a few looks as we emerge from the storage cupboard. Mostly though, it's jealousy. Holding my head up high, I join the back of the queue for the ladies, which thankfully, is shorter than when we passed it earlier, and I allow Theo to wrap his arms around me and kiss my neck while I wait to clean up.

22

THEO

"**P**retty sure I've never seen you smile quite this much before," Seb shouts at me as we're standing at the bar, waiting for another round of drinks.

I shrug, still unable to wipe the smile off my face.

"It's fucking great, man. I'm happy for you."

The moment Emmie emerged from the bathroom earlier, she walked straight into my arms and together we rejoined our friends, who were still grinding it up on the dance floor. Even Nico and Toby had joined, pulling some poor, innocent, unsuspecting girls along with them.

All of them watched our return with knowing smirks on their faces, but fuck it. I don't care. As long as they know that Emmie is mine and one hundred percent off-limits, then that's all that matters.

"You aren't going to get out of it that easily," I warn him.

He holds his hands up in surrender, a wide smile on his face.

"Got you what you wanted in the end, didn't it?" I look over his shoulder to where Emmie is standing with Stella and Calli, each of them in their matching dresses. Obviously, Stella has Seb's name and number on hers. But Calli stuck with Cirillo, giving herself the number one position. I wouldn't have put it past her to put one of the other guys' names on the back just to piss me and Nico off.

As much as I love that my cousin has grown a backbone since meeting Stella and Emmie, I also hate it.

It was easier when she was as quiet as a mouse and did as she was told. But I guess we should have known we were on borrowed time.

"You're so fucking whipped," Seb laughs.

"Fuck off. You're just jealous that I put a ring on it first."

His lips part to argue, but then he looks at Stella and all his argument leaves him. "Yeah, actually. I kinda am."

"What the fuck happened to us, man? Handing our balls over to them two."

"Shit could be worse. Cheers, mate," he says to the barman as my eyes float to Toby, who's leaning back against the railing, his shoulders lowered in defeat and dark circles around his eyes.

Yeah, shit could be worse. Our entire family could have imploded before our eyes.

Grabbing two of the drinks that have appeared before us. I carry one over to him.

"Here you go, bro."

It takes him a beat to realise I'm even standing in front of him, and he barely reacts until he spots the drink in my hand. The second he sees it, his eyes light up and he happily takes it from me, knocking it back in one.

Leaning in so he can hear me over the music, I shout, "Tell me what I can do."

I want to help. I want to make it better for him. But I have no fucking idea how.

"He's having a fucking funeral next week," he slurs. "A fucking funeral. People are going to be crying over him. A fucking scumbag like him. He doesn't deserve for anyone to care that he died. He should be burning in hell, not be laid to fucking rest," he rants.

"I know, man. I know." I grab his shoulder, hoping that he gets some kind of support from it. "But it's not about him. Boss is doing it for other innocent people like you."

"Anyone who loved a piece of fucking shit like that can't be innocent."

I bite back my initial response to point out that his mum must have cared at some point. That is not the kind of support he needs right now.

"He was a master at manipulation. And I get it, I understand why you're hurting. But the man they lost isn't the one you know existed."

"I know, fuck. I know. I just..." The glass in his hand flies toward the floor, shattering around our feet. "I want to burn that fucking church down with them all in it."

"It won't help, Tobes."

"No, it'll make me just like him," he spits in disgust.

"You're nothing like him, man. You're good. So fucking good. And despite all that shit, you've got people around you that love you. A sister," I say, shooting a look at Stella and my girl. "A sister who would raise hell for you, and a real dad. One I'm pretty sure would do anything to make this better."

"They must fucking hate me right now." His voice cracks as he says this, and when I get a look in his eyes, I find them glassy with emotion.

"They don't. I fucking promise you that."

Two girls over his shoulder catch my eye.

"You've got an admirer at four o'clock," I shout.

He turns the second I say it.

"Get out of your head. Take Nico with you," I suggest, knowing what the two of them can be like together when there's too much alcohol involved.

"It just fucking comes back the next day."

"It'll get better, Tobes. I fucking swear to you."

Tingles erupt down my body, and I know why before Toby speaks.

"You should go, your girl is ready to hit the dance floor again."

"Damn, I was hoping she might be ready to hit the hotel room. You fucking seen that dress?"

"Yeah, bro. You're a lucky motherfucker. Both of you are," he says, nodding to where Seb's standing with Stella.

"We'll be saying the same to you one day."

"If I make it that long," he mutters sadly.

"Tobes, don't—"

Warm hands slip around my sides before Emmie nestles into me.

"Hey," she says, looking between the two of us. Her voice is raspy from shouting and slightly slurred from the alcohol. It's hot and has a direct line to my dick, it seems. "Sorry, am I interrupting?" she shouts, a frown marring her brow.

"No, you're good," Toby says, looking over at the girls who are still attempting to capture his attention. They squeal in excitement, one of them pushing the other to make her come over. "Looks like I might have a new friend anyway."

Emmie follows his line of sight before nodding. "Enjoy that then, Tobes. Just remember… you're the good one."

He scoffs at that and takes off.

"Missing me?" I ask, turning to Emmie and wrapping my arms around her waist as hers land over my shoulders.

She presses closer, her breasts brushing against my chest as she reaches up on her toes so she can whisper in my ear.

"Wanna get out of here?"

"Is that a trick question?"

"Maybe. Who knows what devilish plans I've got up my sleeve for when we get back."

"I'm sure I can get on board with every single one."

Unwrapping her arms from my neck, I take her hand in mine and begin marching toward the exit.

"Wait," she shouts. "Stel and Seb are coming too."

"Oh course they are," I mutter.

Glancing back, I see them heading our way.

"What about Calli?" I ask, hating to be the sensible one right now. I should be thinking with my head, not my dick.

"Xander's gonna make sure she gets back in one piece."

I stare at her, my lips parting to argue.

"He won't touch her. We're all too young and innocent for him." She rolls her eyes.

I should probably be grateful that's his opinion, and the reason why he's never gone after my girl, but it still pisses me off.

"If he so much as—"

"He won't," she says, tapping my chest patronisingly.

"Now, let's go. Unless you don't want—"

"Let's go," I snap, finally making it to the stairs with her laughing behind me.

"Desperate much?" she shouts.

"Hellcat," I growl, pulling her in front of me and dragging her arse back against my crotch before we start ascending the stairs. "You have no idea."

"Oh," she laughs. "I really think I do."

Our brief stop to collect her jacket means that Stella and Seb overtake us, and by the time we get outside there's a car pulling up, ready to take the four of us back to the hotel.

"In you get, Princess," Seb instructs before following inside.

"Wait," I bark before Emmie moves forward to join them. Holding her back, I fold my body into the seat and then pull her down onto my lap.

"O-oh no," the driver says in a heavily accented voice from the front of the car, but I'm too lost in my girl's heated eyes to really give a shit about his opinion on this.

"We'll pay you ten times the fare," I bark. "Just drive."

Twisting Emmie around, I sit her so she's straddling my waist, her dress bunching high enough up her thighs to give me a flash of the black fabric that's covering what I really want to be looking at.

"No sex in my car," he hisses, but forgets about his argument about having four of us in the back of his car.

"I like you better when you're getting laid," Seb confesses, his eyes catching mine as he lifts Stella and slips beneath her, mimicking our position.

"I prefer you when I don't have to watch you getting laid," I mutter, turning my attention back to Emmie. "Fuck, I need you," I groan, wrapping my hand around the back of her neck and dragging her down so I can claim her lips.

She slips down my lap, her pussy pressing down on my aching cock as she parts her lips for me, pushing her tongue into my mouth.

A deep, hungry growl rumbles in my chest as she rolls her hips against me.

She gasps when the thickness of my cock hits her just so.

"You wet for me, Hellcat?" I groan into our kiss.

"What do you think?" Her fingers twist in my hair at the nape of my neck, tugging to drag me exactly where she wants me as Stella's wanton moan rips through the air, quickly followed by a curse from the driver.

The fire that's been burning within me since the second I saw her standing in the crowd at the game earlier only gets hotter as she continues grinding down on me, her breathing becoming more and more erratic, our kiss getting messier, dirtier by the second.

"Gonna go for your second hat trick of the day?" she whispers in my ear after ripping her lips from mine and kissing along my jaw.

"I'm gunning for a lot more than three out of you tonight, babe."

My hands tighten on her arse, tugging us even tighter together as I lift my hips from the seat, taking over her pleasure.

"Oh God," she moans, her back arching and her eyes falling closed.

"Eyes on me," I growl, and she immediately rips her eyelids open and stares right at me.

"Shit," Stella hisses, and I glance over just in time to see Seb's hand disappear between their bodies.

Stella's plea rips through the air, echoing around us.

"Girls like doing everything together," Seb laughs, although the roughness of his voice gives away just how badly he needs to sink balls deep into his girl. A feeling I'm more than familiar with right now. "Ready to give our nice driver a lasting impression of his favourite journey of the night?"

"Seb," she cries as Emmie whimpers when I grind against her again.

"Exactly what we thought. Dirty little princesses," Seb mutters.

I want to join in, but I can't. I'm too lost watching the expression on Emmie's face morph to one of undiluted pleasure.

Her eyes are so dark they're practically black, her lids are heavy with desire, her lips parted as she tries to catch her breath and the blush on her cheeks spreads down her neck and disappears beneath her dress.

"Let go," I whisper. It's so quiet I don't think she could have possibly heard me over her ragged breaths, but then her entire body stills for a beat before her release slams into her. Her teeth sink into her bottom lip, her eyes damn near closing, but not quite, and her fingers curl around my shoulders, her nails digging into them through my shirt.

"Fuck," I breathe as I watch her slowly come back to herself, everything else around me a blur. She is literally the only thing I see.

"You two fucking getting out or what?" the deep, familiar voice growls from somewhere outside of the car.

Ripping my eyes from Emmie, I glance out the window, seeing our hotel.

Turning the other way, I find Seb standing on the pavement, looking into the car with a smirk on his face.

"Shit," I hiss, quickly reaching for the handle.

"Don't worry, I've already given our accommodating driver a more than healthy tip for that journey."

Emmie snorts a laugh as I help her off my lap.

"Appreciate it, mate," I say, not risking a glance in the rear-view mirror for fear that I'll see his desire for my girl.

Pretending he was oblivious to what just happened, I follow Emmie out, shoving my hand into my trousers to adjust my painful boner.

"Last ones to the suite are losers," Seb barks before he and Stella take off like idiots, laughing through the hotel lobby and causing more than a few concerned glances from the patrons.

I'm sure this isn't the kind of place they expect sixth form kids to be staying, but fuck them.

We're as entitled to a room here just as much as they are.

The doors to the lift Stella and Seb darted into close a beat before we get there, but I see that as a good thing. We've already shared enough in the past twenty minutes, even if I completely blanked what was happening right beside me as my girl started to fall.

The second the doors to the next lift open, I drag Emmie inside, tapping our suite key to the control panel to allow it to take us right to the top.

The second the doors close behind us, Emmie's palms slam down on my chest and I allow her to back me up into the wall as the air around us crackles with electricity.

23

EMMIE

We both pause for a split second, our eyes locking before I reach up on my toes and slam my lips to his.

The moment I crush the length of my body against his, the thickness of his cock presses against my stomach, making my mouth water and my core ache.

What happened in that storage cupboard and then the short time in the taxi was not enough. Nowhere fucking near. If I were a rational, normal person, then I probably would have put a stop to that situation before it started. But seeing as I claim to be neither, I pushed all the reasons for making it stop aside and jumped headfirst into the pleasure this guy can give me.

After all, it's a hell of a lot better than the pain.

"Shit, Emmie," Theo grunts into our kiss when my fingers brush the skin of his chest as I begin unpopping his buttons, my desperation to feel his skin against mine becoming too much to bear.

He sucks in a sharp breath when my knuckles brush his lower belly as I reach for his waistband.

"Fuck. You want my cock, babe?" he groans as I make enough space between us so I can pop the button and pull down the zip.

I do it all blindly, my eyes sucked into the hungry emerald stare before me.

I see everything. All the emotion and need he tried to hide at the beginning of all this. I feel it in every one of his touches now, and I can't help but wonder if I tried too hard to stop it.

No, never. He deserved it all and then some.

The moment his trousers are undone, I push my hand inside, finding his hard, burning hot skin and wrapping my fingers around it.

"Fucking need you, Hellcat," he moans when I squeeze him. "Jesus. Fuck."

His eyes shoot to the control panel, I assume to take note of how close we are to our floor, but I'm too lost in him to bother looking.

"Yes," he hisses, clearly happy about what he discovers, although I'm not, because not two seconds later does he wrap his hand around my wrist, pulling my hand from his dick.

"Hey, I want that," I whine.

He pushes from the wall, giving me little choice but to back up as his heated eyes bore down into me.

His intensity is almost overwhelming. But knowing that one stroke of my hand or lick of my tongue will be his undoing means I hold steady, daring him—begging him—to do his worst.

"You're mine. Tell me you're mine," he demands, his voice low and terrifying.

My mouth goes dry as my lips part to respond.

I might have already said it tonight, but that was

while he was touching me, playing me like a musician would his instrument. Right now, he's asking when I've got almost a level head. If you ignore the alcohol and desire flowing through my veins.

Holding his eyes steady, I wet my lips and give him the truth. One I feel right down to my soul.

"I'm yours, Theo. Every inch of me."

The lift dings in response, and my heart lurches into my chest, the sound startling me a beat before the doors open.

Theo moves faster than I anticipate, bending over until his shoulder presses against my stomach.

A scream of fright rips past my lips as my feet leave the ground, and in a heartbeat, we're moving.

"Theo," I squeal. "Put me down."

"No fucking chance, Hellcat. You're mine. And I'm making sure you don't do anything stupid. Like run."

A smile pulls at my lips at the thought.

Brushing my hands down his lower back, I take the roundness of his arse in them and squeeze as hard as I can.

He grunts in response, but his steps don't falter.

"You'd fucking love chasing me, and you know it."

"Maybe, but the only place I want you right now is bouncing on my cock, not running in the opposite direction."

"Aw, I love it when you get all romantic."

The moment we appear in front of his suite door, he taps the card to the keypad, and without stopping, he swings the door open and marches us inside.

He doesn't stop to put me down. He just keeps moving until we're shut in the confines of his room.

Twisting around, he finally lowers me to my feet,

but he doesn't release me. Instead, he presses me back into the door, the length of his body aligning perfectly with my much shorter one.

His eyes search mine, the intensity making my stomach knot as he tries to find an answer to whatever his unknown question might be.

"T-Theo—"

"Shh." He presses two fingers to my lips, cutting off whatever I might have said.

"Emmie, I—" He swallows, his Adam's apple bobbing violently before he shakes his head.

Reaching up, I cup his jaw, desperate to tell him that it's okay. To comfort him. To tell him that we don't need words right now. But then he tries again and every single thought falls from my head.

"Emmie, I... I love you."

I suck in a sharp breath, shock at hearing those three little words from him rendering me speechless.

My heart begins to race as our eyes hold.

Part of me wonders if he's expecting me to say it back in return. The reckless, foolish, romantic part of me that I try to keep buried at all times wants to. My lips even part to do so. But then I remember everything else. It flickers through my mind like a bad movie, and I swallow my response down.

Not now. Not yet, anyway.

Thankfully, he very quickly gives me a reason to push my panic aside when he wraps his hands around the backs of my thighs and lifts me from the floor once more. Securing them around his waist, he lines us up perfectly and I groan in response. Wrapping my hand around the back of his neck, I drag his lips down to mine.

I might be unable to say the words out loud, but that doesn't mean I'm not able to show him just how deep my feelings for him run with every move I make.

I kiss him, the ferocity of it being our first and our last all combined into one, and he matches me move for move.

Skimming his hands down my bare legs, he knocks my boots from my feet, letting them thump to the ground before dragging his burning hands back up and over my arse, taking my dress with it.

"Fucking love this dress," he groans into our kiss. "But it's got nothing on what's hiding beneath."

"Please," I beg, shamelessly arching my back off the door, giving him the space he needs to pull it off me.

He doesn't miss a beat, wrapping his fingers around the fabric and tugging it away.

His lips find mine again the second it passes my face, and he discards it somewhere behind him as his hands cup my tits, squeezing with the most dizzying pressure.

My head falls back against the door with a thud, but I don't feel it because Theo tucks his fingers under the cups of my bra and exposes me, ducking down to suck my hard peak into his mouth.

"Yes," I scream, my fingers twisting in his hair and holding him in place. Not that I really think for a second that he's about to go anywhere.

He's had plenty of opportunities to run, to turn his back on me and cut me out of his life—marriage certificate aside—but he hasn't. He's come back time and time again, no matter how hard I've tried to push for the opposite.

"Fuuuck," I scream as he bites down on me, his

teeth sending a bolt of pleasure so strong to my clit that I begin to wonder if he could make me fall from just this alone.

"Can't get enough of you, Hellcat," he groans, switching to the other side and giving that the same treatment.

"Oh God, Theo," I cry, fighting between needing to watch him feasting on me and closing my eyes to focus on the sensation.

"So sensitive, babe," he mutters, lowering my feet back to the floor and dropping to his knees before me.

His nose brushes across the top of the boy shorts Callie demanded I wear to compliment the dress.

"These are different," he breathes, knowing that I have a certain taste in underwear.

"Stop," I command, and he instantly sits back, following my orders.

I stare at him for long seconds, just taking in the sight of him on his knees before me.

To the rest of the world, he's such an enigma, so cold, powerful, dangerous. Yet he's here, kneeling at my damn feet, following my orders. After everything we've been through, the control that he's shown me time and time again that he so badly needs, he's here, handing every ounce of it over.

My head spins to the point that I actually forget why I stopped him.

"Don't walk away, Em. Do not fucking—"

A soft, sympathetic smile plays on my lips, and a frown forms on my head.

My beautiful, broken boy.

"I'm not leaving, Theo. Nothing, and I mean

nothing, could make me walk out of this room right now."

He releases a breath and his entire body relaxes at my words. The actions tell me more about where his head is at right now than his words did.

His relief, his hope, is palpable.

His brow creases when I don't say any more. "So why did you stop?"

"Because," I say, pushing from the door and stalking into the room, "I thought you might want to get a look at this before you rip them from my body."

"W-wha—"

His word cuts off the second I turn around and show him my arse.

"Holy fuck." He barks out a laugh, seeing his name printed across the arse of the knickers. "We're getting more of those made," he announces, getting to his feet and striding up to me.

"I knew you'd ruin these."

"Not replacements, babe. A pair for every day of the fucking week, just to show any motherfucker who might get too close to you that you're fucking owned, Hellcat."

He steps up behind me, one of his hands slipping down my stomach, his fingers dipping under the black knickers until he can part me and circle my clit.

A low growl rumbles in his chest when he finds me soaked for him.

His other hand cups one of my full breasts while his teeth nip my ear.

"Get on the bed, babe. Face down, arse up."

He releases me with a gentle shove, and I

immediately mourn the loss of his fingers as the release he was quickly working me toward fades away.

"Knobhead," I hiss, although doing exactly as I'm told, falling onto the bed on my hands and knees, waving my arse temptingly at him.

"No need to tease me, babe. That arse is mine. It's got my fucking name on it," he states proudly, making quick work of shedding his clothes.

I watch, enthralled, as he loses each item, revealing inches upon inches of perfection. Before finally, fucking finally, he drops his boxers, giving me a look at what I'm really dying for.

Sex in that cupboard in the club was great, don't get me wrong. We fucking needed it. But it has nothing on this.

He stalks closer, one hand wrapped around his massive cock, and the other brushing his hair back from his brow, his eyes locked on his name.

He says nothing as the mattress dips when he joins me, and I startle when his hands land on my arse, palming them roughly.

"Theo," I moan, arching my back in the hope of getting more of his touch.

"Greedy little hellcat," he murmurs before one of his hands leaves me, although not for long.

Crack.

"THEO," I scream, my entire body surging forward with the force.

His palm remains on my burning cheek, rubbing the pain away.

I just start to lean back into him again when he pulls away.

Crack.

"Fuuuuuuck."

My breathing is beyond erratic as he soothes the pain away once more.

"Such a good girl," he whispers, and I swear I only get wetter at his praise.

If anyone had asked me if I'd have liked that patronising phrase during sex before meeting Theo, I'd have told them where to go. Fast. But it turns out, I fucking love it.

When his hand leaves me again, I brace for impact, but the pain never comes. Instead, cool air rushes over my heated skin when he pulls my knickers aside.

He doesn't give me any kind of warning. One second my pussy tingles, knowing that he's staring right at it, and the next, his monster cock is pushing inside.

"Oh God," I whimper when he fills me to the hilt, hitting me so deep I swear I'm going to feel it for a week.

"You feel that, babe? You feel how much I fucking missed you? How badly I fucking need you?" he grits out, his fingers digging into my hips with a punishing grip that I already know will leave bruises behind.

A whimper is the only answer he gets as I try to wiggle in my need to make him move.

"Please," I beg when he makes it more than clear that he's happy just being inside me.

"Please what, babe?"

"Please take me, fuck me, ruin me. I don't care. J-just... do something," I damn near scream.

"Fucking love it when you beg for it."

Crack.

My scream rips through the air once more before he pulls almost all the way out and slams back inside, his grip tightening to stop me from surging forward on the bed.

All conversation subsides. Our moans and grunts of pleasure, along with the slapping of our skin as he takes me hard and fast, are the only things that can be heard.

Releasing my hip with one hand, he skates it up my spine, making my entire body shudder as he pushes me closer and closer to release with his brutal thrusts.

He undoes my bra, and the fabric falls away from my body and makes me moan.

Wrapping my hair around his fist, he drags me upright and pins me against his chest, his breath racing past my ear and making my nipples even harder and my release surge closer.

His fingers find my clit and I groan his name as he plays me, finally pushing me over the edge.

"Theo," I cry as wave after wave of my orgasm slams into me.

His moan of pleasure rumbles against me a second before he slams me back down again with his hand on the back of my neck and fucks me so hard through the end of my release that I see stars.

He comes with an animalistic growl not ten seconds later, his cock jerking violently as he fills me.

"Holy shit," he sighs breathlessly, falling to my side and immediately pulling me into his body.

Our chests are both still heaving as we try to catch our breaths as he claims my lips again.

His arm snakes around my back and his leg hooks over my hip, dragging me closer still.

I gasp when I feel his length pressing against my stomach.

"Again?" I ask into his kiss.

"All fucking night, babe. It's been a long time coming."

Pulling back, I look him dead in the eyes. "Did you really hold off until earlier?" I ask, feeling more than suspicious. I know his self-control is second to none, but not getting off while we were sexting? That takes things to whole new levels.

Something flickers through his eyes and I grin, knowing I just caught his lie.

Ignoring the tug of disappointment that he's still not being totally honest with me, I forge forward. There will be time to fight with him about it tomorrow.

"You're a liar, Theodore Cirillo," I hiss. "Argh," I squeal when I'm suddenly pushed onto my back, my wrists captured in one of his hands above my head, and him between my thighs.

"I'm not," he assures me. "I never actively got off. But..."

His hesitation along with his confession makes something explode within me.

"I swear to fucking God, Theo," I growl. "If you've been with someone else, I'll fucking castrate you before I go and hunt her down and make her—"

The most wicked yet unbelievably happy smile appears on his lips as he stares down at me.

"What?" I hiss, focusing on my anger and not his reaction, which threatens to soften me.

"I've not been with anyone else, babe. The fact that you thought I could even consider it kinda offends me."

"Yeah, but—"

He lowers down, his muscles in his arms pulling and rippling in the most delicious way before his warm breath tickles over my ear.

"I came in my fucking pants like a schoolboy, watching you get off in your bedroom," he confesses.

"Oh my God," I laugh, all the anger and betrayal that washed through me at the thought of him being with someone else immediately disappearing.

"I was barely even touching myself. But watching you... Fuck, babe. I needed you so bad," he groans as if he's still in pain over it all.

"So... what are you going to do about it?" I taunt as he rips my knickers from my body, exposing me fully with my legs wrapped around his back. Tightening my hold on him, I drag him down on top of me.

"Hmm... I've got a few ideas."

He's back inside me before I even blink, and any concern I might have had about his honesty floats off into nothing as I let him prove that every word he's said to me tonight is the truth with every one of his actions, his touches, over and over again.

24

THEO

When we finally succumbed to our exhaustion last night, I pulled Emmie's naked body right up against mine, held her tight for fear she might slip out the second I released her, and fell asleep with a more than satisfied and happy smile on my face.

This girl. This fucking girl.

She's everything I never wanted, yet everything I never knew I needed.

The image of her on all fours on the bed with my name printed across her arse is something I'm pretty sure I'll never forget.

For the first time since I last had her in my bed, I fell asleep almost instantly and stayed that way until morning. I probably would have stayed even longer if I wasn't suddenly woken by a more than a forceful slap on my chest before Emmie tried jumping out of bed.

"Not yet," I mutter sleepily. "I'm not ready to let you go."

"That's cute," she says, although the hard edge to

her tone makes me finally crack an eye open. "But we've got an issue… maybe… I don't know."

Her words have me more than alert in the blink of an eye, and I push up on one elbow and stare at her.

I'm taken aback for a second by just how fucking beautiful she looks.

Her hair is a mess, and the remains of last night's makeup still linger on her face along with a more than suitable amount of stubble rash from my jaw, and her lips are swollen, sending my mind straight into the gutter as I think back to her having them wrapped around my cock at some point last night.

Her brow lifts as she realises that I'm ignoring her issue in favour of checking her out.

"What?" I argue. "My wife is fucking banging, first thing in the morning."

"Firstly, it's hardly first thing, it's almost lunchtime." My brows shoot up at learning that. It's not often I sleep later than seven. My body is usually more than ready to hit the gym and start the day. Apparently, fucking my wife until dawn fucks with not only the tight hold I have on my control but my schedule too. "And secondly, look."

She shoves her phone into my hand and I have to blink a couple of times to make my eyes focus.

Lovell Estate Gangster Found Dead

"Holy shit."

Worry lines have formed on Emmie's brow when I look back up at her.

"What's wrong? Luis was a cunt. Can't say he didn't deserve it." It's true. The prick has been trying to encroach on our territory with his less than stellar products for years, trying to undercut us, break the rules and generally make a fucking pain in the arse of himself. His daddy died in more than suspicious circumstances a few years ago, and Luis's superiority complex took over. He runs things in that estate like a fucking dictatorship. It really is no wonder it's such a hellhole.

Pushing her hair back from her face, Emmie holds my eyes, allowing me to see the torment she's in right now.

"I... Yeah, you're right. He's a prick. But... I dunno, I've just got a bad feeling about this."

I sit up fully, scooting back to rest against the headboard, and I pull Emmie right along with me, letting her pull the covers over us.

"You think this is linked to your mum?"

"I dunno. I might be overthinking it. I'm sure there are a million and one people who'd want him dead. I'm probably just being paranoid after he took me."

Holding her tighter, I drop a kiss to her temple as images from that day continue to haunt me.

"I'm sorry I let you get—"

"No, Theo," she says, pressing her palm to my chest and climbing onto my lap.

The sheets fall from her body as she straddles me and takes my face in her hands.

"That wasn't your fault. They ran us off the road. There wasn't much you could do."

"I should have taken charge of the situation, and I shouldn't have fucking passed out so they could take you."

"It's not your fault," she repeats as guilt begins to eat at my insides, ripping me apart piece by piece. "And it's in the past now. There's nothing we can do about it.

It's just another piece in our slightly broken puzzle of how we got here."

"We're not broken, babe," I say softly.

She smiles at me, compassion oozing from her. "A little dented then, maybe?" she suggests.

Nodding, I lean forward, capturing her lips in a toe-curling kiss.

When we finally part, she looks at me with sadness darkening her eyes.

"I think we should go home."

Disappointment floods me. I was more than happy to spend every single second we could in this place, just the two of us, while we let the rest of the world continue around us.

"Give me a couple of hours before I have to share you again?" I ask hopefully. I understand why she wants to get back, but I'm not ready. It might make me a selfish prick, asking to keep her to myself right now, but I'm confident that I can distract her from the worry that's pinching her brows. "We can order room service. I'll let you do whatever you want to me." I wiggle my brows suggestively and she laughs. "Call your dad, check in with home so you know things are okay. Then I'll take you back later this afternoon, yeah?"

She thinks about my offer for a beat before she nods, biting down on her lip and looking at me seductively through her lashes.

"Something you wanted, Hellcat?" I ask, my voice raspy from sleep and my overwhelming need for her, despite having spent almost all night inside her.

Her hips roll and she shudders when the head of my cock slides across her already more than ready pussy.

"Yeah," she states confidently. "You."

Wrapping my fingers around her hips, I drag her exactly where I want her and impale her on my dick in one swift move.

She cries out at the invasion, and I force myself to hold still. There's no way she's not sore after last night.

"You okay, babe?" I ask, sitting forward, allowing her pert nipples to brush against my chest, making her gasp and her inner muscles clamp down deliciously on my cock. Wrapping my hand around the back of her neck, I rest my brow against hers, staring down into her dark, hungry eyes.

"I am now," she says with a smirk. That simple statement makes my heart soar.

She might not have responded to my confession last night, but to be honest, I wasn't expecting her to. Hell, I wasn't even expecting to say the words. But in that moment, it felt right. I have no other ideas how to make her realise that I really want this. Her.

I've spent the past few months trying to prove the exact opposite and running from the truth. Well, I'm done. I'm so fucking done from running away from what I really want, from listening to that little voice in my head who tries to control me, force me into the life that's been designed for me, not the one I actually want.

"We'll take it slow."

My eyes widen when her hand wraps around my throat, and she smiles in accomplishment that she's been able to shock me.

"Don't you ever fucking hold out on me, Theo. I'm here because I want you. All of you."

I swallow harshly against her hold at the sincerity I see shining back at me in her eyes.

"What if I want to take it slow? What if I want to make love to you?" I ask, my heart thundering in my chest at asking a question I never envisaged falling from my lips... ever.

"Then do it, but because you want to, not because you don't think I can handle anything else."

"Fair enough, babe." I roll my hips on the final word and Emmie cries out as I graze her G-spot, her grip on my throat tightening.

"You like hurting me, huh, babe?"

"Consider it revenge for all the times you've hurt me." There's a little bite to her tone, but I wouldn't have it any other way. I deserve a whole world of pain for the shit I've put her through.

"I don't deserve you."

"Well, fuck," she mutters, moving with me as I lift her from my cock. "Something else we agree oooooon," she screams when I drop her back down.

"Pretty sure we can find plenty of other things. Like how you should be screaming louder."

I flip us, pinning her to the bed and fucking her into the mattress like a fucking wild animal.

By the time I've pushed her over the edge twice, we're both dripping in sweat and I'm pretty sure the trickle I can feel down my back is actually blood from the way she clawed at me.

"We should clean up," I say, pulling out and falling beside her. "In about an hour," I confess weakly. My entire body is lit up like a million fairy lights from that release.

Brushing my fingers up her parted thigh, I find her

swollen core, dipping my fingers inside her again, feeling our joint releases coating her.

She shudders, her fingers wrapping around my wrist and halting my movements.

"Stop, please," she begs. "I can't take any more."

I can't help but chuckle at her.

"I know. I just like knowing you're full of my cum."

"You're an animal," she scoffs, twisting away from me and slowly standing up.

"You okay, babe?" I ask, rubbing at my jaw in an attempt to hide my smirk at seeing her struggling to make her legs work.

I don't do a very good job at covering my delight, because when she looks back over her shoulder, her eyes immediately drop to my grin.

"You're a knobhead, Cirillo," she hisses lightly before taking off toward the bathroom.

"Fine by me," I sigh, falling back on the bed and letting my smile widen.

I've got my girl, and Luis Wolfe is dead. As far as I'm concerned, it's a pretty fucking great day.

"What are you doing?" I ask when I finally find the energy to join her in the bathroom.

Placing her hands on her hips, she glares at me.

"Kinda thought it was obvious. Did I fuck all your brain cells right out of you?" she sasses, her eyes taking a leisurely trip down my body.

Knowing that she was in here naked meant I never really sank my boner after I pulled out of her, and having her staring right at me really doesn't do anything to help that situation.

"Yeah, you might well have, Hellcat. I'll leave you to explain that to my old man. Maybe you can take my place." I wink, weirdly loving the idea of her being the top dog in the Family one day.

"Nah, not sure I'll be able to. I'll be too busy showing the Reapers how it should be done," she quips.

As much as the idea of her being part of another team pisses me off, I can't deny that going head to head with her as rivals doesn't stir something inside me.

We could take over the fucking world, the two of us. Okay, so maybe just the city, but whatever.

"You wanna overthrow Cruz? He might have something to say about that, babe."

I close the space between us and she backs up.

"I'm sure he will. So are you in?" she asks, her eyes shooting to the bath she was drawing.

"You want me to get in a bubble bath?" I ask, although I'm not sure why. Her intentions are more than obvious.

For a second, I swear she actually looks nervous. It's so fucking cute.

Rushing forward, I gather her up in my arms.

"You wanna get all wet and soapy with me, babe?" I ask, loving this more vulnerable side that she only allows me to see.

"After I got home the other day, Stella and Calli looked after me. Drew me a bath and tried to make me feel better, tried to help me forget just how much it hurt watching you walk away from me."

"Em, I'm—"

"No," she says quickly, cutting me off. "I'm not

saying this to make you feel bad. I know why you did it. It was the same reason I've done it to you."

"I was scared you wouldn't want me," I explain anyway, knowing there's no way she could have felt the same the times she turned her back on me. "I was scared of letting you see everything I really wanted and you throwing it back in my face. I was a coward. And I should have been there for you. I should have been the one to take you home, and I should have sat in that bubble bath and helped to erase the memories with you."

Her entire expression softens at the picture I paint for her, and her hold on me tightens.

"Make up for it now then," she suggests, glancing over at the bath once more.

"I can't think of anything I'd rather do," I say honestly, releasing her and holding her hand as she steps into the giant tub.

I climb in straight after her and sink down in the burning hot water, my skin stinging until I'm almost fully submerged.

Emmie remains standing, looking down at me with something akin to awe on her face.

"I tried imagining what you might look like surrounded by fluffy bubbles. Turns out I've got a shitty imagination, because I didn't come up with anything as incredible as this."

"I aim to please, Hellcat." Reaching out a hand, I twist my fingers with hers and tug her down, settling her in front of me and wrapping both my arms and legs around her.

"I'm sorry I've not taken care of you like I should have," I apologise quietly.

"Theo, no. I—"

Pressing my fingers to her lips, I cut her off, needing to get some of this off my chest.

"Deep down, I knew you weren't involved with all that shit with Stella. That you had to know what was going on just because you were a Ramsey and hung out at the club was bullshit. Just like I knew that you never stole from my dad, from me.

"I was furious when he passed me that marriage certificate and contract signed by both him and your mother.

"I'd spent weeks, months trying to convince myself that I didn't feel anything for you other than hate." A laugh spills from my mouth as I think about the little firecracker I met at the beginning of the school year who broke all my rules, and she frowns.

"All my life I've been in training to be the perfect soldier, the perfect heir to this Family. Despite the fact that my dad loves my mum more than his own life, he believes that loving someone, giving a piece of your heart to them makes you weak. It's a distraction, a reason for someone to hurt you.

"I've been brought up being told that meaningless hookups to get what you need and then moving on is the way it should be done. Then when the time comes to make some more little heirs, I should pick a certain kind of woman. Someone who—"

"Does as they're told and makes the perfect housewife," she finishes for me.

"Yeah, something like that," I mutter. "My life has been set in stone from the moment I was born. And I was okay with that. I thought it was what I wanted.

"I mean, it is what I want. I'm a Cirillo, I'm pretty sure it's ingrained in me to want it."

"But..." Emmie prompts, trying to get me to the point.

"But it's not all I want," I breathe. "I don't want to be a cold, loveless monster whose relationship is only fulfilling some fucked-up requirement for me to have kids. I want a life, one I get to choose for myself. I want to spend it with someone I care about, someone who makes me laugh, someone who challenges me, who calls me out on my bullshit and laughs at my need to control every aspect of my life." Her hands glide over my cheek, anchoring us together. "I want you."

All the air rushes from her lungs, the minty flavour from the toothpaste washing over my face.

"If you'll have me," I add when she doesn't say anything for long, painful seconds.

"Did you mean what you said last night, or was it just some heat of the moment reaction?"

"What do you think?" I ask, my eyes bouncing between hers as she tries to figure all this out.

"That's the problem. It's kinda hard to know with you."

Taking her hand that's still resting on my cheek, I slide it down until it's hovering over my heart.

"I fucking swear to you, Emmie. I'll never lie to you again. I know it's an easy thing to say, but I'm going to figure out a way to prove to you that everything I tell you, every confession I make, no matter how hard or painful, will be true.

"I live in a fucked-up world, but you get that more than anyone I've ever met. I can't promise you a life of sweetness, of peace. It's going to be chaotic, and dark, and downright ugly at times, but I'll always tell you everything. All the twisted, fucked-up—"

"I get it," she says, interrupting me. "I was never destined for that nice, idealistic life anyway. I've got Cirillo and Reaper blood running through my veins. My life was always going to be messy and painful."

"How are you so perfect?" I mutter, unable to process how I found this incredible woman in my life.

Her sad laugh fills the air. "I'm far from that, Theo."

"To me, you are. To everyone who loves you, you are."

"Who are you?" she whispers, studying me as if this is the first time she's ever really seen me. To be fair, it might be.

"Your husband."

I surge forward, slamming my lips down on hers and sending a wave of bubbly water sloshing over the edge of the tub.

25

EMMIE

Wrapping a towel around myself, I walk out of the bathroom, leaving Theo standing behind me like a Greek god with rivulets of water running over his insane body and soaking into the towel he has tied around his waist.

Something lights up on the floor as I walk toward the wardrobe, knowing that he'll have unpacked properly even for a weekend stay, and I can steal one of his shirts to wear.

I grab my phone, which must have slid off the bed sometime between me showing Theo the gossip that was all over Facebook and him pushing inside me once more.

I've got a stream of notifications, some from people I haven't spoken to since the day I walked out of Lovell. The sight of them makes my stomach twist painfully.

There's no way this is anything good.

No fucking way.

My hand trembles as I hold my phone before me,

willing myself to unlock it and find out what's happened.

I knew this was going to be bad. The second I saw that Luis had been killed, dread lodged itself so deep inside me that I had no doubt it was about to complicate my life further.

"Oh God," I sob quietly as I think about Dad and Cruz. "Please, please, please," I beg. If they went after this stupid prick because of me and they ended up hurt or worse... No, just no.

Blowing out a slow, calming breath, I swipe the screen and open the first notification. I don't even take the time to see who it's from. I just need to know what's hiding inside and how this newest revelation is going to change my life.

The second I read the headline of the article, my heart jumps into my throat.

"Theo," I call, my voice coated in panic as I try to get my head around what I'm reading.

"What's wrong?" he asks not two seconds later as he comes rushing out of the bathroom. "Emmie?" he breathes in concern when he gets a look at the expression on my face.

"It was my pops." Confusion pulls at his brows for a beat. "He... he killed Luis."

Theo's lips part to respond, but no words come out. Instead, he shakes his head and moves closer, lifting my hand that's still clutching my phone to read the news article I was reading.

"Weapon found at the scene believed to belong to MC President Charles Ramsey. Manhunt is in progress to find... Fuck," he breathes as the article goes on.

"None of this makes any fucking sense, Theo," I

confess, throwing my phone back on the bed. I don't need to read any of the other messages, I'm pretty sure I know exactly what they're going to say.

"I know, babe," he says softly, pulling me into his arms and holding me against him.

Pressing my face into the crook of his neck, I focus on the steady beat of his heart.

"Do you know what happened to Ram after you left?" Theo asks softly, and I shake my head.

"No, Dad didn't offer any details. And mostly, I was happy to live in ignorant bliss. "Dad told me he wasn't an issue and—"

"Didn't he also tell you that about the Wolves?"

"Yeah, but—" I blow out a breath instead of arguing about something I have no clue about.

"When your dad and Cruz turned up at my door after you left, they were covered in blood. Whose was it?"

I frown, remembering them turning back up at the house, looking the same.

My initial reaction was that it was all Theo's, but the second I found out it wasn't, I didn't want to know, although I had my suspicions.

"Honestly, I assumed it belonged to either Pops or Luis or a few of his guys. Dad and Cruz assured me that things had been dealt with, so I tried to push it aside."

He nods, looking down at me with sympathetic eyes.

"We should probably get back." His hand cups my cheek and he stares down at me intensely.

"What?" I ask, reading something in his depths that I don't think I'm going to like.

"I swear to you, Em. I don't know anything."

I nod. "I believe you," I tell him honestly. "Please, tell me what you're thinking."

"I think... I think we should get back. Assuming anything isn't helping anyone."

My heart thrashes in my chest as I stare up at him, the heat of his hands on my face keeping me grounded.

"You don't think it was him?"

"I think there are a lot of possibilities. But..." He blows out a long breath. "The most obvious thing to believe is that he's retaliating after Luis took you. To the outside world, that would seem realistic. But—"

"We're not the outside world," I mutter, starting to predict where he's going.

"Why would he suddenly feel the need to protect you? He sold you. He was more than happy to hand you over, so why would he—"

"Be suddenly coming to my rescue," I finish. "You're right, we need to get home."

Taking a step back, I give him little choice but to release me as I continue toward his wardrobe for something to cover up with while ideas I don't really want to think about flicker through my mind.

But two faces keep popping up, and I'd put money on all of this having something to do with them.

Stella, Seb, Calli, and Xander are all sitting around on the sofas when we walk through the living area of the girls' suite only a few minutes later.

They take one look at me wearing only Theo's shirt and smiles appear on all their faces.

"Yes, bro," Seb shouts, holding his hand up for Theo to high-five. "Man, don't leave me fucking hanging."

With a roll of his eyes, Theo concedes and claps his hand against his friend's.

"You two are fucking idiots," Stella snaps.

"Oh, like you are any better. The second you're alone, you'll be comparing notes about our dick size," Seb announces.

"Theo's is bigger," I blurt, much to his horror.

Pushing to stand, Seb's hands drop to his waistband. "You're only saying that because you haven't properly compared." He just rips the button open when Stella drags him back to the sofa.

"You're an asshole," she hisses. "Leave them alone."

He pouts, but it doesn't stop him from taunting Theo.

"But look how happy he is," Seb teases.

"Right, well. We're out of here. You're gonna have to sort out your own way home," Theo barks.

"You're ditching us for a girl?" Seb asks, his brows shooting up in faux shock.

"No. I'm ditching you for my wife. I'm sure you'll figure it out. You two haven't christened Nico's car yet so—"

"Oh no. They're not going at it if I've gotta be in the back with them," Calli pipes up, looking thoroughly horrified by the thought alone.

"Sorry, baby C. Not our fault that you're not the only one who didn't get laid last night."

"She's right, you know. You are an arsehole," Calli hisses, her eyes narrowing in anger at Seb.

"You can ride on the back of my bike," Xander offers.

Theo's grip on my hand tightens.

"Xander's solid. If she wants to, he'll take good care of her," I tell him.

He doesn't say anything, or give her permission, not that she needs it. Calli is her own woman and can make her own decisions. Although something tells me that she'll choose Xander's bike just to piss the guys off. If I didn't have issues of my own right now, I'd be actively encouraging it.

"Come on. We need to move," I say, tugging Theo in the direction of my room.

"She can't get enough! Look, dragging him off to the bedroom again already."

Flipping off my idiot cousin, I continue forward. He doesn't need encouragement with a response.

Dragging Theo's shirt over my head, I rummage around in my unpacked case—something Theo doesn't miss—to find some underwear.

"I don't like that," he announces when I pull on a lace thong—a really freaking sexy lace thong, I might add.

"Let me guess," I say. "It doesn't have your name on it."

A smirk pulls at his lips as he rests one shoulder against the wall, his eyes locked on my body as I pull my bra on. Anger and darkness radiate from him in the same way they do me as thoughts of what might have happened while we've been here run through my head.

"Dad was keen for me to come this weekend," I blurt, as I drag on a pair of skinny jeans up my legs. "I thought it was weird that he was encouraging me to be out and potentially in danger. With you," I add.

"Your dad loves me," Theo says with a smirk.

"Oh yeah. The mafia prince with blood on his hands is every dad's dream for his little girl."

"Don't forget who your father is, Hellcat. We're kindred spirits, I'm sure."

I shake my head, more than able to picture a younger version of my dad in the middle of a gunfight.

"Yeah. What the hell have I put myself in the middle of?" I mutter lightly.

He doesn't respond, clearly more than aware that I didn't need an actual answer to that question.

We both know what I'm in the middle of. Fucking chaos.

And to think, I believed that I'd move in with my dad and have an easier life.

Pretty sure I couldn't have been any more off the mark there.

Theo doesn't say another word and I pull the rest of my clothes on, brush my crazy half wet hair and pile it on top of my head, out of the way. I do a quick job of swiping some eyeliner and mascara on, shove my feet into my boots, and grab my bag.

"Let's go."

Theo stares at me with wide eyes.

"That was... fast."

"What were you expecting?" I ask, quirking a brow at him.

"A longer wait. I thought girls always took ages."

"Well, I'm not your average girl."

"That you are not, Hellcat."

The second I get to him, he wraps his arm around my shoulder and pulls me into his body.

He doesn't take my bag for me, or even offer, and I love it. I love that he doesn't see me like some damsel in distress who can't look after herself. He knows I'm capable and treats me as such. The knowledge makes my heart flutter and my stomach clench.

The words he said to me last night, and assured me he meant this morning, still ring in my ears, but still, I can't say them back. Not yet.

"Something's going on," Stella says, hopping up from the sofa and placing her hands on her hips the second we appear.

"Uh... What makes you say that?"

"I can just see it on your face. What's happened?"

My eyes shoot over to Xander, and one side of his lips curl up.

He knows.

He knows, and he hasn't said anything.

I grip Theo's waist tighter in the hope that he caught that look too and realises that Xander is as loyal as they come.

"Luis Wolfe is dead," I say.

"Good," Seb spits. "That's less than what he deserves for what he did to you."

"Why are you rushing back? Shouldn't you be celebrating?"

"Yeah, we should," I concede, not wanting to dive into our suspicions yet and incriminate anyone unduly.

"They're saying Ram did it," Theo says when I hesitate.

"Oh shit," Seb gasps. "That's..." A deep frown forms on his brow.

"Yeah," we both sigh together.

"You're right. You should get back. We'll be right behind you."

"No," I argue. "Stay, enjoy the luxury while you've got it. We'll be fine. I'm sure there's no drama."

They all stare at me like I'm insane, and a rush of emotions swells within me for the people surrounding me.

My family.

I might have fought it, with Theo especially, but everyone here, and a few probably still passed out elsewhere in the hotel, have become everything to me.

I left Lovell with nothing, and I fully intended to eventually leave Knight's Ridge the same way after two years of torture there. But that's not what I got. I found myself my ride or dies within the elite and privileged walls of that place, and quite honestly, I wouldn't have it any other way.

All of these guys would take a bullet for me, I have no fucking doubt. And, if I'm being honest, I'd do exactly the same for them.

"Okay, Em," Stella concedes, but I know she's just telling me what I want to hear. The second we walk out of this suite, they're going to be getting ready to do the same.

"Ready, babe?" Theo breathes, tugging me tighter into his warmth and strength.

"Yeah. We'll see you soon, yeah?"

In only minutes, we're back in the lift once more and heading to the basement parking level.

Just like last night, the second the doors close on us, the intensity in the enclosed space almost becomes unbearable.

Pressing his hand to my stomach, Theo pushes me back until I hit the wall.

I stare up at him with my heart racing in my chest,

waiting, begging for him to kiss me. But he never does. Instead, his fingers curl around my hip, grounding me with his sparkling emerald stare.

"Everything's going to be okay, Em," he says reassuringly. "Me, Seb, the guys, your dad and uncle. None of us are going to let anything happen to you."

Sliding my hand up his chest, I wrap it around the back of his neck.

"I know. I... I trust you."

All the air rushes from his lungs as I say those three little words. They might not be as big as the ones he said last night, but after everything we've been through, the lies, the secrets... they feel almost as important.

"Fuck, Em. You wreck me in the best possible way," he breathes before brushing his lips against mine and making me forget my own name with his searing kiss.

When the lift dings to announce our arrival underground, I'm more than ready to hit the close door button once more and head right back up to the top, just to keep reality at bay, and Theo's hands on me a little longer.

Sadly, that's not what happens though, because the second the doors open, Theo steps back, grabs my hand and tugs me forward.

"Keep looking at me like that and we'll never leave this hotel, Hellcat," he growls, using his free hand to rearrange himself.

The desire to drop to my knees for him rushing through me is almost too much to ignore.

"You're a filthy little whore, babe," Theo growls, dragging me along toward his car. "I fucking love it. And," he adds, "I'll totally take everything that's in your head right now. Just later, once I've got you back in my flat, alone and all to myself."

"Who says I'm having a sleepover with you tonight?"

"You can fight it and argue if you want, but we both know you're already wet for it."

My lips part, but I can't find it in me to challenge him. "Damn you, Theodore Cirillo."

"Fuck, I love it when you use my whole name." Faster than I can compute, he spins me, collars my throat and presses me up against the side of his car. "It gets me all kinds of hard, Hellcat."

Just to prove his point, he grinds his length against my stomach.

"You'd let me, wouldn't you?"

"W-what?" I stutter, too lost in him to really grasp what he's saying.

"You'd let me fuck you right here in the middle of the car park."

"Yes," I confess, my voice raspy with desire. "I'm yours."

"Goddamn, babe."

He drops his head to my shoulder and sucks in a shaky breath.

"Dad always told me that love makes you weak," he whispers in my ear, the sensation of his hot breath on my sensitive skin enough to send lightning bolts of desire shooting around my body. "But he was wrong. Because I'd fight through hell for you, Emmie. Anything for you."

"Theo," I breathe, my body sagging back against the car.

"And right now, I'm looking after you and taking

you home. But later, I'll lick, suck, and fuck that greedy little pussy until you can no longer remember your own name." My panting becomes damn near embarrassing as he whispers those wicked words in my ear.

Before I get to respond, he pulls the passenger door open and guides me in.

My head is still spinning and my body burning when he leans in, drags the seat belt across me and brushes his lips against mine.

"Tease," I hiss when he pulls back without giving me what I really want.

"Oh, babe. That's all you. Sit tight." He stands and gives me the delight of watching him try to do something with his boner before he throws my bag that had been abandoned on the floor into the boot and joins me.

He glances over, a knowing smirk firmly in place.

"You know," he says, pushing his finger into the ignition and letting the beast rumble around us, "I think you and I are going to have so much fun, wife." He winks and revs the engine, and I can't help but laugh.

"Yeah," I confess. "I think you might be right."

26

EMMIE

"**D**addy, we're home," I sing the second I push through the front door, but the only thing that greets me is silence.

Theo walks into the house behind me and closes the door.

"Drink?" I offer, walking down the hall after kicking off my boots and hanging my jacket on the hook.

"Yeah, sure."

I make us both a coffee, Theo's eyes drilling into me the entire time before we head through to the living room.

"So what's the plan then?" he asks.

"Wait, I guess. I need to talk to him before we do anything else."

He studies me, his eyes bouncing between mine.

"What if it was him—them?"

"Then... nothing. I'm not going to look at them differently, judge them for it. All that kind of stuff is a part of Cruz's life, my dad's past, your life. I won't criticise any of you for what you do for your families, how you operate your... businesses. I just... I'm a part of them now. Both of them. And I know that I can't always know everything, be involved with everything. But when it involves me, then yeah, I wanna know. I'm not going to put up with being lied to.

"I can handle the dark and the dirty." Theo's lips twitch in acknowledgment. "If this is my life, my future, then I want to embrace it. Not live on the outskirts like I have my whole life."

"It's your life, babe, and you can dive in as deep as you like into the underworld, as long as you're holding my hand while you're doing it."

Threading his fingers through mine, he tugs me until I have no choice but to tumble into his body.

"I'll consider it," I mutter teasingly.

"Yeah, you do that." His lips brush mine with every word he says and tingles spread through my entire body.

I love it when he lets go and forgets about taking life too seriously. Every time I see that easy smile and the sparkle of excitement, I can't help but feel incredibly lucky to be a part of his inner circle. "But right now, we've got this house to ourselves and I think we should make the most of it."

"Oh? Wanna show me what you have in mind?"

Our coffees are long forgotten after I place them on the table. He tugs me so I'm lying beneath him and looms over me, all muscle and strength, making me feel like a little mouse caught up by his power and intensity.

"Mine," he growls, gently knocking his nose against mine.

Reaching for my hand, he lifts it, his eyes flicking to the ring sitting on my finger before he presses his lips to it.

"You really want this, don't you?" I ask, my heart galloping in my chest as he honours the somewhat bullshit union between us.

His eyes seek mine out once more, allowing me to see everything he's feeling in the dark green depths.

"I do. But only if you want it too."

"Don't you think we're too young?"

"For what? Falling in love? Thinking about our future?"

"I-I—"

"We don't need big dresses, white picket fences, and a plan for kids. All we need to be is us. We can carve out our lives as we see fit, one day at a time."

"You're annoyingly sweet and perfect, do you know that?"

He shrugs, an endearing, shy smile playing on his lips.

"I have my moments. Just... don't tell anyone. I'm meant to be a ruthless soldier and heir to this Family, remember? I need to keep my rep as a cutthroat arsehole."

"It can be our little secret," I whisper, pulling my hand from his grip and wrapping it around the back of his neck, dragging him down so our lips finally meet.

———

I'm so lost to Theo's kisses and the way he grinds against me, the friction from our jeans doing insane things between my legs as he rolls his hips that I don't hear the front door slam. Nor do I acknowledge the deep, rumbling laughter that floats down to us. And neither does Theo, as he continues to drown in me as much as I am him.

But I sure as fuck hear the loud throat clearing right behind my head a beat before Theo jumps off me as if he's just been shot.

Tipping my head back, I look at Dad and Cruz through hazy, lust-filled eyes.

"Oh hey, we were waiting for you," I say breathlessly as heat begins to spread across my cheeks and down my neck from being caught. I'm not going to apologise for it though. Hell knows I've caught Dad and Piper making out enough times.

"So we see. Get bored, did you?"

"Dawson, Cruz," Theo grunts in greeting, his voice deep and the bulge in his jeans more than obvious.

"Glad to see you're keeping it in your pants this time, Cirillo," Cruz barks in amusement.

Theo's eyes find mine and something flickers through them that I can't decipher as I drag myself up.

Both Dad and Cruz drop into the two chairs opposite and continue staring at us. I'm not entirely sure what they're expecting, but they don't look entirely shocked when I blurt, "We've seen the news."

"Oh yeah?" Cruz asks, sitting back and spreading his thighs wide as if he's settling in for the long haul. "Motherfucker deserved it."

"Couldn't agree more," Theo agrees, sitting

forward and resting his elbows on his knees. "But Ram, really?" The sarcasm in his tone is heavy and more than lets Dad and Cruz know what he's angling toward.

"His DNA was on the gun the cops found. What more do you want us to say?" Dad says, annoyingly looking as fucking cool as a cucumber.

I glare at him, one brow quirked in irritation.

"How about the truth?" I spit, refusing to have them both lie to my face.

Dad's chin drops, but it's all fake. An act. I know him, I know both of them, better than they think I do.

"Emmie, I—"

"No," I hiss, scooting forward to sit on the edge of the sofa while I continue glaring at him. "Don't bullshit me. This was you, both of you. Admit it."

"Can't do that, kiddo," Cruz pipes up.

I blow out a frustrated breath.

"Stop treating me like a child. I can handle this. Please," I beg.

Dad and Cruz share a look, and it says a million words.

"Okay, so I'll take that as you confirming our suspicions then," I mutter, rolling my eyes hard.

"Kiddo, we can't—"

"I get it, okay? I get it. But just tell me this..." I push to stand so they're both forced to look up at me. "Where is Pops?"

"On the run from the police. And the longer he runs, the worse it's going to get for him."

"You have no idea where he is?"

Dad's lips part but Cruz takes over, probably predicting that Dad's considering lying to me again.

"Not since we let him free for the manhunt, no. He's on his own with hounds chasing his tail."

"Why?" I ask, forgetting that I said I only wanted to know one thing. "Why not just end it?"

"Because..." Cruz hesitates, trying to come up with the right words.

"It would let him off too easy?" Theo offers behind me.

"Bingo," Cruz sings. "He's controlled us, everything around him for too long. He's made himself too many enemies, enemies who want more flesh from him than we do, it seems, and that's saying a lot.

"He's always been a power-hungry cunt, but in the past few years, he's taken it to the extremes. Kissing Damien's arse over the whole Joker situation was a fucking joke, because while he was trying to form stronger allegiances with the Cirillos, he was colluding with Luis to bring the Family down a peg or two, planning on taking over their supply chain."

"What?" Theo roars, surging to his feet to stand. "Does my dad know about this?"

"He does now," Dad says with a nod. "That's where we've just been."

"It's what all of this has been about," Cruz says, waving his hand between the two of us. "Ram and Luis used your mum's connections to the Cirillos for their own gain. They tied you to the Family, to your enemy, in the hope of digging up some dirt, causing some shit. But while your mum's greed played right into their hands, your need for vengeance didn't."

"That's what that guy meant," I mutter to myself.

"What guy?" Theo asks.

Blowing out a breath, I think back to my short time in captivity at someone else's hands other than his. "When I was locked up, there was this guy who came. He was nice. Let me use the bathroom, shower. Spoke to me like a human being. He told me that the reason I was there was because they needed me on side. I had no idea what he meant at the time and he wasn't exactly forthcoming with an explanation. But now it makes sense.

"Did they really want me to be a snake?"

"Yeah," Dad states coolly. "And your pops instigated the whole fucking charade."

"Motherfucker," I hiss under my breath.

"They lured your mum in with promises of the wealth and future she dreamed of for the two of you, all the while waiting to incriminate her and sell you out," Cruz explains, in case it wasn't already abundantly clear.

Dad's fists curls where his hands are resting on his thighs before he pushes from the seat, announcing, "I need a fucking drink."

No sooner has he left the room than Theo drops a kiss on my cheek and takes off after him.

It's not until they've both vanished from sight that I finally fall back on the sofa and blow out a long, calming breath.

"This is fucking insane."

"Welcome to my world, baby girl."

I flip him off at his use of the nickname he uses to tease me.

"What happens next, Cruz?" I ask, my voice sounding utterly defeated even to my own ears.

"Well..." he starts, sitting forward and stealing one

of the very cold coffees from the table. He takes a sip before his top lip curls back in disgust. "This is gross."

"We got distracted."

A knowing smirk twitches at his lips.

"Don't even start. I'm a married woman."

He salutes me and thankfully turns the conversation back to where we started.

"Okay, so as for what's next. The Wolves need a new leader. The Reapers need a new Prez." He winks, and I can't help but laugh.

"God help the world, Cruz is about to be the boss," I mutter lightly.

"Oi, you shut your trap, brat."

I smile fondly at him as I flip him off once more.

"And hopefully," he continues, "we can all work our parts of the city as one big happy family."

"Just like that. Peace on Earth?"

"I'm sure it'll be way more complicated, but that's the idea. What about you? What's next for Mrs. Emmie Cirillo?"

"Ramsey-Cirillo, please."

His brows lift at how quickly I snap that response back.

"So, we're calling off the lawyers then?"

"Am I crazy, Cruz?" I implore. "Like, I am. I know I am. But... Shit. This is insane. I'm actually considering continuing with this."

"Em," he sighs. "I've never had anything close to what you seem to have found with Theo. You're talking to the wrong person for advice on matters of the heart. You need to off someone, I'm your guy. Torture someone, I'll be right there. But love and happily ever afters? Nah, not my bag."

"Helpful, thanks," I mutter, crossing my arms over my chest.

"Look," he finally says after seconds of us just staring at each other. He drags his hand down his face, rubbing at his rough jaw. "Everyone and their wife will have an opinion on what you two should do, on how you should live your lives. But really, the only two people's opinions that matter are the two of yours. Only you two know how you feel. What you really want. Trust your heart, trust your gut, and just hope to fuck everything else falls into place."

"I think... I think I'm in love with him," I confess, letting out the words that have been spinning around my head for a while, even more so since he said them to me.

Cruz's lips part to respond, but before he gets a chance to say anything, a shadow falls over the doorway. My heart slams against my ribs, already knowing who's standing there. Who just heard my confession.

Sucking in a breath and some confidence right along with it, I finally follow Cruz's gaze toward the guy standing in the doorway. And thank fuck I do, because the expression on his face and the shocked disbelief in his eyes floors me.

Nothing is said as the air crackles between us. The only sounds that can be heard is my pounding heart and Cruz's awkward shuffling.

Finally, Theo clears his throat and lifts his hand, pushing his hair back from his brow. "Y-your... your dad said we could have a sleepover." He winks, and all the embarrassment I felt from being walked in on earlier comes flooding back.

"O-oh, okay. Great. That's great," I stutter like a fucking idiot, but I can't help it. Knowing he just heard me confess that to someone else... Fuck.

Regret floods me as I push to my feet.

The only person I should have said those words to is him.

Shit.

Closing the space between us, he watches me closely before stopping me with his burning hot hand splayed on my belly.

"It's okay. I get it," he whispers. "Take your time."

Glancing up at him, my heart tumbles at the understanding that's staring back at me.

"I'll go repack."

"I can help," he offers, a cheeky grin appearing on his lips.

"I don't think so, Cirillo. Come and sit with Uncle Cruz for a bit."

"Really?" I groan, turning back to look at the big scary biker sitting in the chair behind me. "It's a little late for *that* speech. We're already married and... yeah."

"Don't I fucking know it," Cruz mutters, reminding me of that mortifying moment on New Year's Day when I had to ask him for the morning after pill.

"I won't be long," I tell Theo, more than aware of the fact that Cruz won't be convinced otherwise. He clearly has something he needs to get off his chest.

Taking the stairs two at a time with my overnight bag in hand, I intend on switching out my clothes, throwing in some clean, sexy underwear and rescuing Theo as fast as I can.

It almost works, but I get intercepted on the way out of my room by my dad.

"I was just going to save Theo from Cruz's how-to-treat-my-niece right speech," I say lightly when he stops me from slipping past him.

"Theo's a big boy, I'm sure he can cope."

Oh, hell yeah he is.

I lock those thoughts down the second they pop up. Not appropriate to be thinking about while looking at my father.

"Emmie, I really don't want to tell you what to do. You're your own person and I trust you, but—"

I groan in amusement at him but he narrows his eyes at me.

"But," he continues, "I'm open-minded and I have no issue with you staying with Theo. He can even crash here, if he wants," he says through gritted teeth. "But school needs to remain your focus. We have no idea what the future might hold. You two might still be together when you're old and grey, or you might not. Nothing in life is certain, but don't throw away opportunities for something you've not even realised exists yet."

"Dad," I say, a smile playing on my lips. "I'm going to fully embrace Knight's Ridge, and I'm going to leave that place with grades that will make you so fucking proud, I promise. Husband or no husband, I will not let you down."

"It's not me I'm worried about you letting down, Em. It's yourself. You've got so much potential, I want you to embrace it."

"I will. I *am*," I assure him.

"Everything is going to be okay. Your pops will be dealt with, and the Wolves and the Reapers will be under new leadership. And you, and your mum, can restart your lives however you see fit."

I nod, hoping that this Pops thing is over sooner rather than later.

I understand, I think, why they've done what they have. But while he's still out there, even if he is in hiding, then he's still a risk.

"And what about you? What are you going to do next?"

"Same as always, kiddo. My calling is the studio, you know that."

"I do, I wouldn't expect anything else. But with Pops gone, Cruz taking over and the two of you sorting your shit out, I wondered if you might—"

"He's offered me a seat at the table," he blurts, his eyes widening as if he wasn't intending to confess that to me.

"Oh? And are you going to take it?" I ask, aware of how much of a big deal that is. Dad's not been a part of the club for a long time. To be offered a place again, it's huge.

"I don't know. We'll see. He's got bigger issues with taking over than what I'm going to do with my life."

I can't say I'm surprised. I'm sure Pops had plenty of guys on his side in all of this. Cruz has got a lot of work to do to clear out any deadwood that had loyalties to the old man.

"Well, if you want my opinion," I can't help but laugh when his brows lift as if to say, 'You're going to give it to me anyway,' "I think it's time we all just embraced who we are and the families we belong to."

"You gonna try and patch in too, kiddo?"

"Meh, who knows. I'll accept being the first female member. There's way too much testosterone in that place." He shakes his head at me in amusement. "We'll figure it out, old man."

"I love you, kiddo. I'm so fucking proud of you."

"You too, Dad," I say, forcing the words past the lump in my throat.

We hold each other until there's a loud bang from downstairs, and then we both break apart and rush for the door.

"What the hell was that?" Dad barks the second we're both in the living room doorway, staring at Theo and Cruz, who are both sitting there innocently.

"What was what?" Cruz says, with a knowing mischievous look in his eyes.

"Jesus Christ," Dad mutters before dropping a kiss on my head. "Have a good night, kiddo. Be safe."

"You got it, old man. There will be no little biker-mafia heirs quite yet."

"You hear that?" Cruz says, pointing at Theo.

"You got it. No harm in practising though, right?"

"He did not just fucking say that," Dad mutters before disappearing down to the kitchen.

"We should probably go," I say to Theo, who immediately pushes to his feet.

"Look after my girl, Cirillo," Cruz hisses.

"You got it. Call me if anything comes to light."

"Sure thing. Have a good one. Although not that good. I refuse to have a worse sex life than my kid niece."

I flip him off behind Theo's back as he wraps his arm around my shoulders and leads me from the house to the sound of Cruz's laughter.

27

THEO

"**A**re they having a fucking laugh?" I grunt as the knocking of my front door rings out around us.

But I don't make a move to answer it. Instead, I push Emmie's body harder against the wall I've pinned her against. My cock is still aching from that little make out session at her dad's, and I need it to fucking continue before I explode.

"They care," she half says, half moans as I kiss down her neck.

"So do I, about making you come and sinking my cock so deep inside you that you'll feel it until this time next week."

"Theo," she moans when I cup her pussy over her jeans, pressing the seam against her clit. "Oh God."

Then my phone starts ringing.

"Motherfuckers," I hiss.

"Answer the door, Theodore," she instructs, pressing her palms to my chest and forcing me back.

"We'll tell them everything is okay and send them on their way."

"And what if they want to hang?"

She stares at me with a quirked brow. "Has hanging out ever stopped them?"

"Fair point." Pushing my hand into my boxers, I moan as I squeeze my needy cock. "First chance I get, I'm sinking balls deep inside you and having you screaming my name."

"Sounds like a plan, boss."

The knocking starts again, and the sound of a pissed-off Seb filters through the door.

I give Emmie a second to straighten herself out before I march toward the banging.

"Oh hey, man. What's up?" I ask lightly, making his brows pinch in irritation, although understanding flickers through his eyes.

"Good to see you fucking came up for air to let us know you were okay." He rolls his eyes, shoving past me and inviting himself inside.

"We're fine. Everything is good," Emmie assures him as Stella follows him.

"We brought takeout," she announces, holding the bag up.

My eyes immediately find Emmie's. My stomach twists in excitement at the mischief I find staring back at me.

"You... uh... were kinda interrupting something."

"So we see," Seb says with a smirk, dropping his eyes to my crotch.

"Don't let us stop you," Stella offers. "We'll dish up."

"You two are weird," I mutter. Seb smiles, seeing

straight through my bullshit. He knows full well that at this very moment, I'd bend her over the sofa and fuck her right here. I am that desperate.

"Aw, babe," Emmie purrs, stepping up to me. My entire body jolts when her palm rubs over my length through my jeans. "Cock blocked again?"

"Hell yeah," Seb barks like the irritating fuck he is. "Keep going, Em. Make him jizz in his pants like a schoolboy."

Emmie's eyes alight with amusement, knowing that she really does have that power, even without touching me.

"Fuck. You," I hiss, although with the way Emmie's hand is rubbing me, my voice loses some of its bite.

"Can you just give us a minute?" Emmie asks, slipping her other hand into mine. "There's a really pressing issue I have to deal with."

Both Seb and Stella snort a laugh, but I quickly forget they even exist as Emmie starts tugging me out of the room.

I was expecting her to head for the bedroom but she goes in the opposite direction—not that I'm fucking complaining, if the hungry look in her eyes is anything to go by.

A growl rumbles in my chest when she leads me toward my office, her back bumping into the door, making it swing open.

"Lean against your desk, boss," she purrs, looking at me from beneath her lashes.

"Fuck yeah," I growl, doing exactly as I'm told.

The second she's in front of me, I thread my fingers into her hair and crash her already swollen lips to mine, hungrily sweeping my tongue into her mouth. She squeaks in pain as my fingers twist, leaving her with no question about exactly how badly I need this right now.

Pulling back, I stare into her eyes.

"Get on your knees. Now."

Excitement darkens her eyes, and I can't help but wonder if she's taken back to earlier times when the burning hate that sparked between us almost scorched us both alive.

"Yes, boss," she breathes, immediately dropping to her knees, her fingers making quick work of tugging my fly open and dragging my jeans and boxers around my hips.

A pained moan rips from my throat as my cock springs free. But all she does is stare at it.

"I lied before," she confesses, and my heart suddenly slams against my ribs.

I know I wasn't meant to walk in on her telling Cruz what she did. I didn't need her reaction to tell me it was really fucking bad timing. But if she takes it back, fuck.

I stare down at her, really trying to keep my expression blank, because if I don't, I'm afraid of what she might see looking back at her.

"I once told you there was only one part of you I liked." Lifting her head, I groan when she wraps her delicate fingers around me. "I mean, it might still be my favourite bit, but I like other parts of you now too."

I bark out a laugh, more than relieved she's not taking back what she said. Because despite the fact that she didn't say it to my face, and also the fact that she said she *thought* it was how she felt, it still meant more to me. Hearing those words from her lips was more powerful than I ever thought it would be.

I knew the second she walked away from me on New Year's Eve after her impressive breakout skills that what I felt for her wasn't what I'd always tried to convince myself it was. And I understand after everything we've been through together that those words, her feelings might take a little longer, and I'll give her all the time in the world to get her head around this. But fuck, I want it. I want to hear those words fall from her lips as she stares me right in the eyes so fucking bad.

I want her to tell me that I'm not crazy for wanting this when it's the least of what I deserve. I need her to—

Fuuuuuck.

My vision clears as I come back to myself as she licks around the head of my cock, lapping up the precum that's collected at the tip as if she was dying without it.

"Mmmm," she moans, the vibrations from it shooting up my dick.

"Jesus, Hellcat. I'll never get used to watching you do this. You look so fucking good on your knees for me."

"Don't fuck this up and I might just do it fairly often," she quips.

"That's a pretty fucking good incentive, babe," I manage to force out before she sinks right down on my length, taking as much of me as physically possible.

She works me into a fucking frenzy with her fingernails digging into my arse as she takes me.

"Fuck, babe. Fuck," I grunt a beat before my release claims me and my cock shoots ropes of jizz down her throat.

She doesn't stop until I'm done, and only when

she's confident she's got it all, does she sit back on her heels and look up at me.

"Such a good fucking girl," I praise, reaching out to swipe a little cum from her lip and immediately pushing it back into her mouth. Her tongue laps at it, and fuck if my cock doesn't jerk, getting ideas for more already.

Collaring her throat, I lift her to her feet, crashing our lips together. I taste myself on her tongue, but it only makes me burn hotter for her.

Commotion and voices from out in the living area float down to us, and Emmie pulls back.

"Tell me they didn't?" I ask, although I already know it's hopeless.

"Pretty sure they did," Emmie replies with a smirk.

"But I want—" My hand cups her pussy once more.

"Ever heard of delayed gratification, boss?" she whispers, that mischievous glint in her eyes back full force.

"You wanna go hang out with my friends instead of letting me get you off?"

"Firstly," she points out, "they're my friends too. You need to learn to share your toys." She quirks a brow, and a smile forms on my lips. "And secondly, I have every confidence that you'll make it worth the wait."

"No pressure, huh?"

"I'm confident in your skills, Theodore."

"Hmm," I say, dragging her back in for another kiss. "I'm more than confident in yours, you filthy little whore."

"Yours," she mumbles into our kiss.

"Mine."

———

"**O**h look, the sex addicts return," Seb barks the second we emerge from my office.

"Oh that's fucking rich," Alex snaps. "You couldn't even wait to get the tip in before I left your place the other night," he happily announces to the room.

Calli shakes her head while Nico high-fives Seb in excitement.

"When you need it, you need it," Nico explains as if it's fucking necessary.

I'm pretty sure the only one in this room who doesn't know that feeling is Calli. And thankfully, the blush on her cheeks right now only confirms my suspicion.

"You're a dog," she hisses at her brother, slapping him around the head, but his only response is to bark proudly.

Dipping my head, I brush my lips against Emmie's ear. "Just remember, you could have been laid out on my desk with my tongue inside you while you screamed my name right now."

My cock swells at the thought.

"There's always time, big man. Let's go eat. I'm starving."

"Fair enough," I concede, unable to deny that I'm hungry and that the scent of the Chinese Seb and Stella have covered my dining table with smells insane.

"So," Emmie starts, and I groan, knowing that I'm not going to like what's coming next. "How was your ride with Xander?" she asks Calli, poking her tongue into her cheek. "What?" she gasps innocently when I elbow her in the ribs.

Every guy around the table stiffens at her suggestive question—even Toby, who's sitting silently at the other end looking like he'd rather be anywhere else in the world right now.

Pain slices through me once more at the anger and hopelessness that surrounds him.

"Oh, it was great," Calli beams, dragging my eyes from Toby. "It was... rough," she suggests with a smirk.

"Callista, you are not falling for a fucking biker," Nico snaps, his fist curling on the table, his knuckles turning white.

"Fuck you, Nico," she hisses back. "I'll fall for who I want." Something passes through Calli's eyes as she says that, but it's gone so fast I wonder if I imagined it.

"Jesus fucking Christ," he mutters to himself before reaching for his beer and downing it in one.

"All right, man?" I say, leaving my girl behind and squeezing Toby's shoulder.

"Yeah," he grunts unconvincingly.

"Have a good time with those girls last night?"

"Fucking pussy got wasted before the good shit happened," Nico answers for him. "Had to man up and entertain them myself. It was a challenge, but lucky for them, I was man enough for the job."

"You're a hypocrite," Calli spits. "I can't ride on a bike of some guy who has zero interest in me, but you can sit there proudly telling us all about spending the night with two girls."

"Children, children," Alex sings. "We all know Nico needs all this attention to make him feel like a man. He can't help it, baby C."

"What the fuck did you just say to me?"

"Nico," Toby pipes up. "Shut the fuck up, man. You wouldn't want me to tell everyone how you couldn't get it up that time."

"Oh my God," Alex and Seb howl in delight. Even Calli snorts a laugh at that announcement.

And just like that, everything is normal once more.

I look around at everyone as Emmie comes to sit in the empty chair beside me and I can't help but smile.

There might be a lot of fucked-up things surrounding each of our lives, but they're my family, and I'd take a bullet for every motherfucker around this table.

"Did anyone invite the devil incarnate to this little gathering?"

Alex's lips part to respond, but he doesn't need to. Guilt is written all over his face.

"He's probably busy," Seb says.

"Or he's downstairs selling his soul?" Nico adds.

"You're a bunch of pricks," I mutter, pulling my phone from my pocket and shooting him a message.

It's read immediately, but he never replies or even starts typing.

Pushing it aside, I drop a kiss on Emmie's cheek, which makes the guys groan.

"Pussy-whipped motherfucker," Alex barks around a mouthful of chow mein.

Flipping him off, I reach for the closest container, ready to start filling my plate.

"This is... weirdly nice," Emmie whispers in my ear when I offer her the food first.

"Yeah. It is. Welcome to the family, wife." I wink.

"Oh, didn't you notice? I've been a part of it for a while. You just tried to ignore my presence," she quips.

"Babe, you're impossible to ignore. I used to know where you were every second."

"Stalker," she hisses.

"Certified. You wouldn't have it any other way."

She holds my eyes, a wicked smile pulling at her lips. "I forgot to tell you. I recorded you in the hotel room Friday night."

My eyes widen in shock, but all I do is shrug. "Enjoy it, Hellcat. Just make sure you film your reaction to watching it for me."

"I didn't stop it from recording when I walked out."

My mind spins for a moment. "You mean you've got..."

"Pretty sure, yeah."

"Do not give that fucking tablet back to Seb," I growl.

"Don't give me what?" he asks, having heard his name.

"Nothing," I hiss, although I can't deny that this whole conversation is giving me ideas. Dirty, cock-stirring ideas.

He glares at me suspiciously, but like fuck am I letting him in on the images that are playing out in my head.

Thankfully, a knock at my door stops him from questioning me, and everyone looks in my direction.

"I'll go then," I say with a laugh when no one else even attempts to move.

"You're an idiot," Emmie mutters as I push my chair back and head for the door.

"You came," I say the second I pull the door open and find Daemon standing on the other side.

"You said there was Chinese," is his only reasoning, but secretly, I think he feels more left out than he wants to show. And now we all live in the same building, he's hardly got an excuse to avoid us. Well, not as big of one.

"Come on, Seb and Stella ordered a feast."

Alex is the only one who makes a deal about him showing his face, but then I guess that can be expected seeing as they're twins.

Everyone else just continues as if he was always here.

Exactly as it should be.

"You look happy," Emmie whispers in my ear as I sit and watch everyone enjoying themselves, my dinner still sitting mostly untouched on my plate.

Wrapping my arm around her shoulders, I lean in closer.

"I am, I confess. What more could I need?"

"Well, now you put it that way," she teases before I collar her throat and kiss her like we're alone while the others whoop and holler like fucking idiots around us.

28

EMMIE

"**W**ho are you messaging?" I ask, dropping down beside Calli on Theo's sofa.

He's with Alex, Nico, Toby, and Daemon in the kitchen, talking business. Business which involves the quickest way they can find my Pops and put an end to all this bullshit. I probably shouldn't have gotten bored listening to them, but I'm fed up of it. I want to forget about all that and enjoy myself.

Calli moves so fast that she actually fumbles with her phone. It lands in my lap, but she comes to her senses quick enough to snatch it up before I get to it.

"Jesus. Is he that hot?" I ask with a laugh.

Her cheeks burn bright red and she stares at me with wide eyes.

"No, no. It's no one."

"Fuck off, Cal. That is not no one. Oh my God," I gasp, lowering my voice. "Is it Xander?"

"What? No." She sounds horrified by even the suggestion.

"He's hot. I'd totally get it if you—"

"I don't. I mean, yeah. He's totally hot. But no. Not my type."

"Okay so who is your type? Because I'm yet to figure it out."

Her mouth parts to respond, but she changes her mind.

"Come on, Cal. This is me. You can tell me anything."

Her eyes shoot to the guys, her brows pulling in concern.

"It's no one. Honestly. Just a bit of stupid fun."

"Even more reason to tell me. Are you sexting?" I ask, wiggling my brows suggestively.

"No."

"Okay... so... is it someone I know?"

"No, it's not. It's really no one."

"Okay, fair enough." She looks at me as if she's already feeling guilty about cutting me out. "Don't do that, Cal. If you don't want to tell me, it's totally fine." Taking her hand, I squeeze gently. "But if you need to talk, I'm here. Okay? You can tell me anything."

Her eyes glisten with tears, which makes my stomach knot with concern.

What the hell are you up to, Callista Cirillo?

The music that's pumping through the hidden speakers throughout Theo's flat suddenly gets louder—so loud it actually makes Seb drag his lips from Stella's on the other sofa for a second.

The hairs on the back of my neck stand on end, letting me know that he's close two seconds before the sofa cushion compresses behind me and his hands slide from my shoulders to my breasts, squeezing in the most teasing way, reminding me of exactly what he owes me.

"Dance with me, wife," he growls in my ear.

Unable to deny him, I push from the sofa as he hops over the back and pulls me into his body.

"Hey, dickhead," he mutters, slapping Seb around the head. "Fuck off home if you can't keep your cock out of her. I don't want your bodily fluids on my sofa."

Seb flips him off over his shoulder, not ripping his lips from Stella's for a beat.

"They're in love, leave them to it," I chastise, brushing my lips along the roughness of his jaw.

"Hmm... Me too," he moans as I suck on his neck hard enough to leave a mark.

"It's not a bad place to be, it seems," I whisper in his ear.

Dragging my head back with his fingers twisted in my hair, he stares down at me, his eyes searching mine.

"It's better than that, Em. It's fucking everything."

His lips find mine, everything and everyone around us ceases to exist as our tongues duel and our hips grind to the beat.

I lose all sense of time as he consumes me, driving me crazy with his burning touch, his kisses, and his downright filthy promises.

The songs all blur into each other as my body burns up, my need for him to return the favour from earlier too much to ignore.

Reaching up on my toes, I brush my lips against his ear. "I can't wait any longer. I want your mouth on my pussy right fucking now."

His grip on me tightens as a growl of need rumbles deep in his chest.

"Let yourselves out," Theo booms over the music. Before I have a chance to say anything, he throws me over his shoulder, his palm coming down on my arse so hard a scream rips from my throat.

I look up just in time to catch Stella's eye before we disappear. 'Have fun,' she mouths.

———

"What?" I ask nervously as Theo stares down at me the next morning with an intensity that makes my breath catch. "Did you..." he hesitates, and that doesn't make my heart rate lessen at all. "Did you really ask Cruz to get you the morning after pill?"

I gasp, ripping my eyes away from him. Shame twists at my insides, although I'm not sure why. I shouldn't feel like that. I did the right thing. I was being sensible. Unlike him. Although, I guess if I really were being a sensible adult like I claim to be, then I shouldn't have let him screw me bare when I knew there was a risk.

"Emmie," he growls, his warm fingers gripping my chin. "Don't try and hide from me." His nose nudges mine. "You already know that I'll find you eventually."

"I know, I just..." I blow out a breath. "Yeah, I did ask Cruz to get me the morning after pill. You locked me down in the basement without my birth control. And then..."

"You seduced me," he growls with a smirk pulling at his lips.

"I was probably overreacting, nothing probably would have happened, but..."

"It was the right thing to do."

It's stupid, but hearing those words from his lips

slices me open. My eyes fill with tears and a lump the size of Australia clogs my throat.

Theo's eyes widen in horror as I quite obviously fall apart right in front of him.

"Em, what's wrong?"

"I-I d-don't know," I stutter as my bottom lip trembles.

A deep frown forms on his brow as he wraps his arm around me and pulls me tighter into his body.

"Do you think you made a mistake? Did you want... Do you want..."

"No. No, I don't want kids. Well, not right now. In the future, maybe. I just..."

"Hey," he says softly as my first tear finally falls. Dipping down, he captures it with his lips. "It's okay, I've got you. Whatever it is, you can talk to me."

I suck in a shaky breath and hold his worried eyes.

"Walking away from you that night was all I'd been able to think about. From the second I woke up and found myself locked up in the basement, my entire focus was getting away from you.

"But the second my plan played out." I swallow thickly. "I regretted it. Seeing the disbelief on your face when I stepped between Cruz and Xander... it fucking killed me, Theo. The moment I walked away with them, I knew it was wrong."

"So why did you go through with it? You could have changed your mind at any point."

"Because... it was the right thing to do," I explain. "What we have—had—it was toxic, Theo. You can't argue with that. All the lies, the secrets. All the things we did to hurt each other. It wasn't right. Being locked up in here. All of it was so fucking twisted.

"We needed to be apart. I needed to know how much it hurt to walk away.

"All these weeks, months, we've danced around each other like this connection between us meant nothing. But that's not true. This... what we have. It's everything, Theo.

"And I walked away and then I put pay to anything that might have come out of it. Whether or not it was the right thing to do, I made that decision alone. That's not how it should be. I should have waited. I should have told you, but I was so fucking angry at both of us that I could barely think straight.

"I wanted to hurt you as much as you hurt me. But I didn't realise at the time how I would hurt myself in the process.

"But now, being here with you... I walked away and potentially aborted what could have been our pregnancy without so much as a second thought."

"Stop it," Theo snaps, the deepness of his voice shocking me before he tries again. "Stop it, please." This time, he sounds as broken as I am right now.

"Everything you did... Everything. It was right. All of it.

"I deserved to watch you walk away. Twice. I deserved it all and then some.

"I wanted to believe so badly that you were the enemy so that I wouldn't have to deal with how I really felt. And that was wrong. So wrong. And I deserve all your wrath for it."

Turning onto my side, I line our bodies up, hooking my leg over his hip, ensuring there's no space between us.

"We both fucked up, Theo. We've both made

mistakes, ruined what we really wanted and intentionally hurt each other. We're both to blame for how everything went down."

He shakes his head. "No, you're—"

"Shh," I say, pressing my fingers to his lips. "Enough. It's our past, our story, some of which we might be able to relay to our kids one day. Who knows." His lips twitch with the beginnings of a smile. "But right now, we're young. Too young to have been through all the shit we have. How about we just take a step forward and look toward the future instead of obsessing about what's already gone before."

Wrapping his fingers around my wrist, he drags my hand out of the way and captures my lips in a searing kiss that makes my heart sing and my toes curl.

"Is that a yes?" I ask when he finally pulls back to catch his breath.

"It's more than a yes, babe."

After spending all day at Theo's, he reluctantly agreed that I should go home so that I could sleep in my own bed before going back to reality tomorrow.

To be honest, I was more than happy to stay and have him escort me to school in the morning.

Going back after breaking Sloane's nose would certainly be easier if I were tucked under his arm. No one would dare say a word to me about it all with him right beside me.

But that's not the kind of girl I am. I don't run from adversity and confrontation, and I don't intend on doing it now from some entitled little rich bitch. Although, if what Theo has discovered is true, then she's no longer a rich bitch. Oh, how the mighty fall.

"I could just bring you back in the morning to get your uniform." Theo pouts at me, pulling out all the stops with his puppy dog eyes.

"Stop that," I say, swatting his thigh. "You know it's the right thing to do."

When I brought up starting over this morning, I meant really starting over.

I wasn't going to suddenly pack up my life and move in with him. Yeah, technically we're married. But we're still young. We've got plenty of time to play house. For now, I just want to be... normal. Despite the fact that that thought is laughable after everything. I know it's the right thing to do. Even if Theo is in a bit of a pissy mood about it.

"I'll see you in the morning."

"You could leave your window open. For old time's sake. I love watching you sleep. It relaxes me."

I pretend to think about it for a few seconds. "Maybe I will," I tease.

"You're killing me, babe."

"It'll be worth it. I promise. Now go, your mum, brother, and sisters are waiting for you."

"They're gonna be pissed when I turn up without you."

"Next time," I promise.

As if she knows we're talking about her, Theo's mum pops up on the screen as his phone rings through the speakers.

"I'm late," he confesses.

"I know. Go. We'll talk later."

"We will." Something wicked twinkles in his eyes, but the second his lips find mine, I forget all about it.

I climb out of the car the second he releases me for fear that I'll just tell him to drive and take me with him.

Stay strong, Emmie. Don't lose your mind over his dick.

"Hello?" I call after letting myself in and waving Theo off.

"Living room," Dad calls.

Dropping my bags, I follow his instruction and find him and Piper curled up on the sofa, watching what looks like a nature program. *Oh, the ways that woman has changed my father.*

"What's so funny, kiddo?"

"Um..." I look between him and the TV. "Are you really watching a documentary about trees?" I ask, quirking a brow.

"No, not really. It was just background noise."

"For?" I realise my mistake the second the word falls from my lips. My eyes drop to the blanket covering them before I lift them to the ceiling. "Just pretend I never said that. I'm gonna go shower and get ready for school in the morning."

"Oh, so you remembered that you live here then?" Dad quips, making a show of lifting his hands from beneath the blanket to show me nothing untoward was happening.

"Yeah. This is my home, and school is my priority," I state proudly. "All the rest, I'll figure out along the way."

Both Dad and Piper smile at me.

"And what does Theo think of all this?" Piper asks after a few seconds.

"Well, his need to control everything around him and keep me safe is freaking him the hell out right now. I've sent him to Selene. Hopefully, she'll sort him out."

"I'm pretty sure the only person in the world that boy really listens to is you, Em," Dad mutters with amusement.

"Why do you think he's heading toward his mum's?"

"Fair play."

"So are you together or..." Piper probes, clearly wanting the gossip.

"Yeah, we are," I confirm. "But we're taking a few steps back, starting over. Being teenagers."

"Sounds smart."

"Well, I am your daughter," I sass.

"Pain in the arse. Theo needs all the luck he can get, being tied to you."

"Love you too, Dad," I say with a smile, backing out of the room.

"Do you want dinner?" Piper asks before I disappear.

"If it's okay with you."

"Always, Emmie. You know that."

"Thank you," I say, holding her eyes, hoping like hell she knows just how much I mean that.

"You're more than welcome, sweetheart."

"I'm going to be staying at Theo's at the weekends. Get out of your hair." They both nod in agreement. "But most school nights, I'll be home."

"Just let us know if anything changes."

Feeling a little of the emotional meltdown that hit me this morning beginning to resurface, I continue to back up until I'm able to run up the stairs and lock myself in my room.

It feels weird, being alone in here again. There's a part of me that wonders if it was all a really fucked-up dream. But then I look down at my ring and recall just a few of the memories, the bad and the good from the past few weeks, and I'm reminded that all of it was very real. And I wouldn't have it any other way.

I lie in bed later that night, waiting for Theo to message me back.

The tracker that he synced to my phone shows me that he left his parents' place not so long ago and that he's heading home.

I feel weird, stalking him after all the grief I've given him about him following me. But it's weirdly comforting, seeing his little dot moving, knowing that he's safe, knowing where he's heading. Although, I must admit that I'm a little disappointed he's not heading this way to check the situation with my window—which, of course, is open.

I blow out a breath, my exhaustion starting to get the better of me, but I refuse to give in until I know he's home and I've spoken to him.

Those intentions are great and all, but when my phone finally vibrates in my hand, it scares the shit out of me and makes my eyelids fly open.

His Lordship: Do you have that tablet Seb gave you to hand?

I blink at the screen as my vision clears.

"Shit," I breathe, realising that I've actually been asleep a while.

Emmie: Yeah, hang on.

Throwing the covers off, I pad across the room, shivering as I go with the coldness from the open window, and pull it from my bag.

I've already got a message waiting for me when I get back.

His Lordship: You dressed for me. Do you have any idea how hard that makes me?

My stomach flips at his words, and my heart begins to race, knowing that he's watching me.

Emmie: I thought you'd like it, boss.

His Lordship: I'd prefer to see it on the floor.

Turning to where I now know one of the cameras is, I bite down on my bottom lip and lift the hem of my cami, exposing my belly to him.

He starts typing immediately.

His Lordship: You're a tease, Mrs. Cirillo.

Poking my tongue out at the camera, I snuggle back into the warmth of my bed as a set of instructions comes through, telling me to find a certain app on the tablet and open it up.

Theo gives me the password, and in only a few minutes, I've got a black screen with a little wheel spinning in the middle.

Emmie: It's loading…

His Lordship: It'll be worth it. Trust me.

I wait, and then the screen begins to flicker to life. It's pixelated at first, but even still, I know exactly what I'm looking at.

"Oh my God. Theo!" I gasp when I get a very clear image of him laid out naked on his bed.

"Hey, babe. Figured it was only fair you get to watch me too. Keep an eye on me and make sure I'm not jerking off every second of the day to thoughts of my hot-as-fuck wife."

"Shit, I need headphones," I say in a panic, reaching for my drawer. The last thing I need is Dad or Piper walking past my bedroom and hearing Theo and his dirty mouth.

"I know something else in that drawer you could make use of."

"You're wicked."

"You wouldn't have me any other way."

Finding my AirPods, I pop them into my ears and connect the tablet to them.

"Okay, please continue."

"Nah, this is your show, babe. You tell me all the things you want to watch. I'll even pretend you don't know I'm watching. Kinda make it fair."

My heart swells, knowing that all of this is about righting a few more of his wrongs.

"I love you," I blurt, my brain not even realising the words were about to fall out of my mouth.

He sits bolt upright in bed, his hand immediately releasing his hard dick.

He blinks at the camera as if he couldn't have possibly heard those words through the speaker.

"Say it again," he whispers. The softness and vulnerability in his voice make my heart ache.

Fuck, why didn't I say this earlier when we were face to face?

"I love you, Theo," I say again, my voice cracking with emotion.

"Shit, Emmie," he sighs, pushing his hair back out of his face and tugging until it has to hurt. "I don't fucking deserve you. I don't deserve to hear those words from your lips."

"Let me be the judge of that. Now," I say, getting this back on track. "sit back against the headboard and wrap your hand around that massive dick." My cheeks burn saying the words to a screen, but I can't deny that I'm not burning up inside. I can only imagine how hot it was, watching me when I didn't know. Jesus, I'm as fucked up as my husband.

"Like this?" he asks, needing my praise.

"Yeah, just like that."

Throwing the covers back, I make a show of pushing my hand into my shorts and gasp loudly when my fingers connect with my needy clit.

"Fuck, babe. You're so fucking perfect."

"Good job I'm your wife then, huh?" I moan out as

I push my fingers inside, my eyes locked on the screen where he works himself.

"You know, if I can't have you in my bed, this is definitely the next best thing."

A whimper rips from my lips as he starts running his hands over his taut abs.

Jesus, how is my husband so fucking hot?

"You're just lucky, I guess," he groans, answering the question I wasn't aware I said out loud. "Fuck, I love you, Em. The best thing you ever did in your life was walk directly into mine. Fuck," he grunts again, the muscles in his forearm pulled tight as he pumps himself almost violently. "I'm never gonna let you go, Hellcat. Never."

"Never," I cry, losing my fight with my orgasm at the same time he groans my name, and I get to watch as he shoots hot ropes of cum over his stomach.

"I love you, I love you, I love you," I chant as my body sinks back into exhaustion.

We both clean up and stay on camera as we snuggle into bed, still connected as I drift off to sleep with his voice in my ear.

And we do the same thing for the next few nights as he keeps his promise to take things slow, despite his desire to come and implant himself right in the middle of my life.

"Hey, kiddo. You had a good day?" Dad asks as I walk through to the kitchen after school on Thursday afternoon.

"Uh..." Images of Theo dragging me into the boys' locker room and making out for the entirety of his free period fill my mind, and I cringe when my cheeks start to burn. "Yeah, it was okay."

He eyes me suspiciously but doesn't say any more.

"Here," he says, choosing to ignore it. "This came for you."

My eyes drop to the white envelope on the table, and I don't think much of it until he pushes it my way and I get a look at the handwriting on the front.

"It's from Mum," I breathe, too shocked to keep it in.

"Yeah," Dad agrees.

"What does it say?" Stupid question, but the blood is racing past my ears and my anger is surging as all the reasons why I should take this outside and burn it flicker through my mind.

"It's addressed to you, Em. I wouldn't—"

"I know. I'm sorry. I just wasn't expecting..."

He looks down at his watch, and I realise that he should already be at work.

"You want me to stay and open it with you?"

"No," I say confidently. "It's just a letter from my mum, how bad can it be?"

Dad smiles in response, but it's forced at best. He's more than aware of how bad it potentially could be.

"Go, Dad. Honestly, I'm fine. And Piper will be home soon, should anyone need to stop me from going and killing her." It's a joke, but from the grimace on Dad's face as it falls from my lips, I'm thinking it was a poor one. "It'll be fine. It's just a letter.'"

His brow lifts as he stares at me in concern.

"Call me if you need me."

"Dad, I'll be fine. I can deal with harder shit than this."

"I know you can, kiddo. But I'm your dad, it's my job to worry."

"I've got this. All of this," I promise.

"I know."

He holds my stare, and my lips part to ask if he's heard anything from Pops, but the words get stuck in my throat. It's been five days since he's been on the run for Luis's murder, and the only news is all the new evidence of crimes against him that seem to keep magically popping up. So now murder is only one of the things he really needs to worry about. Theo and the guys are still doing everything they can to find him. I've not been brave enough to ask what they intend to do once they do find a location, but I know how they work. He hurt me, which means in turn he hurt them. It's not going to have a good outcome. And weirdly, I'm okay with that.

For years, he's been hurting those I love most. Maybe it is time for him to meet his maker and for a new reign of power to fall over this side of the city.

"Go to work. Zach will string you up if you're late." He rolls his eyes at me but doesn't comment.

"Call me," he urges.

"I'll be fine."

"I know. Call me anyway. You might be all grown up and married and shit, but I still worry."

"I'll shoot you a message," I promise, not wanting to get in the middle of his night.

After dropping a kiss on my head, he quickly leaves the house, proving that he is actually late.

I stand there and stare at the envelope for the longest time.

It's not until my stomach starts growling that I finally move.

Grabbing some snacks, and the letter, I take it all up to my room.

Theo is at football training with the guys. Stella and Calli are doing gym, and I've got a ton of homework to do if I want to be on top of everything to spend the entire weekend in Theo's bed, exactly as he promised earlier.

I put the letter on the side and try to push it from my mind as I work, but it's easier said than done, and with each minute that passes, I feel its presence more, as if it's a person in the room staring at me.

"Fuck it," I mutter, standing from the bed and swiping it from the side.

I rip it open as if the content has already offended me.

Pushing my laptop and books aside, I rest back against my headboard and pull the sheet of paper from inside.

My heart thrashes against my chest with my need for Mum to explain everything and make me understand. Even after everything, I'm still desperate for her to be a good person, the one I thought she was when I was a naïve little girl.

Trying not to think too much into my issues surrounding Mum, I hold the letter before me, taking in her familiar yet awful handwriting.

A smudge in the ink catches my eye, and my heart jumps into my throat. She was crying when she wrote this.

All the promises I've made myself over the past few weeks to stop putting her on this special pedestal come crashing down around me.

No matter how much of a fuck-up she is, she's still my mum, and I'm not sure I'm ever going to shed that connection, that feeling. It might be time for me to come to terms with the fact that I'll always want her to get better, all the while she continues to disappoint me.

Blowing out a long breath, my eyes find the beginning.

Emmie, my sweet, sweet girl,
I want to say I'm sorry. But those words just aren't big enough to encompass all the ways I've hurt you.
All I've ever wanted is a better life for you. I wanted to do right by you the second I discovered I was pregnant.

*I was terrified but so excited. I made myself all these
stupid promises for how I was going to give you the best
life, be the best mother, and offer you the world.
I've always been good at lying to myself.
But I've screwed it all up, time and time again. And I'm
sorry, I truly am.
I should have tried to get clean years ago, but I knew it
would mean leaving you and I was too scared.*

My chest aches as I think of Mum over the years and all
the things we've been through together. The pain
bleeding in her words, her regret is palpable, and it
makes my eyes burn with tears.

*I thought Damien was our way out. And it might have
been, if my greed and desperation for that new, better life
didn't take control of everything.
The day Luis Wolfe offered me a deal, I should have told
him no. I should have walked away.
But I couldn't. Not when he promised me a way to give
you the life I craved.
I was naïve, I'll admit that. But I was a mess, strung out
on God knows what at the time, and when he handed me
a wad of cash, I was gone.
But with each week that passed, the more I realised that
I'd sold my soul to the devil. But it was too late, and I
panicked.
I believed your father, grandfather, and Damien would
have protected you. I never, ever thought that Ram
would have been on Luis's side.
I'd like to say that if I knew, I'd have done things
differently, but honestly, you know as well as I do that I
probably wouldn't.
I gave Damien your name, knowing that he'd look after*

his own, and I had to trust that he'd lay down his life for you, just like I knew your father would and hoped Ram would.

But Luis and Ram's need to topple the Cirillo empire ran deeper than I ever could have imagined.

I never wanted to hurt you, Emmie. But I screwed up, I tried taking the easy way out.

I promise you, I'm going to do my time here. I already feel better than I have in years, and then I'm going to restart my life. I'd love to have you in it. Theo too, if you can forgive me. But I also understand you might not be able to, or even want to. And that's okay.

All I want is the best for you, and if that means I need to be out of your life then so be it.

I love you, Emmie, and I hope they're giving you the world, because you deserve it and then some.

All my love,

Mum x

Big, fat, ugly tears slide down my cheeks as I stare at Mum's words, the pain of the past ripping through me like a tornado.

"Fucking hell," I mutter to myself, wiping my face with the backs of my hands.

The urge to grab some paper and reply is huge, but I force myself to lock it down.

Just like I've enforced taking things slow with Theo, something tells me that it's going to take even more time to discover a healthy relationship with Mum. Too many years have passed, filled with hurt and pain.

She made a mistake, trusted the wrong people. I get that. I even understand her desperation for more. But to be manipulated by a snake like Luis when she knew that ultimately I would pay the price? That's going to take a while to digest.

When I look back at everything that's happened because of her desperate decisions, I realise just how much worse it could have been. The fact that I'm still breathing after she stole from Damien and sold her soul to the devil is a freaking miracle. And I have every reason to believe that if I weren't a part of the Family by blood, then I'd no longer exist. Mum either.

It's a sobering thought, and one that almost makes me grateful for everything I have suffered through. I'm still here. I'm still fighting. And the rightful leaders are beginning to emerge.

Once my tears have subsided, I reach for my phone, finding a message that came through unnoticed a while ago.

His Lordship: Dad's called me in. Talk later. Love you. x

A smile curls at my lips and a lightness washes through me.

If all of the pain and heartache that came before was all in a quest to lead me to Theo, then I'm pretty sure it might have all just been worth it. Because he's everything.

Everything I didn't know I needed.

My deviant knight who lets the world see his impenetrable shell, but for some reason chose me to see the soft, caring, lovable guy beneath.

Emmie: Okay, I'll be waiting…

His Lordship: I wish I could hold you.

A laugh falls from my lips as I look at the camera and blow him a kiss.

Emmie: All weekend. I'm okay, I promise. Just dealing with some ghosts.

His Lordship: You've got this, babe. There isn't anything my girl can't handle.

I lower my phone with a wide smile on my face.

Closing down our conversation, I find another number, one I've not rung in a long time.

I hesitate for a beat but quickly pull up my big girl panties and hit call.

"Emmie," a deep growl rumbles down the line. Not so long ago, the timbre would have done things to me. But not now. That was the old me.

"Archer," I sigh. "How are you doing?" I ask, refusing to spill the I'm-sorry-for-your-loss bullshit. He hated his brother. I hated his brother. I'm pretty sure no one is actually sorry he's gone.

But I have no doubt his death has had a massive impact on Archer's life. And we used to be friends at one time, and hell, we're connected in an entirely different way now. If the Cirillos, the Reapers, and the Wolves want a peaceful future, then we all need to find a way to get along.

"I'm..." he hesitates. "I'm sorry, Emmie. If I knew what he was doing, if I had any idea then—"

"Stop, Arch. It's not your fault. I don't blame you for any of it."

"The second I found out, I tried to help, tried to—"

"Oh my God," I gasp, realisation slamming into me. "It was Jace," I breathe, sagging back against the headboard once more.

"Yeah," he says with a chuckle. "And he assured me you were fine. Sassy little brat you've always been."

"Arsehole," I mutter.

"Whoa, careful. Are the Family taming you? You might have Greek blood running through your veins, girl. But don't you forget where you come from," he mocks.

"Nah, I'll always be the girl from Lovell, Arch. You know that. So what happens now?" I ask.

"Ah, they got you on a snooping mission?"

"No," I say, not leaving any question in my tone. "I don't follow orders from them."

"I'm teasing, Em. I can't see you ever taking orders from anyone. But things are good. I always knew this day would come. I'll figure it out the best I can. And I've got Dax and Jace by my side, so what could go wrong?"

I snort a laugh, thinking of the dumb shit the three of them have done over the years. "Oh yeah, what could go wrong? What about Misha? I'm sure she'll—"

"We're over," he cuts me off.

"Oh."

"It was just a bit of fun. Whatever, right?"

"Right," I agree. Although I detect an undercurrent

of hurt there. "Sorry if I interrupted anything, I just... I got a letter from Mum and I—"

"Missed me?" he teases.

"I was feeling nostalgic," I confess. "But I'm glad I called. Thank Jace for taking care of me. I appreciate it."

"I just wish I could have got there sooner."

"It's in the past, Arch. It's all too late. Focus on the future. Something tells me that yours is going to be busy, Mr. Wolfe."

He blows out a long breath, and I can imagine him scratching at his rough jaw as he considers what his life is now.

"If you need anything, you know where I am, yeah? I might not follow orders, but I'm happy to dish a few out for old time's sake."

"You're one of a kind, Em. You know that?"

"Life would be boring otherwise. Apologise to Dax for me."

"Sheesh, that motherfucker deserved it for touching something that didn't belong to him. Plus, it was only a flesh wound."

"I'm glad. But seriously, Arch. We're on your side okay? Shit gets tough, just shout." I have no idea what I'm really offering here, but something tells me it's the right thing to do.

Archer's wanted to clean up the Wolves for years. Well, now might just be his time. And I'm sure the guys would be well up for helping him remove a bit of trash. Hell, I know I am.

"You got it, girl. Take care, yeah?"

"Yeah, you too, Arch."

I hang up with a smile on my face once more as everything that's been up in the air recently starts to settle around me in nice, tidy piles.

My phone lights up again.

His Lordship: I love you, Emmie Cirillo.

30

EMMIE

Something warm tickles down my cheek, rousing me from sleep, and I lift my hand to swat it away. But instead, I find my fingers twisted with someone else's as warmth rushes down my arm.

"Theo," I breathe happily, still half asleep.

"You need to wake up, Em," he whispers in my ear, sending goosebumps racing across my entire body.

"Or you could just join me. Sleepy sex is the best."

He chuckles as he tugs on my arm, rolling me onto my back.

"As fucking amazing as that sounds, Hellcat, it's not why I'm here."

Confusion makes my eyes finally open, and when they do, they widen at the sight before me.

Oh holy hell, my husband is fine.

My mouth goes instantly dry as I take in his perfectly cut black suit. I swear it's been damn near sculpted onto his body. I dread to think how much it must have cost. The dark shirt and tie only add to the appeal, and the whole dark lord of death look makes his green eyes sparkle with danger.

"W-what's going on?" I ask, not missing the split knuckles and dried blood that coats his right hand.

Dropping down to his haunches, he reaches out and cups my face. I flinch at the coolness of his skin, but I don't move away.

"We found him, Em."

"Y-you..." I hesitate as my brain tries to catch up with the situation. "You found him. Where?"

"I'll explain all in a bit. We're going now. You need to get up."

I push myself up so I'm sitting and sweep my hair out of my face.

"What time is it?'

"Four am."

Yep, that makes sense.

"O-okay... u-um..." I stutter, not having a clue what I'm meant to be doing right now.

"Get dressed. I brought you clothes." He throws the bag on the bed, and I'm too shocked to say anything.

He grasps the bottom of his shirt that I'm wearing and drags it up my body.

"Fuck, babe," he groans, taking in my bare chest and bright red lace knickers.

Before I know what's happening, he's got my nipple in his mouth and I'm crying out his name as electric sparks shoot straight to my clit.

"Oh God, Theo."

Reaching up, he covers my mouth with his hand but doesn't stop, in fact, he ups the ante by twisting his fingers in the side of my underwear, tugging until they rip and fall from my body.

"What the hell are you— argh," I mumble against his hand as he runs two fingers through my pussy, dipping them straight inside and stretching me open.

"So wet for me, Hellcat."

One second I'm standing before him, the next I'm on my back with my thighs spread and his tongue lapping at my clit.

"Holy fucking, yesssss," I cry, my back arching as pleasure engulfs me. "I-I thought we were going—"

"We've got time for this," he says against me, his fingers driving deeper and finding my G-spot with ease. "Grab the pillow, babe. This is gonna be quick."

The cocky smirk on his face as he says those words should really put a damper on this, but it doesn't, not at all. Mainly because I know he's about to fulfil that promise and have me screaming in seconds.

Doing as I'm told, I smother myself with the pillow as he gets back to work. His tongue and teeth assault my clit as his fingers hit the right spot over and over until I'm chanting his name and quickly screaming out my release only a minute later.

I pull the pillow from my face just in time to watch him wipe my juices from his chin with the back of his hand.

"Fucking addicted, babe," he confesses, looming over me and stealing a kiss that would have made my knees weak if I could actually feel them. I groan as I taste myself on him, and my hips roll in my need for more.

But he doesn't give it to me.

Instead, he stands and takes a step back.

"How? How do you still look like a fucking god?" I

spit, knowing that I look like a wrung-out, panting whore right now.

My eyes run down the length of his still perfect suit until I find the massive bulge in his trousers.

Heat floods me and my mouth waters.

"No time, babe," he growls, his voice raspy and full of need. "Get dressed."

"You're no fun," I mutter, sliding from the bed and praying my legs hold me up.

He watches me with amusement. "I beg to differ, Hellcat."

Turning my back on him, I upend the bag he brought, my curiosity more than piqued about what he thinks I should be wearing for this little mission.

There's a part of me already groaning, thinking there's a sleek black dress in here that will make me look like a fucking mafia Barbie.

But I'm soon proven wrong, and I can't help but smile as I realise just how well he knows me.

"Someone's been busy," I mutter, grabbing the underwear from my pile and pulling it up my legs.

"You should see my wardrobe. It's all ready for my wife."

I glance over my shoulder, needing to know if he's serious or not. Of course, he totally is.

"Theo, I don't need you buying me things."

"I know. But I want to. There's a massive difference."

I start to argue but quickly shut it down. Now is not the time.

He watches my every move as I pull on the silk and lace bra, followed by the slim-fit black trousers and perfectly fitting blazer, which shows off a healthy amount of the bra beneath.

"Fuck. I have no chance of sinking this boner with you looking like that."

A satisfied smirk pulls at the corner of my lips before I sit in front of my dressing table, quickly pulling my hair back into a messy yet stylish bun and applying my makeup, complete with blood-red lipstick.

"Now?" I ask, standing before him, ready to go and deal with my enemy first hand.

"Like my best fucking fantasy come to life. My wife is a fucking bad-arse."

"Well, obviously. Shoes?" I ask, not seeing any with the clothes.

"I thought you'd probably castrate me with them if I bought you heels."

"Wise."

"Grab your boots, babe, and let's go deal with this for good. Then," he takes a step toward me, "you can spend until sunrise on your knees for me. Just like you're picturing." He pinches my chin between his forefinger and thumb and holds my eyes. "Fucking love you, Em."

"I love you too. Your cock more, though."

"Careful, babe. Or I won't give you this intel and just spend the night inside you."

"Big words, boss. Now, let's go."

I glance at the open window I know he entered through but think better of it. The stairs and front door seem like a much better option.

I'm not expecting anyone else to be in Theo's car, so when voices hit me after I open the door, it startles me.

"We thought he'd changed his mind and got in bed with you instead," Seb laughs. "I know I would have."

Stella's slap rings out through the car. "She's your cousin, you sick fuck," she hisses.

"With you, Princess. I meant to get in bed with you."

I look up to the mirror just in time to see his eyes roll.

"So to what do I owe this pleasure?" I ask them before they start either fighting or fucking, and Theo drops into the driver's seat.

"You think we were gonna let you do this alone, cous? Nah, we're in this shit together."

My entire body lights up, knowing that they're with me.

"Thank you," I breathe, continuing to hold Seb's eyes in the mirror.

"Has Theo told you the plan?" I ask.

"Sure thing. We're following your lead and just here for emotional support and inappropriate jokes."

"Appreciated."

While I might not have known that tonight was going to be the night, Theo and I have talked in depth during our nighttime calls this week about what I wanted to happen when they did find him.

As I expected, Theo was all for putting a gun to his head. And at the beginning of all this, I can't say that I was hugely opposed to the idea. He might be my grandfather, but he's hurt too many people I care about to put much consideration into sparing his life.

But as each new crime came to light along with all the evidence that Dad and Cruz have somehow been leaking over the past few days, it occurred to me that death would be the easy way out.

He's spent his life playing with the fate of others.

It's time to lose all of that control and finally pay for his crimes. The proper way.

"Where is he?" I ask as Theo starts to head toward the other side of the city.

Seb groans at the question, which makes me even more curious.

"He's with the Italians," Theo confesses.

"What?" I gasp.

"Clearly he's not screwed them over yet, and I can't say I'm surprised they're willing to protect him—badly, I might add—for a little intel on us. The Italians have been building to make their move for a while. They think we're not watching them. They're also stupid motherfuckers."

"Right, so..."

"They've got him in an unsecured apartment building. We can just walk right in." Theo tucks his hand into his jacket. "Even got the key," he says proudly, holding it up between us.

"How the fuck—"

"It's not what you know, it's who you know, cous. And we fucking know them all," Seb announces, rubbing his hands together.

"Right. Well..." I trail off, not really knowing what to say to any of that.

The second we pull up, Theo and I get out of the car, leaving the other two behind. They don't even try to convince me to let them join, which I'm grateful for, because while I might look confident in what I'm about to do, inside I'm shaking like a fucking leaf.

Theo's hand presses to the small of my back before we get to the main entrance.

"Are you sure about this?" he asks, his eyes searching mine.

"Yes. It's the right thing to do."

"You don't have to face him if you don't want. We can just sit out here and watch it play out."

I smile softly at him, understanding why he might want to give me an out. But I've made my decision and I'm sticking with it. I'll regret it otherwise, and I don't ever want to live with those motherfuckers.

"I know. But I need to do this."

"Fair enough. Take this then." He reaches behind him and pulls a gun from his back.

I frown, staring at the weapon as he holds it out for me.

"Is that wise?"

"Trust me," he urges. "I need to know that you can protect yourself should this go wrong."

"It won't go—"

"Just in case," he says, pressing the gun into my palm.

"Okay." I've had enough lessons with Cruz to know how to handle it, something Theo clearly knows because he doesn't so much as flinch at giving me a deadly weapon.

I tuck the thing in my waistband, and after nodding at Theo, we head for the building, my stomach in knots and my heart thrashing like a wild beast in my chest.

We come to a stop outside a flat and Theo checks his watch. "We've got three minutes."

"All I need," I confirm as he pulls the key out again and pushes it into the lock.

The second the door is open, I have to fight not to cough at the pungent smell that hits me clean in the face.

"Jesus," I grunt.

"This place is basically a squat," Theo whispers. "We won't be staying long."

The room is in darkness, but I've got enough vision to make out a bed and the lump that's sleeping on top of it.

I walk over, adrenaline pumping faster around my body as I approach the man responsible for all of this.

He might be cast in shadows and living a life on the run, but the man I've known all my life looks entirely different.

I stand there for a beat, wondering how I ever thought he was worthy of anything in his life, let alone the love he received from his family.

In a spur of the moment move and with the support of my husband right behind me, I pull the gun from behind my back and press it to Ram's forehead.

"Wake up, motherfucker," I bark, pressing harder to ensure it hurts.

The lights flicker on above us and Ram's eyes open wide—even more so when he acknowledges who's holding a gun to his head.

A deviant smile curls at my lips, one I'm sure he'd be proud of in any other situation.

"Hey, Pops. How's it going?" I ask, my voice light and airy, at complete odds with the dark need for revenge that's eating me alive inside.

"E-Emmie?" he stutters and tries to shift in the bed.

"Move and I'll pull the trigger." He stops instantly, and the knowledge of just how powerful I am right now slams into me like a truck. "W-what are you... How did you..."

"Tsk. And here I was thinking you knew the Cirillos better than this, Pops. Or is that why you planted me in the middle of them? Because you really are fucking clueless?"

"N-no, I—"

"Not interested," I spit. "There's only one thing you need to know about the Cirillo Family before we end this. And that... is that they are better than you in every single fucking way. So thank you, Granddad," I sneer, "for showing me what family should really be about, for opening my eyes to who I really am, and for setting me free. Something I'm sure a simple conversation could have achieved—but points for creativity, old man. Now," I say, spotting something moving outside the dirty window, "I've got a few friends who'd really like to get to know you better, and right now, it seems you're down in the friend department. You'll be pleased to know they've promised to treat you as the fucking scum of the earth that you really are."

Movement sounds out from behind me as Theo breathes, "Hellcat."

"I wish you a really pleasant stay in hell, Ram. I'm sure your bloodthirsty enemies will really enjoy themselves."

I take a step back and lower the gun a beat before bodies all dressed head to toe in black flood the room.

"Charles Ramsey, we're arresting you for the murder of Luis Wolfe. You do not have to say anything. But, it may harm your defence if you do not mention when questioned something which you later rely on in court. Anything you do say may be given in evidence."

A strong arm wraps around my waist and I'm hauled backward into a familiar solid body as the officers drag my grandfather from bed before throwing him back down on his front and slapping cuffs on him.

"I'm so fucking hard for you right now," Theo confesses, causing a manic laugh to erupt from my throat as the officers continue their job right in front of us.

"You're fucked up, Cirillo."

"Takes one to know one, Hellcat."

We don't move until they've frog-marched Ram out of the room, leaving one officer behind.

"Cirillo." He nods at Theo, who discreetly takes the gun from my fingers and tucks it away before holding his hand out to shake with the officer.

"Always a pleasure, Burton," Theo grunts.

The guy nods before turning his back on us and following his unit out.

"Holy shit," I breathe the second we're alone.

Theo finally releases me and I stumble forward, barely able to believe what I just did, what I just witnessed.

"How are you feeling?" Theo asks tentatively.

"On top of the fucking world. I need a drink. Can we get a drink?"

The most incredible smile pulls at Theo's lips.

"You're fucking unbelievable," he says, shaking his head. "And you're all mine."

Pulling his phone out, he taps at the screen for a beat before sweeping me up in his arms.

"You were made for me, Emmie Cirillo. And I'm never fucking letting you go again."

"Good. Because I'm not going anywhere."

The desire to let him kiss me forever lingers, but the stench of the room is stronger and after only a few seconds, Theo takes my hand and leads me out of the building.

Seb and Stella have moved and are now in the front, I assume ready for a quick getaway if it was needed.

"Well you two look happy," Seb announces.

"Emmie has officially joined the Family. I'm pretty sure she just made the Reapers Prez piss his fucking pants. It was fucking beautiful," Theo states proudly as warmth spreads through my chest. "Now, let's go. My woman wants a drink to celebrate, so that's what we're going to give her. I've already called the guys."

"It's five am," I blurt.

"It won't be the first time we started the party this early, babe, and I'm pretty sure it won't be the last."

31

THEO

"Are you sure this place is open?" Emmie asks as I push the door open to let her walk into the bar first.

"Trust me, Hellcat." I spank her arse as she walks ahead and she squeals in delight. "You like that, babe?" I ask, quickly stepping up to her, wrapping my arm around her waist and pulling her back against me.

"I'd prefer it if there were fewer clothes involved."

"Mmm... Revenge makes you playful."

Spinning in my arms, she looks up at me with her huge dark eyes which have the power to totally disarm me.

"Are you going to be my playmate, boss?"

"I'll be anything you want me to be," I murmur, leaning forward to capture her lips as voices float down to us.

"Emmie's a fucking bad-arse bitch," Alex booms, making her laugh into our kiss.

I'm hardly surprised they beat us here. They were

only sitting around the corner from the building entrance just in case things went south after all.

As always, we're in this together.

Emmie is ripped away from me as Alex engulfs her in a bear hug.

"I bet you were so fucking hot, ripping that wanker a new one," Alex announces.

"Fucking smoking," I confess. "And mine," I add.

"Oh, unknot your fucking knickers, Cirillo. I'm not stealing your girl, jeez."

He passes Emmie back to me as the five of us head deeper into the club where Nico and Daemon are sitting at the bar, surrounded by shots of vodka.

"This is a Cirillo bar then, I assume?" Emmie asks me, looking around.

"Yep. And we cleared it out for a private party."

"Impressive," she says teasingly, taking the shot glass when I hand it to her.

"Gotta win you over somehow," I mock.

"Oh, and your wealth and status hit me right in the feels."

Throwing my head back, I bark out a laugh. "Pretty sure I could be the richest guy in the world and you'd be utterly unimpressed."

"Bingo, baby. I don't give a fuck. All I want," she says, laying her hand on my chest right over my heart, "is right in here."

"Drink up, kids. We need to be wasted before dawn," Nico shouts, pulling us both from the trance we'd fallen into.

With a wicked smirk full of dirty promises of things to come, Emmie places her glass against her lips and throws her shot back in one.

As if on cue, the music starts up around us, and after two more shots each, we hit the dance floor, Seb and Stella close behind us while Alex pouts like a toddler because he's got no playmates.

"Where's Toby?" Emmie shouts in my ear over the music.

I glance over at Alex and Nico again, and while Alex broods about lack of female attention, Nico is sitting with a scowl set firmly in place. And I know why. I feel it too.

"It's Jonas's fake funeral tomorrow. He's... not in a good place."

Emmie stops dancing, her hands framing my face.

"He'll get through it. You, Nico, Stella, all of us. We won't let him drown."

"I know, I just wish there was more I could do."

"Just be there. He'll find his way again."

"He doesn't want us there tomorrow."

"I didn't mean literally. Let him do what he needs to do, but always be there for him to fall back on afterward."

"Fuck. You're amazing."

"I spoke to Archer," she blurts.

A smile twitches at my lips, loving that she feels she needs to confess.

"You're allowed friends. A life outside of me, no matter how much it might pain me to admit it."

Her eyes narrow in suspicion. "You already knew because you watched me make the call."

I shake my head. "No, I know because he was with me when you did it."

Her chin drops in shock. "But you said you were with your dad."

"I was, and Archer and Cruz too." Cupping her jaw, I brush my thumb along her bottom lip. "That fresh start you wanted is happening, babe. From here on out, everything is going to be different."

"What about the Italians?" she asks.

"Fuck them, we're better than them. And with the Reapers and Wolves having our backs, they don't stand a fucking chance." Lowering my lips to hers, I breathe. "Bring it on. Bring it all the fuck on."

"There's something really wrong with you." Although, despite her words, a wide smile spreads across her face.

"Yeah, but you love me for it."

"I do." Her eyes soften, and it makes my chest ache in the most incredible way. "I love you, Theo Cirillo."

"I love you too, Emmie Cirillo. You're mine, for better or worse, richer or poorer."

"I'm pretty sure I can get on board with that." She throws her arms around my shoulders and presses her lips to mine. "But right now," she says into our kiss, "I want to see you at your worst, boss."

Spinning her around, I walk us to a dark corner of the club and push her up against the wall.

"You can scream as loud as you like in here, Hellcat."

"My hero."

My laughter is swallowed by her kiss as I set about proving to her how I'm anything but.

Toby

My blood burns me from the inside out as I stand in the shadows, just watching.

My heart pounds and my hands tremble as I stay frozen, watching people all dressed in black walking into a church as if the person they're going to say goodbye to is actually worthy of ever being inside a fucking place of worship.

But maybe they do think he's a good man. Maybe they believe all the lies, they don't see the manipulation.

I guess we didn't understand the depth of it, so why should they?

Who even is this man they're all mourning? What lies has he spun them over the years? What do they think he does for a job that has allowed him enough time to ruin mine and Mum's lives while living a secret one on this side of town?

My head spins from the whisky I sank last night in the hope I could sleep through this entire day, but I knew it was wishful thinking. I knew I'd be standing right here, watching this car crash play out.

The others only started their party at dawn, celebrating the demise of another of our enemies, but I couldn't bring myself to see the joy on their faces. And plus, they didn't deserve to have me dampening the mood with my misery.

All of them have been through too much recently to be brought down by me and my bullshit.

It shouldn't be this hard.

We're free from that sick son of a bitch. I should be able to turn my back on him and walk away.

But I can't.

It's why I still turn up to visit him most days of the week to sate my inner monster so that I can rest a little at night, knowing he's getting exactly what he deserves for the way he treated my mum all these years.

I should be at home spending time with the sister I never knew I had, or my actual biological father. But I can't. Not while *he's* taking up all my headspace.

Until he's hurting like he's hurt those I love, I can't do anything else. I can't see anything else.

I might not be his son, I might not share his vindictive blood, but that doesn't mean I haven't learned from him over the years, or from the training he enforced on me in his quest to make me his perfect protégé.

And just like he taught me, I'm not going to back down until the job is done, until I've destroyed every single inch of my enemy, he who did me wrong. And then, and only then, will I look forward to what our lives can be like without such a poisonous snake living among us, controlling us.

A large black hearse comes to a stop at the end of the path that leads to the church, and my heart leaps in my chest.

Is there even a person in that coffin? How much effort has Damien really put into this farce?

It's a joke, a fucking joke that he even considered doing this for a second, but as much as I don't understand, doing this has brought me one step closer to my goal.

A second funeral car pulls up and I wait, my heart racing and my skin prickling with anticipation as the driver gets out and pulls open the door for the people sitting inside.

I lean forward, more than ready to get my eyes on the one person I've come here for.

An older lady emerges first, followed by another young woman I recognise from all the research I've done.

My teeth grind, thinking that she's not with them. But then a black shoe and a smooth calf emerges.

My heart jumps into my throat as I wait for the rest of her to be revealed.

My new target.

My new enemy.

My ultimate vengeance.

Toby's story starts in One Reckless Knight. Grab your copy now for FREE

Need more of Emmie & Theo, and maybe a little Stella & Seb thrown in for good measure? DOWNLOAD DEVIANT FIGHT NOW!

HATE YOU PROLOGUE

Tabitha

I stare down at my gran's pale skin. Her cheeks are sunken and her eyes tired. She's been fighting this for too long now, and as much as I hate to even think it, it's time she found some peace.

I take her cool hand in mine and lift her knuckles to my lips.

"It's Tabitha," I whisper. I've no idea if she's awake, but I don't want to startle her.

Her eyes flicker open. After a second they must adjust to the light and she looks right at me. My chest tightens as if someone's wrapping an elastic band around it. I hate seeing my once so full of life gran like this. She was always so happy and full of cheer. She didn't deserve this end. But cancer doesn't care what kind of person you are, it hits whoever it fancies and ruins lives.

Pulling a chair closer, I drop onto it, not taking my eyes from her.

"How are you doing today?" I hate asking the question, because there really is only one answer. She's waiting, waiting for her time to come to put her out of her misery.

"I'm good. Christopher upped my morphine. I'm on top of the world."

She might be living her last days, but it doesn't stop her eyes sparkling a little as she mentions her male nurse. If I've heard the words 'if I were forty years younger' once while she's been here, then I've heard them a million times. She's joking, of course. My gran spent her life with my incredible grandpa until he had a stroke a few years ago. Thankfully, I guess, his end was much quicker and less painful than Gran's. It was awful at the time to have him healthy one moment and then gone in a matter of hours, but this right now is pure torture, and I'm not the one lying on the hospital bed with meds constantly being pumped into my body.

"Turn the frown upside down, Tabby Cat. I'm fine. I want to remember you smiling, not like your world's about to come crashing down."

"I know, I'm sorry. I just—" a sob breaks from my throat. "I don't know how I'm going to live without you." Dramatic? Yeah. But Gran has been my go-to person my whole life. When my parents get on my last nerve, which is often, she's the one who talks me down, makes me see things differently. She's also the only one who's encouraged me to live the life I want, not the one I'm constantly being pushed into.

That's the reason I'm the only one visiting her right now.

When my parents discovered that she was the one encouraging my 'reckless behaviour', as they called it, they cut contact. I can see the pain in her eyes about that every time she looks at me, but she's too stubborn to do anything about it, even now.

"You're going to be fine. You're stronger than you give yourself credit for. How many times have I told you, you just need to follow your heart. Follow your heart and just breathe. Spread your wings and fly, Tabby Cat."

Those were the last words she said to me.

HATE YOU CHAPTER ONE

Tabitha

The heavy bass rattles my bones. The incredible music does help to lift my spirits, but I find it increasingly hard to see the positives in my life while I'm hanging out with my friends these days. They've all got something exciting going on—incredible job prospects, marriage, exotic holidays on the horizon—and here I am, drowning in my one-person pity party. It's been two months since Gran left me, and I'm still wondering what the hell I'm meant to be doing with my life.

"Oh my god, they are so fucking awesome," Danni squeals in my ear as one song comes to an end. I didn't really have her down as a rock fan, but she was almost as excited as James when he announced that this was what we were doing for his birthday this year. Although I do wonder if it's the music or the frontman who's really captured her attention. She'd never admit it, but she's got a thing for bad boys.

I glance over at him with his arm wrapped around Shannon's shoulders and a smile twitches my lips. They're so cute. They've got the kind of relationship everyone craves. It seems so easy yet full of love and affection. Ripping my eyes from the couple, I focus back on the stage and try to block out that I'm about as far away from having that kind of connection with anyone as physically possible.

I sing along with the songs I've heard on the radio a million times and jump around with my friends, but I just can't quite totally get on board with tonight. Maybe I just need more alcohol.

"Where to next?" Shannon asks once we've left the arena and the ringing in our ears has begun to fade.

"Your choice," James says, looking down at her with utter devotion shining in his eyes. It wasn't a great surprise when Shannon sent a photo of her giant engagement ring to our group chat a couple of months ago. We all knew it was coming—Danni especially, seeing as it turned out that she helped choose the ring.

Shannon directs us all to a cocktail bar a few streets over and I make quick work of manoeuvring my way through the crowd to get to the bar, my need for a drink beginning to get the better of me. The others disappear off somewhere in the hope of finding a table

"Can we have two jugs of..." I quickly glance at the menu. "Margaritas please."

"Coming right up, sweetheart." The barman winks at me before his eyes drop to my chest. Hooking up on a night out isn't really my thing, but hell if it doesn't make me feel a little better about myself. He's cute too, and just the kind of guy who would give both my parents a heart attack if I were to bring him home. Both his forearms are covered in tattoos, he's got gauges in both his ears, and a lip ring. A smile tugs at the corner of my mouth as I imagine the looks on their faces.

My gran's words suddenly hit me.

Just breathe.

My hand lifts and my fingers run over the healing skin just below my bra. My smile widens.

I watch the barman prepare our cocktails, my eyes focused on the ink on his arms. I've always been obsessed by art, any kind of art, and that most definitely includes on skin.

I'm lost in my own head, so when he places the jugs in front of me, I startle, feeling ridiculous.

"T-Thank you," I mutter, but when I lift my eyes, I find him staring intently at me.

"You're welcome. I'm Christian, by the way."

"Oh, hi." A sly smile creeps onto my lips. "I'm Biff."

"Biff?" His brows draw together in a way I'm all too used to when I say my name.

"It's short for Tabitha."

"That's pretty. So... uh... how do you feel about—"

"Christian, a little help?" one of the other barmen shouts, pulling Christian's attention from me.

"Sorry, I'll hopefully see you again later?"

I nod at him, not wanting to give him any false hope. Like I said, he's cute, but after my last string of bad dates and even worse short-term boyfriends, I'm happy flying solo right now. I've got a top of the range vibrating friend in my bedside table; I don't need a man.

Picking up the tray in front of me, I turn and go in search of my friends. It takes forever, but eventually I find them tucked around a tiny table in the back corner of the bar.

"What the hell took so long? We thought you'd pulled and abandoned us."

"Yes and no," I say, ensuring every head turns my way.

"Tell us more," Danni, my best friend, demands.

"It was nothing. The barman was about to ask me out, but it got busy."

"Why the hell did you come back? Get over there. We all know you could do with a little... loosening up," James says with a wink.

"I'm good. He wasn't my type."

"Oh, of course. You only date posh boys."

"That is not true."

"Is it not?" Danni asks, chipping in once she's filled all the glasses.

"No..." I think back over the previous few guys they met. "Wayne wasn't posh," I argue when I realise they're kind of right.

"No, he was just a wanker."

Blowing out a long breath, I try to come up with an argument, but quite honestly, it's true. My shoulders slump as I realise that I've been subconsciously dating guys my parents would approve of. It's like my need to follow their orders is so well ingrained by now that I don't even realise I'm doing it. Shame that their ideas about my life, what I should do, and whom I should date don't exactly line up with mine.

Glancing over my shoulder at the bar, I catch a glimpse of Christian's head. Maybe I should take him up on his almost offer. What's the worst that could happen?

Deciding some liquid courage is in order, I grab my margherita and swallow half down in one go.

I'm so fed up of attempting to live my parents' idea of a perfect life. I promised Gran I'd do things my way. I need to start living up to my promise.

By the time I'm tipsy enough to walk back to the bar and chat up Christian, he's nowhere to be seen. I'm kind of disappointed seeing as the others had convinced me to throw caution to the wind (something that I'm really bad at doing), but I think I'm mostly relieved to be able go home and lock myself inside my flat alone and not have to worry about anyone else.

With my arm linked through Danni's, we make our way out to the street, ready to make our journeys home, and Shannon jumps into an idling Uber while Danni waits for another to go in the opposite direction.

"You sure you don't want to be dropped off? I don't mind."

"No, I'm sure. I could do with the fresh air." It's not a lie—the alcohol from one too many cocktails is making my head a little fuzzy. I hate going to sleep with the room spinning. I'd much rather that feeling fade before lying down.

"Okay. Promise me you'll text me when you're home."

"I promise." I wrap my arms around my best friend and then wave her off in her own Uber.

Turning on my heels, I start the short walk home.

I've been a London girl all my life, and while some

might be afraid to walk home after dark, I love it. I love seeing a different side to this city, the quiet side when most people are hiding in their flats, not flooding the streets on their daily commutes.

My mind is flicking back and forth between my promise to Gran and my missed opportunity tonight when a shop front that I walk past on almost a daily basis makes me stop.

It's a tattoo studio I've been inside of once in my life. I never really pay it much attention, but the new sign in the window catches my eye and I stop to look.

Admin help wanted. Enquire within.

Something stirs in my belly, and it's not just my need to do something to piss my parents off—although getting a job in a place like this is sure to do that. I'm pretty sure it's excitement.

Tattoos fascinate me, or more so, the artists.

I'm surprised to see the open sign still illuminated, so before I can change my mind, I push the door open. A little bell rings above it, and after a few seconds of standing in reception alone, a head pops out from around the door.

"Evening. What can I do you for?" The guy's smile is soft and kind despite his otherwise slightly harsh features and ink.

"Oh um..." I hesitate under his intense dark stare. I glance over my shoulder, the back of the piece of paper catching my eye and reminding me why I walked in here. "I just saw the job ad in the window. Is the position still open?"

His eyes drop from mine and take in what I'm wearing. Seeing as tonight's outing involved a rock concert, I'm dressed much like him in all black and looking a little edgy with my skinny black jeans, ripped AC/DC t-shirt and heavy black makeup. I must admit it's not a look I usually go for, but it was fitting for tonight.

He nods, apparently happy with what he sees.

"Experience?" he asks, making my stomach drop.

"Not really, but I'm studying for a Masters so I'm not an idiot. I know my way around a computer, Excel, and I'm super organised."

"Right..." he trails off, like he's thinking about the best way to get rid of me.

"I'm a really quick learner. I'm punctual, methodical and really easy to get along with."

"It's okay, you had me sold at organised. I'm Dawson, although everyone around here calls me D."

"Nice to meet you." I stick my hand out for him to shake, and an amused smile plays at his lips. Stretching out an inked arm, he takes my hand and gives it a very firm shake that my dad would be impressed by—if he could look past the tattoos, that is. "I'm Tabitha, but everyone calls me Biff."

"Biff, I like it. When can you start?"

"Don't you want to interview me?"

"You sound like you could be perfect. When can you start?"

"Err... tomorrow?" I ask, totally taken aback. He doesn't know me from Adam.

"Yes!" He practically snaps my hand off. "Can you be here for two o'clock? I can show you around before clients start turning up. I'll apologise now for dropping you in the deep end, we've not had anyone for a few weeks and things are starting to get a little crazy."

"I can cope with crazy."

"Good to know. This place can be nuts." I smile at him, more grateful than he could know to have a distraction and a focus.

My Masters should be enough to keep my mind busy, but since Gran went, I can't seem to lose myself in it like I could previously. Hopefully, sorting this place's admin out might be exactly what I need.

"Two o'clock tomorrow then," I say, turning to leave. "I'll bring ID. Do you need a reference? I've done some voluntary work recently, I'm sure they'll write something for me."

"Just turn up on time and do your job and you're golden."

I walk out with more of a spring in my step than I have in a long time. I'm determined to find something that's going to make me happy, not just my parents. I've lived in their shadow for long enough.

I look myself over before leaving my flat for my first shift at the tattoo studio. I'm dressed a little more like myself today in a pair of dark skinny jeans, a white blouse and a black blazer. It's simple and smart. I'm not sure if there's a dress code—D never specified what I should wear. With my hair straightened and hanging down my back and my makeup light, I feel like I can take on whatever crazy he throws at me.

With a final spritz of perfume, I grab my bag from the unit in the hall and pull open my door. My home is a top floor flat in an old London warehouse. They were converted a few years ago by my father's company, and I managed to get myself first dibs. They might drive me insane on the best of days, but at least I get this place rent-free. It almost makes up for their controlling and stuck-up ways... almost.

Ignoring the lift like I always do, I head for the stairs. My heels click against the polished concrete until I'm at the bottom and out to the busy city. I love London. I love that no matter what the time, there's always something going on or someone who's awake.

The spring afternoon is still a little fresh, making me regret not grabbing my coat, or even a scarf, before I left. I pull my blazer tighter around myself and make the short journey to the shop.

The door's locked when I get there, and the bright neon sign that clearly showed it was open last night is currently saying closed.

Unsure of what to do, I lift my hand to knock. Only a second later, the shop front is illuminated, and the sound of movement inside filters down to me, but when the door opens it's not the guy from last night.

"Oh... uh... hi. Is... uh... D here?"

The guy folds his arms over his chest and looks me up and down. He chuckles, although I've no idea what he finds so amusing.

"D," he shouts over his shoulder, "there's some posh bird here to see you."

My teeth grind that he's stereotyped me quite so quickly, but I refuse to allow him to see that his assumptions about me affect me in any way.

"Ah, good. I was worried you might change your mind."

"Not at all," I say, stepping past the judgemental arsehole and into the studio reception-cum-waiting room.

"That's Spike. Feel free to ignore him. He's not got laid in about a million years, it makes him a little cranky." I fight to contain a laugh, especially when I turn toward Spike to find his lips pursed and his eyes narrowed in frustration. All it does is confirm that D's words are correct.

"Is that fucking necessary? Posh doesn't need to know how inactive my cock is, especially not when she's only just walked through the fucking door. Unless..." He stalks towards me and I automatically back up. I can't deny that he's a good looking guy, but there's no way I'm going there.

"I don't think so."

"You sure? You look like you could do with a bit of rough." He winks, and I want the ground to swallow me up.

"Down, Spike. This is Tabitha, or Biff. She's our new admin, so I suggest you be nice to her if you want to stop organising your own appointments and shit. I don't need a sexual harassment case on my hands before she's even fucking started."

I can't help but laugh at the look on Spike's face. "Don't worry. I'm sure you'll find some desperate old spinster soon."

He looks me up and down again, something in his eyes changed. "Appearances aside, I think you're going to get on well here."

I smile at him. "Mine's a coffee. Milk, no sugar. I'm already sweet enough." His chin drops.

"I thought you were our new assistant. Why am I still making the coffee?"

"Know your place, Spike. Now do as the lady says. You know my order."

"Yeah, it comes with a side of fuck off!" He flips D off before disappearing through a door that I can only assume goes to a kitchen.

"I probably should have warned you that you've agreed to work around a bunch of arseholes."

"I know how to handle myself around horny men, don't worry."

After finishing my A levels, before I grew any kind of backbone where my parents were concerned, I agreed to work for my dad. I was his little office bitch and spent an horrendous year of my life being bossed around by men who thought that just because they had a cock hanging between their legs it made them better than me. I might have fucking hated that year, but it taught me a few things, not just about business but also how to deal with men who think they're something fucking special just because they're a tiny bit successful and make more money than me. I've no doubt that my time at Anderson Development Group gave me all the skills I'm going to need to handle these artists.

"So I see. So, this is your desk. When you're on shift you'll be the first person people see when they're inside, so it's important that you look good. But from what I've seen, I don't think we'll have an issue. I've sorted you out logins for the computer and the software we use. Most of it is pretty self-explanatory. I'm pretty IT illiterate and I've figured most of it out, put it that way."

D's showing me how they book clients in when someone else joins us. This time it's someone I recognise from my previous visit, although it's immediately obvious that he doesn't remember me like I do him. But then I guess he was the one delivering the pain, not receiving it.

"Biff, this is Titch. Titch, this is Biff, our new admin. Be nice."

"Nice? I'm always nice. Nice to meet you, Biff. You have any issues with this one, you come and see me. He might look tough, but I know all his secrets." Titch winks, a smile curling at his lips that shows he's a little more interested than he's making out, and quickly disappears towards his room.

It's not long until the first clients of the afternoon arrive, and I'm left alone to try to get to grips with everything.

Between clients, D pops his head out of his room to check I'm okay, and every hour I make a round of coffee for everyone. That sure seems to get me in their good books.

"I think I could get used to having you around," Spike says when I deliver probably his fourth coffee of the day. "Only thing that would make it better is if it were whisky."

"Not sure the person at the end of your needle would agree." He chuckles and turns back to the design he was working on when I interrupted.

My first day flies by. D tells me to head home not long after nine o'clock. They've all got hours of tattooing to go yet, seeing as Saturday night is their busiest night of the week, but he insists I get a decent night's sleep.

Continue reading Tabitha and Zach's story
HATE YOU!

ABOUT THE AUTHOR

Tracy Lorraine is a *USA Today* and *Wall Street Journal* bestselling new adult and contemporary romance author. Tracy has recently turned thirty and lives in a cute Cotswold village in England with her husband, baby girl and lovable but slightly crazy dog. Having always been a bookaholic with her head stuck in her Kindle, Tracy decided to try her hand at a story idea she dreamt up and hasn't looked back since.

Be the first to find out about new releases and offers. Sign up to my newsletter here.

If you want to know what I'm up to and see teasers and snippets of what I'm working on, then you need to be in my Facebook group. Join Tracy's Angels here.

Keep up to date with Tracy's books at
www.tracylorraine.com

ALSO BY TRACY LORRAINE

Falling Series

Forbidden Series

Rebel Ink Series

Trick You #2

Defy You #3

Play You #4

Inked (A Rebel Ink/Driven Crossover)

Rosewood High Series
Thorn #1

Paine #2

Savage #3

Fierce #4

Hunter #5

Faze (#6 Prequel)

Fury #6

Legend #7

Maddison Kings University Series
TMYM: Prequel

TRYS #1

TDYW #2

TBYS #3

TVYC #4

TDYD #5

TDYR #6

TRYD #7

Knight's Ridge Empire Series
Wicked Summer Knight: Prequel (Stella & Seb)

Wicked Knight #1 (Stella & Seb)

Wicked Princess #2 (Stella & Seb)

Wicked Empire #3 (Stella & Seb)

Deviant Knight #4 (Emmie & Theo)

Deviant Princess #5 (Emmie & Theo

Deviant Reign #6 (Emmie & Theo)

One Reckless Knight (Jodie & Toby)

Reckless Knight (Jodie & Toby)

Reckless Princess (Jodie & Toby)

Ruined Series

Ruined Plans #1

Ruined by Lies #2

Ruined Promises #3

Never Forget Series

Never Forget Him #1

Never Forget Us #2

Everywhere & Nowhere #3

Chasing Series

Chasing Logan

The Cocktail Girls

His Manhattan

Her Kensington

Printed in Great Britain
by Amazon